"PLEASE DO NOT MAKE ME FALL IN LOVE WITH YOU," SABINA CRIED.

"Isn't it too late?" asked the gipsy quietly. "If you are honest with yourself, you already love me a little."

"No! No!" Sabina whispered. "It isn't true!"

"And I am telling you, Sabina," he continued, "that it is too late. I am not even touching you and yet you are quivering as if I were holding you in my arms."

For a moment she could only tremble and then she felt a sudden flame of ecstasy shoot through her. Then the world stood still and they were, in that second, so close to each other in spirit that the confines of the body were completely broken.

Books by Barbara Cartland

A SONG OF LOVE
A HAZARD OF HEARTS
DESIRE OF THE HEART
THE COIN OF LOVE
THE ENCHANTING EVIL
LOVE IN HIDING
CUPID RIDES PILLION
THE UNPREDICTABLE
  BRIDE
A DUEL OF HEARTS
LOVE IS THE ENEMY
THE HIDDEN HEART
LOVE TO THE RESCUE
LOVE HOLDS THE CARDS
LOST LOVE
LOVE IS CONTRABAND
THE KNAVE OF HEARTS
LOVE ME FOREVER
THE SMUGGLED HEART
SWEET ADVENTURE
THE GOLDEN GONDOLA
THE LITTLE PRETENDER
STARS IN MY HEART (also
  published as STARS IN
  HER EYES)
THE SECRET FEAR
MESSENGER OF LOVE
THE WINGS OF LOVE
THE ENCHANTED WALTZ
THE HIDDEN EVIL
A VIRGIN IN PARIS
A KISS OF SILK
LOVE IS DANGEROUS
THE KISS OF THE DEVIL
THE RELUCTANT BRIDE
THE UNKNOWN HEART
ELIZABETHAN LOVER
WE DANCED ALL NIGHT
AGAIN THIS RAPTURE
THE ENCHANTED MOMENT
THE KISS OF PARIS
THE PRETTY HORSE-
  BREAKERS
OPEN WINGS
LOVE UNDER FIRE
NO HEART IS FREE
STOLEN HALO
THE MAGIC OF HONEY
LOVE IS MINE
THE AUDACIOUS AD-
  VENTURESS
WINGS ON MY HEART

BARBARA CARTLAND'S
  BOOK OF BEAUTY &
  HEALTH
A HALO FOR THE DEVIL
LIGHTS OF LOVE
SWEET PUNISHMENT
A GHOST IN MONTE
  CARLO
LOVE IS AN EAGLE
LOVE ON THE RUN
LOVE FORBIDDEN
BLUE HEATHER
A LIGHT TO THE HEART
LOST ENCHANTMENT
THE PRICE IS LOVE
SWEET ENCHANTRESS
OUT OF REACH
THE IRRESISTIBLE BUCK
THE COMPLACENT WIFE
METTERNICH THE PAS-
  SIONATE DIPLOMAT
JOSEPHINE EMPRESS OF
  FRANCE
THE SCANDALOUS LIFE
  OF KING CAROL
WOMAN THE ENIGMA
ELIZABETH EMPRESS OF
  AUSTRIA
THE ODIOUS DUKE
PASSIONATE PILGRIM
THE THIEF OF LOVE
THE DREAM WITHIN
ARMOUR AGAINST LOVE
A HEART IS BROKEN
THE RUNAWAY HEART
THE LEAPING FLAME
AGAINST THE STREAM
THEFT OF A HEART
WHERE IS LOVE?
TOWARDS THE STARS
A VIRGIN IN MAYFAIR
DANCE ON MY HEART
THE ADVENTURER
A RAINBOW TO HEAVEN
LOVE AND LINDA
DESPERATE DEFIANCE
LOVE AT FORTY
THE BITTER WINDS OF
  LOVE
BROKEN BARRIERS
LOVE IN PITY
THIS TIME IT'S LOVE
ESCAPE FROM PASSION

BARBARA CARTLAND

5
THE CAPTIVE HEART

ALSO PUBLISHED AS THE ROYAL PLEDGE

A JOVE BOOK

THE CAPTIVE HEART
(also published as THE ROYAL PLEDGE)

Copyright © 1956 by Barbara Cartland

Seven previous printings
First Jove edition published September 1980

10 9 8 7 6 5 4 3 2 1

Printed in the United States of America

Jove books are published by Jove Publications, Inc.,
200 Madison Avenue, New York, NY 10016

THE CAPTIVE HEART

CHAPTER ONE

"DAMME, we might be a funeral procession."

Sabina spoke the words out loud and then gave a little gurgle of laughter at the sound of her own voice. Her mimicry of the Squire's quite audible muttering as he escorted his daughter up the aisle to be married always made her sisters dissolve into helpless giggles, although Papa would have been both distressed and displeased if he had known of his eldest daughter's witticism.

It was true, however, that the horses pulling the old and creaking hackney-carriage over the rough roads seemed to be getting slower and slower. Sabina looked through the window, the glass of which could have done with a clean, and saw that darkness had fallen and the stars were coming out and being reflected, shimmering and iridescent in the sea below them.

After so many delays and accidents it seemed as if she would never arrive at Monte Carlo and yet, at the same time, it was absurd to worry.

She drew in a deep breath of delight as she looked down at the sea far away below and at the dark shadows of the trees which, silhouetted against the sky, seemed exotic and strangely shaped. She was in France. She was travelling towards the place which only two months ago she had never expected to visit even in her wildest dreams.

'Glory to goodness, I am a lucky girl!'

Sabina whispered the words, then laughed again. How ridiculous she was, talking to herself! Anyone would think she was as crazed as the idiot boy in the village at home, who had always made her shudder when she met him wandering vacantly down the twisting lanes, talking in a high-pitched voice.

How far away Cobbleford and Gloucestershire seemed now, and yet it was only a few days ago since she had left. At this moment the family would be sitting in the drawing-room having long ago finished their plain, rather

7

light meal, which Papa insisted on calling supper although Mama always referred to it as dinner.

The girls would be busy—Harriet at work on her embroidery, which always brought exclamations of admiration from everyone who saw it, while Melloney would be painstakingly trying to copy her and not succeeding, poor darling, however hard she tried. Perhaps Angelina would be at the piano—Papa always liked to hear how she was getting on with her pianoforte lessons—and Clare would be in bed, because until they were fifteen none of them were allowed to stay up to dinner.

Mamma would be sitting in her favourite chair, the lamplight on her pretty hair which was beginning to show grey threads amongst the gold. And Papa, if he had finished preparing his sermon for Sunday, would come in from the study and sit down on the other side of the hearth, opposite Mamma, and join in the conversation. There would be lots of things to talk about although they had been together all day, and perhaps, at this very moment, one of them was saying: 'I wonder how Sabina is and if she has arrived yet at Monte Carlo?'

If only they knew, Sabina thought. How horrified Papa would be to know that she was not yet at Monte Carlo but travelling alone in a hackney-carriage! But really there was nothing else she could have done.

When Miss Remington fractured her leg stepping out of the train at Nice, Sabina had felt, for one shameful moment, as though it was entirely a trick of some evil demon to prevent her reaching her destination. She had been horrified at the selfishness of such a thought a few seconds later, as she coped as best she could with the commotion which the accident caused.

Miss Remington, who was a cousin of the Bishop and a woman of sensible age or else she would never have been entrusted with the task of chaperoning Sabina, had behaved, the latter thought secretly, in a very foolish fashion. She had screamed and cried and then swooned away, so that Sabina had the greatest difficulty in bringing her back to consciousness with smelling-salts, a cold-water compress and even the smoke of a few feathers burnt under her nose.

The feathers Sabina had procured with great ingenuity. Some crates of live fowls were standing on Nice Station waiting for a train to transport them to Monte Carlo.

8

Sabina had seen the label as she slipped her fingers between the slats to pick up the fallen feathers. Worried though she was about Miss Remington, she could not help the leap of her heart at the inscription and a feeling of irritation that her journey there must now be delayed until Miss Remington could have medical attention.

It had taken ages for a doctor to be fetched, while Miss Remington lay on the hard, uncomfortable bench in the waiting-room, crying out at the pain she was suffering and swooning at least a dozen times before a heavily bearded Frenchman with a small black bag came in through the glass door.

Sabina was glad then, as she had been during the whole journey, that she had a considerable knowledge of the French language. Mamma had been most particular that she should be punctilious about her studies whatever else was neglected, and she rejoiced too, with a vanity that could not be repressed, that her accent was impeccable.

"I must apologize, *monsieur*, for incommoding you in any way," she began. And the doctor, who had been looking cross and irritable, and was undoubtedly in a hurry, took off his hat with what, she privately thought, was a most courtly gesture and even forced a smile to his lips.

"I was informed that there had been an accident, *mademoiselle*."

"That is unfortunately true," Sabina answered. "My friend, who is accompanying me to Monte Carlo, fell when dismounting from the train. She is not a lightweight, as you can see, and I am afraid that her leg is broken."

"This is indeed a grave misfortune, *mademoiselle*," the doctor said, still watching her and seeming, she thought, in no hurry to attend to his patient.

Miss Remington, however, made sure of drawing his attention to herself by uttering a little squeal of pain, and when he turned towards her, promptly swooning again. Sabina hastened to her side.

"It is best to examine her leg while she is unconscious," she said practically. "Otherwise she cannot bear it to be touched."

The doctor made a very cursory examination.

"A bad fracture," he said. "We must get *madame* to the hospital."

9

"The hospital!" Sabina repeated in dismay. She had hoped that the doctor would be able to bandage up Miss Remington's leg and they could proceed on their journey.

"The leg will have to be set," he said, "and put in splints."

"Will that take a long time?" Sabina asked.

"*Madame* should be able to leave the hospital in perhaps three weeks," the doctor replied.

"Three weeks!" Sabina exclaimed.

"It is very fortunate," the doctor agreed.

"But very," Sabina cried. "Miss Remington was to have gone to Italy tomorrow. She was chaperoning me as far as Monte Carlo and then she had made all arrangements to proceed to Rome."

"I am afraid *madame's* visit will have to wait," the doctor said. "But you, *mademoiselle*, will be able to proceed to Monte Carlo."

"Yes, yes, of course."

Sabina felt her anxiety lighten at the words. Yes, of course she would go on. No one would expect her to stay with Miss Remington. Besides, it would be impossible for, as it was she had only just enough money for the journey.

It was money that was worrying Sabina some hours later when she left the hospital and went back to the station. By that time Miss Remington had her leg in splints and was tucked up in bed in a small but pleasant room from the windows of which she could see the sea.

The nuns who ran the hospital had been most kind, but at the same time Sabina felt rather depressed by the obvious poverty of the hospital and the lack of any luxuries. However, the patients she saw in the wards seemed cheerful enough, and Miss Remington, when she felt well enough to speak, assured Sabrina in a whisper that she would be quite all right.

"I don't like leaving you," Sabina said.

"But you must go on at once," Miss Remington said. "You cannot stay alone in Nice. Think what your father would say. Besides, I have heard stories that make me feel sure it is not at all a place for a young girl."

Sabina had felt relieved that Miss Remington's idea was the same as the doctor's that she should continue her journey to Monte Carlo. At the same time, because she was so eager and willing to go, she felt a decided prick of conscience at leaving poor Miss Remington, white-faced and tear-stained, alone and friendless.

"I shall be quite all right," Miss Remington protested when Sabina voiced her fears. "Take the next train and explain to Lady Thetford how sorry I am not to accompany you on the last part of your journey. I would not wish her, or indeed your dear parents, to think I have failed in my duty."

"Oh, Miss Remington, how could you help what happened? It was a horrible accident and all the fault of the station authorities who have made the platform far too low for the trains. It seems so inefficient somehow."

"Hush, dear, we must not criticize other countries or judge them by our own standards," Miss Remington said. "At the same time, there is no doubt that most things are much better arranged in England."

Sabina bent to kiss her good-bye.

"I will try to come over and see you in a day or so," she said. "I am sure Lady Thetford will be only too willing to let me come when she hears where you are. I do hope you will not be miserably uncomfortable."

"These things are sent in life to try us, my dear!" Miss Remington said.

In the face of such resignation Sabina could only once again feel guilty that she had ever thought Miss Remington had behaved foolishly and in a somewhat uncontrolled manner on the railway station.

She said good-bye to the nuns and told the Mother Superior that she felt sure that the Dowager Lady Thetford, with whom she was going to stay in Monte Carlo, would wish to be informed at once if Miss Remington required anything special or should there be any deterioration in her health.

The Mother Superior, unworldly though she might be, seemed suitably impressed at Lady Thetford's name, although when she heard that Sabina's destination was Monte Carlo she murmured a few words in Latin which Sabina understood to be a prayer for the safety of her soul.

It was only when she left the hospital and walked quickly down the narrow streets which led her back to the station that she realized how late it was. It was not entirely the setting sun and the fading sky that told her that the afternoon was far spent, but also an aching stomach which reminded her that she had not eaten for a long time. She was, indeed, conscious of feeling extremely hungry, and when the delicious fragrant odour of coffee came to her nostrils she paused outside a *pâtisserie* and, after a moment's hesitation, went in.

The coffee was as good as it smelt, the *gâteaux*, rich with cream and chocolate, were even more satisfying than they looked. It was only after she paid the bill that Sabina looked with a feeling of dismay at the dwindling coins in her purse.

She had tipped the porters who had carried Miss Remington to the carriage which the doctor had summoned. Then there had been the carriage to pay for, and when they reached the hospital, the doctor had asked bluntly, and with what Sabina thought was a lamentable lack of delicacy, for his fee. It had not been a large sum but it was quite a lot of money to Sabina. She had thought, of course, that Miss Remington would pay her back, but when she went into her room after the doctor had set her leg and saw her so weak and shattered, all thought of money had vanished from Sabina's head.

She had enough, however, she had thought to herself consolingly, because her railway ticket carried her through to Monte Carlo.

Her hunger satisfied and feeling impatient now to get on with her journey, Sabina left the *pâtisserie* and almost ran down the street to the station. There was an air of quietness and emptiness about the platform, which in itself was a foreboding of the news that was to come.

It took her some time to find any officials, but finally she ran to earth a resplendent-looking individual covered in gold braid whom she took to be the station-master.

"Pardon, *monsieur*, but can you tell me what time is the next train to Monte Carlo?" Sabina asked.

"Nine o'clock tomorrow morning, *mademoiselle*," was the reply.

"Tomorrow morning!" Sabina cried. "But there must be one tonight."

"I regret, *mademoiselle*, the last train for Monte Carlo left over half an hour ago."

"There must be some mistake. . . ." Sabina began, and then realized it was no use arguing.

The station-master had already turned his back on her and was deep in some abstruse calculations amongst the

12

papers that littered his very untidy desk. She walked out of the door and then turned back again.

"How else can I reach Monte Carlo tonight?" she inquired despairingly.

"*En voiture*," he replied, without raising his head.

Of course, a carriage, Sabina thought with relief. How stupid she was to imagine that there was no other way of reaching Monte Carlo except by train! Indeed she remembered that Papa had told her how, before the railway was built four years ago in 1868, *Monsieur Blanc*, who had made Monte Carlo so fashionable, had hired a steamer carrying 300 people to ply its way daily between Nice and Monte Carlo. And Papa went on, had also arranged for a fleet of hackney-carriage with first-class horses to bring the gamblers to what, before his advent, had been the inaccessible and almost bankrupt capital of Monaco.

The steamer would have left by now, Sabina thought, but a carriage could carry her to Monte Carlo in little over two hours if Papa's story had been correct!

She found a porter, a small man smelling strongly of garlic, to carry her round-topped trunk and black tarpaulin railway basket to the entrance of the station. There she commanded him to find her a carriage.

"For which hotel, *m'selle*?"

"For Monte Carlo."

"Monte Carlo!" He repeated the words, then smiled and wished her good fortune at the tables.

"I am not going to gamble," Sabina answered. "I am going to stay with friends. But as I have missed the train I must have a carriage to take me there."

"I will find *m'selle* one with two good horses—very fast!" the porter told her.

He was turning away when Sabina called him back.

"One moment," she said. "How much will it cost?"

The porter shrugged his shoulders, then quoted a sum which made her cry out in despair.

"Oh no, not so much as that!"

"*Ce dépend*," the porter said reassuringly. "A very smart carriage, many francs; not such good horses, not such a smart carriage, not so many francs."

Sabina told him the most she could afford and the porter put the luggage on a truck and led her to where a row of carriages waited. What followed seemed to her a nightmare of argument, expostulation and what, at times, bordered very near to abuse. But the porter had taken her under his wing. He went down the row bargaining with each coachman in turn. They spoke with an accent which Sabina found, at times, hard to understand, she guessed that on the whole it was a good thing she could not understand more.

Finally, several things transpired from the conversation. First, that there had been a fall of stone on the Lower Corniche Road, which meant that anyone travelling to Monte Carlo that night must go by the Upper Corniche—the old road, high, twisting and rough-surfaced which had been practically abandoned since the railway had been built and with it the Lower Corniche Road from Nice to Monte Carlo. Secondly, the sum Sabina wanted to pay would not entice the coachmen to take their horses on a long, tiring journey when, as they pointed out forcibly and with much gesticulation, they could, in all probability, pick up twice the amount in Nice itself.

They had reached the end of the row of carriages and Sabina was beginning to despair of ever finding a coachman who would take her, when a man with two thin, miserable looking pieces of horse-flesh and a rickety, old-fashioned hackney-carriage with the paint peeling off the doors, agreed to make the journey.

The porter heaved her trunk up on the roof, and before Sabina could look doubtfully at the horses and even more doubtfully at the interior of the carriage, she found herself inside with the door shut upon her. The porter waved his cap apparently pleased by his *pourboire* although Sabina felt it little enough for all he had done to help her, and they set off at a trot amid an ironical cheer from the other carriagemen who had all refused to carry her.

The horses soon gave up any effort to hurry and, despite the crack of the coachman's whip, moved slower and slower until Sabina longed to get up on the box and try handling the reins herself.

She could drive the pony-cart in which her mother travelled about the countryside, but then the horses which were housed in the stables at home were well-fed and properly looked after, for whatever other economies were made in the Vicarage, the Reverend Adolphus Wantage took good care that his horses did not suffer.

It must have been seven o'clock before Sabina started off from Nice, and even allowing for the slowness of the horses and the fact that they had to go by the longer, more difficult route, she reckoned that she should arrive by ten o'clock.

But her calculations were thrown out by the fact that even before they left the outskirts of Nice there was trouble with one of the wheels and the carriage was forced to pull up at a blacksmith's shop. It was nearly half an hour before they started off again.

It seemed to Sabina, sitting impatiently inside the carriage, that there was far too much conversation and too many arguments in France before anything got done. However, a new pin, or whatever was needed for the axle, was brought and finally, after an exchange of compliments, good wishes and many other pleasantries, they recommenced their journey.

By this time the sun had sunk. The beauty of the sky and the glimpse Sabina had while she was waiting—of mimosa trees in full bloom; of oranges and lemons growing profusely in every garden; and of purple bougainvillaea trailing over grey walls, made her forget everything else. It was almost unbelievable to see with her own eyes what before she had only read about in books.

'Oranges growing on the trees just like apples!'

She could hear herself saying the words to her sisters at home, and adding:

'If you want a lemon, you only have to go out and pick one.'

How she wished that she could tell them now about her journey. As the miles passed slowly she began rehearsing to herself the impersonation she would give of Miss Remington, screaming as she lay on the platform. It might be unkind to take off the poor injured lady, but it would make the girls laugh, and they always said that Sabina's imitations were so life-like that no one could mistake the person she mimicked.

She would show them, too, how the porter had bargained with the coachmen and would mimic the doctor with his black bag and shabby top hat. What fun it would be, when she got home again! Most of the fun of doing things was to be able to talk about them afterwards.

Sabina stopped suddenly. She was forgetting—indeed she had forgotten—about Arthur. In four months' time, after the beginning of June, there would be no more going home because she would be a married woman living in a

15

house of her own. Sabina clasped her hands together. She was conscious of a very strange sinking feeling in her breast. Then she shook herself determinedly.

How ridiculous she was to feel apprehensive. It was all due to Arthur that she was here at this moment in the middle of the most wonderful adventure that any girl could have. It was Arthur who had made everything possible, who had made Mamma so pleased and delighted with her, who had taken away that terrible fear that had lurked for so long in the back of her mind—that she was a failure. It was Arthur whom she was going to marry!

There was a sudden lurch of the carriage and Sabina was thrown with some violence into the corner, bruising her arm and hitting her head so that her bonnet tipped forward over her nose. She heard a shout and knew that the carriage had come to a jerky standstill.

For a moment she felt dazed then she pulled off her bonnet and struggling to her feet opened the door. It swung back and she put her head out to see that the coachman had already clambered down from the box.

"What has happened!" she asked.

He let forth a voluble flow of language from which she gathered that the blacksmith from whom they had parted so cheerily was the darkest villain in all Christendom, a crook and a fraud and an evil-intentioned idiot who was not capable of sweeping a crossing let alone attending to the wheel of a carriage.

Sabina clambered out on to the road and saw, as she had expected, the wheel tippled drunkenly in the dust, the carriage down on its axle. She looked round. It was lighter than she had expected it to be and she saw that the brightness was due to the moon, which was rising slowly up the star-strewn sky.

They were high up on the mountain-side. The sea seemed very far away. On one side of the road there was a sheer precipice; on the other there were trees and rough scrub-land fading away into the darkness towards rocks and high cliffs.

"What can we do?" Sabina asked.

The coachman shrugged his shoulders and then burst into another volley of abuse and recrimination.

Sabina looked around her. Perhaps there was a house, she thought, from which they could obtain help. She moved a little away from the ranting coachman and then, for the first time, saw there was the bright golden light of a fire a little way from them. She interrupted the coachman to point it out to him.

"Perhaps there is someone who can help us."

He looked in the direction to where she pointed with a little shrug, as if he almost resented that there could be any solution to their problem.

"It is impossible to leave the horses," he muttered surlily.

"I will go and see if I can get help," Sabina said.

She picked up her reticule, which contained her purse, from the floor of the carriage where it had fallen, and then set off, lifting her skirts and picking her way over the rough grass and stones to where the fire gleamed like a beacon.

The flames seemed to leap higher as she drew nearer to it. It was further than she thought and more than once she stumbled against a rough tuft of grass or the stones with which the ground was littered. But as she got further from the road, the way became smooth, and as the fire grew brighter she saw there were people in a circle around it—people and wagons.

She came within the light of the flames before she could see clearly, and then, as she still moved forward, she heard music—the music of a violin, of a guitar and of other instruments that she could not recognize.

It was a gay, wild tune that was being played; a tune that seemed to Sabina an invitation to dance, so that almost unconsciously the worry and anxiety she had been feeling about the accident to the carriage was forgotten. She felt her spirits lighten and her feet quicken, as though they wished to keep time to the melody that was swelling louder and louder until it seemed to Sabina that it filled her head and her whole body with its throbbing harmony.

She stepped into the light of the fire; and as she did so she saw clearly, for the first time that it was a party of gipsies who were camped there. She had not, however, expected to see so many of them or that they would be so colourful.

There was a large company of men and women sitting round the fire and on the steps of the wagons which were drawn up behind them almost in a full circle. In the space round the flames a woman was dancing. The gold embroidery on her bodice, her ear-rings and her bracelets

17

flashed in the firelight and her long dark hair swirled out behind her as she twisted and turned, her bare brown feet moving swiftly over the ground.

The rest of the company were watching her in silence. The music was not loud, it only throbbed like the pounding of one's own blood in the ears or the beating of an excited heart. There was the soft tinkle of the dancer's bracelets, the sudden crack of her fingers as she snapped them as a Spaniard might snap the castanets, and then, suddenly, as she swirled her skirts and bent her body towards the flames she caught sight of Sabina and stopped dead.

The music stopped too, and Sabina saw every head turn towards her, saw the dark suspicious faces, the flashing eyes glinting in the firelight, and the sudden movement of colours—red, orange and green—as people moved, rising, as it seemed, as if to come towards her.

It was then, for the first time, that Sabina was frightened. She had never been frightened of people before.

She had known gipsies; talked to them when they had camped on the outskirts of the village at home. The same tribe had come year after year so that the locals got to know them and even to welcome their return. True, the farmers said their chickens disappeared and the eggs were scarce that week, but on the whole the gipsies were harmless.

Brown-skinned men who would occasionally give a hand in the harvest and sloe-eyed women who came to the kitchen door selling clothes pegs, skilfully woven baskets or broom handles, and who offered to tell the fortunes of those who crossed their hands with silver.

But these people staring at her now bore little resemblance to the gipsies Sabina had known. They were well dressed for one thing. The men wore full-sleeved white shirts embroidered with braid and ribbons; the women were bejewelled with gold ornaments, their skirts brightly coloured over a profusion of vivid petticoats, their low-cut black velvet bodices laced tightly over low-necked blouses. Yet there was something wild and primitive in their expressions and in their swift panther-like movements which made their clothes seem superfluous.

The sudden cessation of the music and the fear that she was intruding on something secret and forbidden made Sabina shiver and feel that her hands were trembling.

18

And then, as she stood there, unable to speak, in a silence that seemed to grow deeper and more poignant every moment, a man rose from the further side of the fire and came towards her.

He was dressed like the gipsies in skin-tight trousers and a shirt with wide sleeves skilfully embroidered. He had a wide sash round his waist and into it was stuck a knife with a jewelled handle. He was extremely handsome and his skin was almost golden, and it drew its colour from the sun; and he had dark penetrating eyes beneath strongly marked eyebrows, and a mouth that was firm yet sensitive.

He was a gipsy and yet there was something different about him; something which made Sabina realize immediately that here was the chief, but also at the same time here was someone of whom she need not be afraid. She did not know why. There was an air of authority, of command, about him—in the very way he moved, in the proud manner in which he carried his head—and yet the moment he came towards her her trembling ceased and she was no longer speechless.

She parted her lips, but before she could say anything he had spoken first:

"*Mademoiselle* needs help, perhaps?"

She felt utterly relieved that he spoke to her in French and not in some Romany tongue that she could not understand.

"Yes, indeed, I am in need of help," she answered. "The wheel has fallen off the carriage in which I am travelling to Monte Carlo. I should be most grateful for any assistance that you or your people could give me."

"But of course. My men will see what can be done," he said. "In the meantime, *mademoiselle*, will you not come near the fire and warm yourself?"

The cold of fear had gone, but Sabina was aware that her hands were, indeed, chilly and the warmth of the day had given way to a night that had undoubtedly a touch of ice in it. It comes from mountains, she thought, and smiled as she answered:

"I should like to sit near the fire for a moment, if I may. I can only hope there is nothing very seriously wrong with the wheel."

He gave an order in a language Sabina could not understand and two or three men ran off immediately in

19

the direction of the carriage. A little shyly Sabina walked round the fire to where the gipsy indicated an improvised couch. A bearskin was flung over what Sabina guessed to be a pile of bracken and leaves. She sat down and almost instantly the gipsy handed her a glass filled with wine.

Sabina shook her head.

"No, thank you."

"Drink it, *mademoiselle*," the gipsy insisted, "it will ease away the fatigue of your journey."

Sabina felt it would be ungracious to refuse, and taking the glass, she sipped the wine, which had a smooth, delicious flavour and which instantly made her feel warmer and a little less shy.

It was only then, as she sat there, that she realized that she was bare-headed, and putting up her hand to her hair she tried to tidy the curls which she felt must appear unruly and dishevelled.

"Do not worry, it is beautiful," the gipsy said quietly.

Sabina turned to look at him, her eyes wide, hardly believing she could have heard his words aright. And then, as she saw the expression on his face, her eyes shyly dropped before his. She had never encountered such an expression in any man's eyes before. Such bold, unreserved admiration made her feel uncertain and unsure of herself.

She felt the blood rise in her cheeks and told herself that it was the grossest impertinence on the part of the gipsy, whatever his nationality, to look at her in such a way. Even without looking at him she could feel his eyes on her hair—the pale gold hair which she had inherited from her mother—and now he was scrutinizing her face.

She had small fine features, Sabina knew that, although her cheeks were often too pale and she thought her whole appearance too thin and too fragile for real prettiness. She had wished so often she was tall like her father and plump and robust like Harriet, who always seemed to be admired when she went to parties and never lacked a partner at any dances.

'Nobody notices me!' Sabina had said often enough. And yet Arthur had noticed her; and how grateful she had been to him! But Arthur had never looked at her as this gipsy was looking, his eyes narrowed a little, yet none the less seeing and taking in everything about her, so that instinctively her hand went to her breast.

Because she felt so embarrassed, she rushed into speech:

"I have to reach Monte Carlo tonight," she said. "Unfortunately I missed the last train in Nice and so I had to hire a hackney-carriage."

"But why, *mademoiselle*, did you come by the upper road?" the gipsy inquired.

"I was told in Nice that there is a fall of stone on the Lower Corniche," Sabina answered.

"Ah, that accounts for it," he exclaimed. "But this road can be dangerous at night unless you have an experienced coachman and good horses."

Sabina smiled.

"I am afraid no one could call the horses that I am travelling with good. They look under-nourished and in all probability they are ill-treated, poor things."

"Then surely it is almost cruelty to take them on such a long journey?" the gipsy suggested.

"I agree, but what else could I do?" Sabina asked.

"You could have stayed in Nice for the night and taken the train in the morning."

"But I couldn't stay alone in an hotel," Sabina exclaimed.

"And yet, are you not travelling alone now?" he commented, and she felt uneasily that she must immediately explain the apparent unconventionality of her behaviour.

"Yes, I am alone," she answered. "But it is only because my chaperon, the lady who was escorting me to Monte Carlo, had an accident. She fractured her leg stepping out of the train at Nice. That is why I am travelling so late."

"I understand. That explains it. I thought it very strange for a lady, and an English lady at that, to be alone at night. It could be dangerous."

"If you are thinking of robbers and bandits," Sabina smiled, "I am told that Monsieur Blanc has eliminated such terrors for anyone who wishes to visit Monte Carlo. Such lawlessness would not be good for the gambling, would it?"

"I do not think even Monsieur Blanc's precautions cater for beautiful young girls who travel alone after dark," the gipsy commented a little dryly.

"I am not afraid," Sabina retorted. "Nobody could rob me of anything because I don't possess very much."

"I was not thinking of money," the gipsy said.

"Then what else could robbers want of me?" Sabina asked innocently.

There was a smile at the corner of the gipsy's mouth as he said:

"*Mademoiselle* is safe with us."

Sabina hesitated a moment, then in a low voice, she faltered:

"I think ... it is only right to tell you ... that I cannot pay you for repairing my wheel. . . . I have very little money left."

"What the gipsies do they do for kindness or . . . for love."

There was a little pause before the gipsy said the last two words, and once again there was something in his eyes which made Sabina blush and look down so that her eyelashes swept her cheeks.

"Do you think the wheel will be mended by now?" she asked still not looking at him. "I just be getting on. My hostess ... the mother of my *fiancé* will be wondering what has happened to me."

"You are engaged to be married?" the gipsy asked.

Sabina nodded.

"To an English nobleman."

"He is fortunate," the gipsy said. "Does he realize, I wonder, how very fortunate he is?"

"I think I am the lucky one," Sabina replied with her usual impulsiveness, and then realized that she was talking of her intimate affairs to a stranger and to a gipsy. It was the kind of thing that Papa disapproved of in her and for which she had been rebuked often enough.

"I am sure it is time to go," she added hastily.

"You cannot go until your wheel is mended," the gipsy amended. "And you must forgive me, we are forgetting to entertain you."

He gave a snap of his fingers and instantly the music began again, the gipsy who was playing the violin moving forward into the firelight so that Sabina could see his dark lined face, the glittering gold ear-rings, the coloured sash around his waist, the wide sleeves of his shirt swinging with every movement of his body. But the dancer who had been dancing when Sabina arrived stood leaning insolently against the steps of a wagon. Her feet were still, her full red lips sulky, her eyes smouldering.

22

Sabina meant to keep silent and listen to the music, but her curiosity got the better of her.

"Are you French gipsies?" she asked.

Her host shook his head.

"That would be an insult if you were not a stranger," he replied. "We are Hungarian. A very ancient tribe known throughout the length and breadth of Europe."

"And are you their chief?"

"Their ataman or perhaps as you would say their king."

"Oh, how exciting!" Sabina exclaimed. "I have always wanted to meet a king of the gipsies. My sisters and I read a book once about the counts of Lesser Egypt—isn't that what you call yourselves?"

"Sometimes."

"We were so interested when we read about the gold goblets which you keep preserved from generation to generation, and which are used at all your ceremonies. And now I have met a king—how envious they will be!"

"You will meet many more influential titles in Monte Carlo."

"But not so romantic," Sabina replied quickly.

He laughed at that.

"Now I have told you who I am," he said, "won't you tell me your name?"

"My name is Sabina . . . Sabina Wantage."

"Sabina! It is a lovely name, and it suits you. Do you know what I thought when I saw you first, standing over there in the light of the fire?"

"No, what did you think?"

"I thought for a moment that the music Zsika was playing had conjured up one of the sprites or nymphs who lived here long before the Romans and the Phoenicians came, before civilized man discovered the lure of the Mediterranean Sea. You looked so very small and white and your hair was shining gold in the firelight, and I thought, for a moment, that your feet were bare and that you had a wreath of roses in your hand—a crown which, laid on the head of some poor mortal, would make him, for the night, immortal like yourself."

His voice was very low as he spoke and when he finished Sabina drew a deep breath.

"How lovely!" she exclaimed. "I only wish it had been true. I wish, indeed, that I had been some nymph walking

23

into your life to bring you something magical you had never known before."

"Perhaps that is just what you have done," the gipsy said very quietly—so quietly that she thought she had not understood his words.

For a moment he held her eyes with his; then, with a little effort, she looked away from him. She felt as if there was some magnetism about him, something which was compelling her, holding her; something which was drawing her against her will—and yet she was not sure why or for what reason.

"I must go," she faltered, and somehow it was a plea rather than a statement of fact.

As if he understood the sense of panic rising within her, he looked to where the three gipsies who had gone to mend the carriage had returned and stood on the edge of the crowd gathered about the fire.

"Your carriage is ready when you are."

"Oh, they have mended the wheel. Thank you so very much."

Sabina got to her feet.

"Thank you," she said again, and held out her hand.

He took it and raised it to his lips.

"Allow me to see you to your carriage."

"Please, there is no need . . ." she began, only to find her voice dying away as, still holding her hand, he led her through the crowd of gipsies to the darkness outside the light of the fire. As he helped her over the rough ground, Sabina was conscious of the strength of his hand. There was a vibration coming from him which could not be ignored. It disturbed her and yet she was not afraid of him—only of the look in his eyes.

They walked in silence until ahead of them she could see in the moonlight the carriage waiting, the tired horses with their heads bent forward, the coachman sitting upright on the box, the candle lanterns flickering feebly and ineffectually against the light in the sky.

As they reached the carriage, Sabina had a strange feeling almost of regret that she must take her hand from his. She looked up at him. It was hard to read the expression on his face, and yet she knew what it was.

"Good night," she said, "and thank you. Thank you so very much for all you have done for me."

Once again he raised her fingers to his lips. She felt the

warmth of them and a little shiver ran over her whole body.

"We shall meet again," he said.

She wanted to answer him but, somehow she could not find the words, and almost too quickly the door had closed behind her, the coachman had whipped up his horses and they were driving away.

She waved her hand and then she turned to look back at him out of the little window at the back of her seat. He was standing just where she had left him; she could see the whiteness of his shirt against the darkness of the trees.

She watched that patch of white until the horses, moving relentlessly along the twisting road, carried her out of sight.

CHAPTER TWO

IT was nearly midnight when the tired horses brought Sabina into Monte Carlo. For the last two miles she had been rehearsing to herself the apologies she must make for waking everyone up at such a late hour, but to her surprise when they drew up at the Villa Mimosa it was to find lights streaming from the open windows and servants waiting at the door to hurry down the broad stone steps to assist her to alight.

She felt tired and travel-stained when she stepped into the square, brightly lit hall, and was uncomfortably conscious of the contrast she was, with her creased dress and wind-swept curls, beside the smart liveried servants, the elegant gilt furniture and the exquisitely arranged bowls of flowers which rested on every table.

She could catch a glimpse of herself reflected and re-reflected in the many mirrors which graced the walls in beautifully carved frames; but before she had time for more than a cursory glance, the butler had opened one of the huge polished doors and announced her name.

"Miss Sabina Wantage, m'lady," he proclaimed in the stentorian tones of an English-trained servant, and Sabina hastily passed by him and entered a room where she found half a dozen people seated round the fireplace.

For a moment she had only a chaotic impression of pale walls ornamented with fabulous pictures and mirrors, of chandeliers shining iridescent from the light of a hundred candles, of china, glass and ornaments of jade and silver, of soft silk hangings, cushions and carpets, all so rich, so priceless, that instinctively Sabina realized they were each in their own way unique.

And then her attention was focused on the people to whom and to one person in particular, all this was but a background. She had wondered so much what Lady Thetford, her future mother-in-law, would be like, and yet her imagination was very far short of the reality.

A tall, thin woman rose from an armchair and came towards her. She was exquisitely graceful and moved in a manner which made one think that she glided over the surface of the carpet rather than that she had feet to propel her along. She was dressed in a gown which left her neck and shoulders bare and which made Sabina wonder what Papa would think if he saw it, and she was so covered in jewellery that she literally glittered.

There were diamonds in her ears and round her wrists, a high dog-collar of brilliants which reached nearly to her chin, and beneath it a great dazzling pendant of stones the size of shillings resting low down on her bosom. There were diamonds in her hair, too; hair which was a colour that Sabina had never seen before—riotously and flamboyantly red, and somehow as artificial as the face which lay below it.

For a moment, as Sabina looked at the woman advancing towards her, she felt that this could not be Arthur's mother. She had known that some women to whom she must never refer used cosmetics. Her brother, Harry, had whispered to her once that the women at the music halls in London had lips that were as red as pillar-boxes and eyelashes that were blackened to stick out half an inch from their eyes. But those, too, were the type of whom she must not speak.

Ladies were different. Ladies never powdered their faces—except in secret or so surreptitiously that it was hardly noticeable. Ladies had pale lips and if their eyelashes were fair or sandy it was just a regrettable accident on the part of nature and there was nothing one could do about it.

So Sabina had believed until this moment; and now, as she looked into the face of her hostess, she saw that nature could certainly be improved when one was brave enough to attempt it.

It was a beautiful face that was looking into hers—or rather a face that had once been very beautiful and was now aging a little so that the contour of the chin was blurred and there were dark lines under the mascaraed eyes and wrinkles on the white forehead that had once been so serene. Even skilfully applied rouge on the cheekbones and the red of the smiling lips could not disguise the fact that youth had departed. Yet the Dowager Lady Thetford was still lovely!

"My dear child!" she exclaimed, holding out her hands to Sabina. "I had given up expecting you. I thought there was no possibility of your getting here until tomorrow."

"I came by carriage," Sabina answered.

"By carriage!" her hostess repeated. "How exhausting! It is such a very long journey and you must be utterly fatigued. Come and sit down, but first let me introduce you to my friends."

She turned to the assembled company, who were staring at Sabina with quite undisguised curiosity. There were two women, who were as resplendently dressed as their hostess herself, and three men, none of them young, but all of them, in their way, having some air of distinction and authority about them.

Sabina hardly heard their names or their titles. Shy and embarrassed, she wondered what they thought of her appearance. She knew only too well how unmodish her dress must appear to them. She had learned that she was unfashionable on another occasion and she had no illusions now about the work of the village dressmaker who had fashioned the plain gown of pale blue tarlatan and the little pelisse that went over it.

"Come to the fire, dear child," Lady Thetford entreated her, and led the way, her train of embroidered satin rustling softly over the carpet as she moved.

"Now tell us exactly what happened," she said. "We were expecting you early this afternoon; but when the last train came in and you were not on it, I felt something terrible must have happened."

27

"Miss Remington had an accident," Sabina began.

"There, I was sure it was an accident of some sort," Lady Thetford interrupted. "Didn't I tell you, Julie, that that was what I expected?"

"You did, indeed," one of the ladies answered. "You are getting uncannily right in your predictions, Violet. I only wish you could apply your powers to the numbers on the table."

"Indeed I wish I could," Lady Thetford replied. "But go on, child. What happened to Miss Remington?"

Sabina told of the accident on Nice Station and how Miss Remington was now in the hospital.

"Poor soul, I am sorry for her having to stay there!" Lady Thetford exclaimed. "The nuns are kind enough women, but they have so little money with which to do their work and I am told that the food is pitiably inadequate."

"It depends by what standards you judge it," one of the gentlemen said. "A man I know had to go there after an accident on his yacht, and he was really quite pleasantly impressed!"

"I am sure I would rather die than go into a hospital!" one of the women exclaimed, in what Sabina thought was rather a foolish manner, and Lady Thetford, ignoring such exaggeration, begged Sabina to go on with the story.

"After I had got Miss Remington settled I went back to the station," she continued. "But the last train had gone and so there was nothing for me to do but to try and get a carriage to bring me here."

"But why should you have taken so long?" Lady Thetford asked.

"We were delayed because the wheel came off."

"There, haven't I always told you those carriages aren't safe!" exclaimed the guest who had been referred to as Julie. "I remember once, when we were travelling at a tremendous pace, a rein broke. It was just sheer inefficiency, of course, but typical of the French. I often declare I am afraid to go in their trains in case they are tied together by string."

"As usual, Julie, you are over-dramatic," Lady Thetford smiled. "How did you get the wheel mended, Sabina?"

"I was afraid, at first, I should be there all night," Sabina answered, "because the accident happened in a very isolated place. Fortunately, however, there were some gipsies. . . ."

Before she could go any further she was interrupted by a chorus of voices ejaculating, "Gipsies!"

"Yes, gipsies," Sabina went on. "They were camping near where we broke down."

"Gipsies on the Lower Corniche Road!" one of the gentlemen exclaimed. "I should have thought that was a most unlikely place for them to be."

"Oh, but we were not on the Lower Corniche Road," Sabina told him. "There had been a fall of stone, so we had to come by the Upper Road."

"You came over the Upper Corniche?" There was no mistaking the horror in the voices now.

"But my dear child," Lady Thetford said when she could make herself heard. "This is the most terrible thing I have ever imagined. The Upper Corniche Road is not safe. No one travels by it now. The road itself is sadly in need of repair, apart from the fact that there might be robbers and all sorts of horrible creatures waiting to waylay one."

"And you actually spoke to the gipsies?" one of the ladies said, in terms of awe. "Weren't you terrified?"

"Not really," Sabina answered. "They were very kind. They asked me to sit by the fire and gave me some wine. Their king sent three men to repair the wheel."

"King, indeed!" a gentleman snorted. "They are all rogues and vagabonds, the whole jack-pack of them. I won't allow them on my estate in Dorset, I can tell you that. I have warned them off for good and all. There wasn't a thing that was safe from their thieving fingers when they were allowed there in my father's time."

"Sabina, dear, they might have murdered you!" Lady Thetford exclaimed.

"It would not have been worth it," Sabina replied, with a sudden smile. "I had not got much money with me, you see."

"But you were young and alone! Well . . . well . . . they might have done anything."

Lady Thetford looked across the room at the other women. There was no mistaking the message which passed between them.

"They were courteous and very kind," Sabina insisted.

"All I can say is that you are a jolly lucky young

29

woman," another gentleman interposed. "I wouldn't trust myself within a mile of the gipsies, especially the sort you are likely to find on the Upper Corniche Road. You say one of them called himself a king! You can take it from me he was much more likely to be a horse thief."

"They did not seem poverty stricken, or indeed in need of money," Sabina said. "They helped me for nothing."

Even as she said the words she remembered the gipsy; looking down into her eyes and heard his voice saying: 'What the gipsies do they do for friendship ... or for love.'

"Well, if they are not in need of money all I can say is there is somebody in the neighbourhood who is poorer tonight. How did you manage to speak their language?"

"The gipsy who called himself their king spoke French," Sabina said. "But he told me they were Hungarians."

"Did he, indeed? Oh, well, I expect if the truth were known, they find it easy to assume any nationality and to speak any language which suits their purpose. If you want to communicate with them and they do not want to listen, they become as dumb and as deaf as an imbecile."

"But I believe some of the Hungarian gipsies are quite romantic figures," one of the ladies cried. "Indeed, when Bertha, my sister, went to stay in Hungary last year, she was thrilled with the gipsy orchestra which came every night to play in the castle where she was staying."

"I wouldn't have any gipsies in my castle, that's all I can tell you," a gentleman retorted. "Not if I didn't want everything pilfered before they left."

"I think we can be very grateful that you have come here safely, despite all the terrible dangers you have undergone," Lady Thetford said quietly to Sabina. "And now, here is Bates with some food for you, after which I expect you would like to go up to bed. I am sure you never slept a wink the last few nights. I can never close an eye when I am travelling."

"Who can in those abominable dirty trains?" Julie cried.

Sabina found the soup, chicken and fresh peaches that the butler brought to her on a tray, both delicious and satisfying. The coffee and cakes that she had had in Nice had not really been very sustaining; and while the wine she had drunk with the gipsies had made her feel warm and excited for a little while after she had drunk it, by the time she reached the villa she was well aware that her feeling of fatigue was, in most part, due to hunger rather than from physical exhaustion.

Now she devoured everything she was given, and though it was a little embarrassing to eat while Lady Thetford and her friends plied her with questions and compliments, she was too hungry to disguise the fact and only when she had finished the very last mouthful did she remember that she had always been told it was polite to leave something for 'Mister Manners'.

"Now, dear, I will take you up to your bedroom," Lady Thetford said. "I don't suppose you feel like coming out with us this evening. Besides, there are many things for you and me to do before you appear in public."

"You are going out tonight, at this hour?" Sabina asked, round eyed.

One of the gentlemen laughed.

"You won't get Violet to bed until she has had the cards in her hand."

"Are you going to the Casino?" Sabina inquired.

"Yes, of course, to the Casino," Lady Thetford said, with a little smile. And now let me show you the way upstairs."

The villa, Sabina had discovered, was built on only two floors, but it was spread out over a wide area and contained what seemed to her a formidable number of rooms, the best of them all arranged so that they looked out over the sea. There was a balcony running along the top floor and Lady Thetford opened the long french windows of Sabina's bedroom on to it.

"You can have breakfast out here in the sunshine," she said. "Ring when you wake and tell Yvonne what you require. My maid-servants are French and so, of course, is my chef; but Bates, the butler, and most of the footmen are English."

"It is so kind of you to have me," Sabina said.

"My dear, don't you think I was longing to see whom Arthur had chosen for a wife? Besides, I have known your mother ever since she was a child."

"Mamma sent you so very many messages of affection."

"I remember Evelyn when she was your age," Lady

31

Thetford said reflectively. "You are not really like her although your hair is the same colour."

"Mamma was lovely," Sabina said warmly. "Everyone always says that she was the loveliest débutante of her year."

"She was, indeed," Lady Thetford said. "And you will be lovely, too, when I show you the dresses that I have got for you from Paris."

Sabina clasped her hands together suddenly.

"From Paris," she breathed, hardly above a whisper.

"Yes, of course," Lady Thetford said. "When I wrote to your mother and said that I wanted my present to my future daughter-in-law to be a *trousseau*, not only for her wedding but for her visit here to me in Monte Carlo, your mother was wise and sensible enough to accept my offer. She posted me your measurements and I sent them at once to a famous *couturier* in Paris, in fact to the fashionable Mr. Worth, who, as you know, dresses the Empress Eugénie."

"Oh, how kind," Sabina exclaimed. "How very, very kind."

"You shall see all the things tomorrow," Lady Thetford promised her. "And now, when Yvonne has finished unpacking for you, get into bed and sleep well. I will send my maid to call you when I am awake and then we must talk together and make plans. Good night, my child."

Lady Thetford bent and kissed Sabina's cheek. There was a sweet fragrance of an exotic perfume, the glitter of her diamonds, the rustle of silk, and then she moved with an almost swan-like elegance from the room.

Sabina sat down on the bed and put her hands up to her eyes. She could hardly believe it. She was here—here in Monte Carlo—and she was to have new clothes, fashionable clothes, clothes from Paris!

She had hardly believed it was true when her mother had told her that Lady Thetford had written suggesting such an idea. Mamma had called her into the morning-room after breakfast and told her to shut the door behind her. She was holding the letter in her hand and for a moment Sabina was afraid that it was something unpleasant that Mamma had to impart to her.

"I have had a letter from Lady Thetford, Sabina," Lady Evelyn began. "Arthur has told her of your engagement and of course, as you know, there can be no formal announcement until you have met his mother and obtained her consent."

"Arthur was not sure that such permission was necessary," Sabina said.

"I cannot believe that that was really Arthur's idea," Lady Evelyn replied firmly. "His mother is a very old friend of mine. I have known her since I was a child, and Papa and I would not feel at all happy if you were not introduced to and approved of by Arthur's nearest relative."

"I would like to meet her, of course," Sabina said.

"I feel sure you would, dear," Lady Evelyn approved.

It was difficult for Sabina to explain, but somehow she had had the impression that Arthur was not at all anxious for her to meet his mother. She could not think why and he had not put it into so many words, but she had been sure there had been a kind of reluctance on his part, not only to talk about his mother but even to write and obtain her consent to his marriage.

It was Mamma who had been so insistent.

"Your father and mother used to come and stay at my home for the hunt balls," she said to Lord Thetford. "I remember when I was quite small peeping over the banisters and watching your mother walk downstairs. She looked like a queen, and when I grew older I used to long for her to come and stay so that I could watch her and think her the most beautiful person I had ever seen."

"I am sure my mother will be most gratified that you have remembered her," Arthur said in his precise, rather cold voice.

"I am delighted, Sabina," Lady Evelyn went on now, "that Lady Thetford has asked you to stay. She never comes to England, and instead she has invited you to go to her at Monte Carlo where she has a villa."

"Monte Carlo! Oh, Mamma!" Sabina exclaimed.

"We must hope that Papa won't be too shocked at the idea," Lady Evelyn said. "There is something else that she suggests, Sabina, which I think it would be wisest not to mention to him. Gentlemen don't understand how much clothes mean to a woman. Papa is very proud, so I think we had best keep it a secret between ourselves, you and me, but Lady Thetford has offered to give you your clothes, both for your visit to Monte Carlo and for your *trousseau*."

33

"Oh, Mamma, how wonderful! You know . . ." Sabina hesitated and Lady Evelyn continued:

"Yes, Sabina, I do know! There has never been enough money, as you are well aware, for such frivolities as fashionable costumes. I know that. I made a mistake in sending you to London without ensuring that you were correctly and properly dressed. But really, there is so much to pay for and things seem to get more expensive year by year."

Lady Evelyn wrinkled her brow and impulsively Sabina put out her arms.

"Dear Mamma, you are so sweet to us. We do not really worry about what we look like—at least not much."

"I know, dear, but clothes do make a difference. We can't deny that. Men always think that women are vain, but clothes not only cover our bodies, they do things to our minds. They give us courage and self-confidence; they even make us feel intelligent and charming and perhaps in some ways better spiritually than we should be if we were ill-dressed."

"Oh, Mamma, you do understand," Sabina exclaimed. "It was so . . . so awful in London!"

"Yes, yes, I know," Lady Evelyn answered. "But don't let us talk about it. After all, everything has come right now, hasn't it, darling?"

"Yes, indeed it has," Sabina replied.

She was thinking of going to Monte Carlo and her new clothes, as she spoke, but Lady Evelyn had been thinking of Arthur.

It was Arthur who was really responsible for all this, Sabina thought as she got into bed and laid her head down on the soft pillow and felt the downy comfort of the mattress, soft as a cloud, beneath her.

But somehow her thoughts would not stay focused on Arthur. Once again she saw the tall, dark-haired gipsy king looking towards her, the firelight on his face. Thieves and robbers she was told they were, and yet she could not believe it. And then, as she thought of it, she suddenly sat up in bed.

The moonlight was coming through the open windows from which she had drawn back the curtains. Sabina did not wait to light a candle but ran across the room to the dressing table. Her hands began searching feverishly—

34

moving her hairbrush, her comb, little trinket trays, the hair-tidy and heart-shaped pin cushion. After a second or so she opened the drawers. There were her things lying tidily as the maid had unpacked them. She stared at them and shut the drawer again abruptly.

It must be there, it must! If only she could remember taking it off. Running now with her bare feet across the room she pulled open the door of the wardrobe. Her blue dress was hanging there, but there was no sign of the brooch where she knew it had been pinned, above the top button on her bodice.

Sabina shut the door of the wardrobe and walked across the room to the window. The glory of the moonlight lay over the palm trees, the luxuriant garden, the palace with its towering roofs and the shimmering sea—but she saw none of them. She was remembering when she had last put her fingers to feel the little diamond brooch safe at the base of her neck. In the shape of a star it had belonged to her mother, and Lady Evelyn had given it to her the morning before she left for Monte Carlo.

"I would like to think you were wearing something of mine, darling," she said. "And I know you will take care of it. My father gave it to me when I was twenty-one. I have treasured it ever since."

"But it is your very best brooch, Mamma," Sabina protested.

"I had bigger and grander ones once," Lady Evelyn smiled. "They have all been sold to pay for governesses or Harry's schooling, and one went to repair the roof. It was better to sleep dry in our beds than for me to have diamonds to wear on Sundays and when we go out to dinner."

"Oh, Mamma! And this is the only one you have left!"

"The only one," Lady Evelyn said. "So bring it back safely to me. I am fond of my little star; I always feel that it brings me luck and I want it to bring you luck, too."

"I am so lucky already."

"You will find there is always room for a little more," Lady Evelyn laughed, and pinned the brooch to Sabina's travelling frock.

Harriet, Melloney, Angelina and Clare were waiting

35

when she came into the hall ready dressed for the journey.

"You look wonderful, Sabina," Harriet whispered as she kissed her.

Miss Remington was there too, fussing about the luggage and looking incessantly at the tickets as if she were afraid they would vanish into thin air if she took her eyes off them for one moment.

Sabina had felt tearful for a moment as she said goodbye, but once they had started down the road which led to the station she had put her fingers up to her brooch fancying that everyone she met must look at her and envy her for being in possession of such fine jewels.

But now it was gone! It had been there when she was at Nice because she had caught a glimpse of it sparkling in a mirror on the wall of the little *pâtisserie* where she had her coffee and cakes. She remembered putting up her fingers to test the clasp to see that it was really firm.

Thieves and robbers! Could it be really true that having said they would mend her wheel for friendship they had taken her diamond brooch in payment? It was hurtful and somehow very bitter to think that this was the truth.

"You are beautiful," the gipsy kind had said, and he had not been pretending the admiration in his eyes—no man could have pretended as well as that. And yet he had taken her brooch! Perhaps as they had walked hand in hand across the rough ground towards the carriage; perhaps as he handed her in and raised her fingers to his lips. She had been so ready to trust him, so gullible, so stupid!

Sabina turned away suddenly from the window. She felt as if some magic, some wonder that had been attendant on her ever since she left home, had vanished. She felt suddenly depressed and unhappy. It was because she had lost her mother's brooch, she thought, and because sooner or later she would have to tell her that the little star she had been so fond of was gone. But in her heart of hearts she knew it was more than that. It was the disillusionment which hurt her, unaccountably, in a manner that she dare not even explain to herself.

Sabina buried her face in the pillow. It must, of course, have been because she was tired, but there were tears in her eyes and rolling down her cheeks on her first night in Monte Carlo. . . .

Youth, however, has an elasticity which makes it difficult to remember, in the morning, the sadness of the night before. Sabina awoke to find the sun pouring into her room, turning everything—the walls, the furniture, the carpet—into a blaze of gold. It blinded her eyes.

She sprang out of bed and ran to the window and then, as she felt the warmth of the sunlight touch her cheeks and her body through the fine lawn of her nightgown, she wanted to cry aloud at the wonder of it.

There was colour everywhere—colour such as she had never believed existed outside a box of paints. The vivid blue of the sky; the deeper tones of the sea; the green of trees; the golden and yellow fruit; the flowers—purple and pink, heliotrope and petunia—filling the beds below in the garden, climbing luxuriantly over the walls and up the side of the house. It was like a dream of a rainbow-splashed earth. Sabina hardly knew whether to laugh or cry at the loveliness of it.

She glanced at her watch and found it was eight o'clock; a late hour for her to be wakened, for she always rose at seven at home and usually managed to have a ride before breakfast. Now she hesitated shyly before ringing the bell in her room and summoning the maid, as Lady Thetford had told her to do.

One thing that Sabina always found difficult was to force herself to give commands to servants. They had so few of them at the vicarage—only old Nanny, who had been with them since Harry, Lady Evelyn's first child, had been born and had looked after all the others and who now did the cooking; and Gladys, the girl whom Lady Evelyn painstakingly instructed in her tasks.

There had been a series of Gladys's ever since Sabina could remember.

"It is no use, Adolphus," Lady Evelyn would say, when her husband remonstrated at their departure. "As soon as they are trained, they can get more money, and they know it. Unless we can afford to give them bigger wages they are bound to leave to better themselves."

"It seems to me unfair, after all you have taught them," the Reverend Adolphus Wantage protested once.

"My dear, it would be unfair to keep them. The pittance we can give them as a weekly wage can hardly keep them in hairpins!"

Lady Evelyn had spoken lightly and Sabina, who had been present at this conversation, had expected her father to laugh. Instead he had risen from the breakfast table and walked round to his wife's side. He put his hand under her chin and tilted her face up to him.

"I have told you before, you ought never to have married a penniless parson," he said.

There had been a note in her father's voice that Sabina had never heard before, and she waited almost breathlessly for her mother's reply.

"Do you think I regret it?" Lady Evelyn had asked softly. "Darling, I am the richest woman in all the world."

Her father bent his head at that and kissed Mamma's forehead, but Sabina had seen his face as he had left the room and she had noticed the hurt in his eyes and the tight lines of his mouth.

It was so easy to hurt Papa. He was hurt if they were naughty or people complained about them, if Mamma hadn't got enough money for the tradespeople, or if the groom who looked after the horses gave notice because he had got too much to do.

"Papa may be a saint," Harriet had said once, "but saints ought really to live in heaven and not mess things up because they are on earth."

Harriet had been in a rage when she said it because of something Papa would not let her do. But Sabina had often thought afterwards there was a lot of truth in what she said. Being a saint did make things uncomfortable, just because Papa didn't understand the difficulties of earthly existence.

How lovely, Sabina thought now, to have enough money to afford plenty of servants! Dozens of them ready to run upstairs with a beautifully cooked breakfast, ready to take away and press the dress one had worn yesterday, ready to stand attentively in the background until it was necessary to arrange one's hair, to bring forward the right shoes, handkerchief, belt or a collar—or whatever was required.

It was over an hour later and Sabina had bathed, dressed, had her breakfast and explored the garden before Lady Thetford sent for her. She felt excited by the summons and followed the lady's maid, with her rustling silk dress and small white silk apron, into the big bedroom where Lady Thetford still lay in bed.

Sabina stood open-mouthed at the magnificence of the

room, with its great arched ceiling, the silver bed shaped like a vast sea-shell, its mother-of-pearl ornaments, its silver dressing-table mirror with entwined cupids holding high a crown, and its curtains and carpets of soft forget-me-not blue which Sabina realized matched her hostess's eyes.

"You slept well, child?" Lady Thetford inquired.

There were soft muslin curtains drawn to diffuse the light and make the room glow rather than shine, in contrast with the brilliance outside. But even so, the light revealed the crow's-feet round Lady Thetford's eyes, the raddled neck, the soft, drooping corners of her mouth and the slightly yellowing texture of her skin now that she was unrouged and unpowdered.

Before Sabina could reply, she added:

"How young you look! Your skin is very white, you must be careful not to get it sunburned."

"I never seem to burn," Sabina told her. "Harriet freckles most dreadfully. Mamma is always speaking to her about spoiling her complexion before she comes out, but my skin has always remained white—too white I am afraid."

"Yes, a touch of rouge would improve you a great deal," Lady Thetford said critically. Sabina looked uncomfortable.

"I am afraid Papa. . . ."

Lady Thetford laughed.

"I know exactly what Papa would say," she exclaimed. "Don't look so shocked, child. Marie shall put it on so skillfully that not even the most critical or censorious person could guess it was not natural. She won't make you look painted—as I do, I promise you that."

Sabina blushed as though she herself had said something uncomplimentary, but Lady Thetford laughed again.

"I saw your face last night when you first looked at me," she said. "I had forgotten that in England one still thinks it is ladylike to appear *au naturel*. In Paris it is very different, and here too. I have lived abroad so long that I have almost forgotten the conventions and the pruderies of English society."

"Do you like living abroad?" Sabina asked.

"Most of the time I am as happy as I could be anywhere," Lady Thetford replied. "But at others I am

39

homesick. Yes, homesick for England and the grey skies and the rattle of traffic down Park Lane and my friends sitting in the park gossiping maliciously about each other!"

"You never go back?" Sabina asked.

"No, I never go back," Lady Thetford answered.

There was so much finality in her tone that Sabina was silent. After a moment her hostess said:

"But let us talk about you. Marie!" She raised her voice and clapped her hands. "Marie, Marie, where are you?"

The dark-haired Frenchwoman who had brought Sabina to Lady Thetford's bedroom came hurrying through one of the doors.

"Oui, madame."

"The clothes, Marie. The clothes for *mademoiselle*. Let us see if they fit her. If they don't, you are going to be very busy."

Marie went from the room and came back a few seconds later with her arms full of clothes. She set them down on a satin-covered sofa and Sabina stood staring. Lady Thetford said briskly:

"Now, slip off that perfectly hideous dress, in which I see indisputably the fell hand of the village seamstress, and put on those clothes which have been made by an *artiste*, a master of his craft."

"Which shall we try first, *madame*?" Marie asked.

"The gown for tonight, Marie. Now, let me think. The turquoise chiffon with the bands of lace round the skirt. I want *mademoiselle* to make an impression; I want people to look at her. The turquoise chiffon is, in its own way, sensational."

"Are we going somewhere special tonight?" Sabina inquired.

"But, of course. A party is being given for you by my good friend the Comtesse de Beaufleur. We will dine at her villa and afterwards we will go to the Casino."

"Oh, how wonderful!" Sabina breathed, her eyes shining like lighted candles.

"Not unless the dress fits you," Lady Thetford said. "A first impression is of the utmost importance. Put it on now."

Sabina could hardly breathe for fear the dress which Marie slipped over her head should prove too big or too small or not to Lady Thetford's taste. But it fitted exact-

40

ly, framing her figure, making her waist incredibly small and giving her soft curves and beautiful lines where she had never suspected she had them.

Sabina stared at herself in the long mirror which stood beside Lady Thetford's dressing-table, and then she turned with a catch in her voice towards the woman who watched her from the bed.

"It ... it is perfect," she stammered. "But how can I thank you? I have always longed for a dress like this, something that really fitted me, something which looked as if it came out of a fairy tale. Oh, what can I say?"

"Don't thank me," Lady Thetford said. "I have enjoyed shopping for you as I have seldom enjoyed shopping for myself. Do you think that Arthur will like it?"

Only for a moment Sabina hesitated before she replied:

"But, of course! I am sure he will. How could he help it?"

"Are you really sure?" Lady Thetford asked. "Oh, well, I must take your word for it. I feel convinced that you know Arthur's taste better than I do."

Sabina stared at herself in the glass. She felt as if a little shadow passed across the glory of the sun. Would Arthur think that she looked too dressed up? That the gown was too elegant? Too expensive? And then resolutely she brushed the thought away. He would want her to look smart and beautiful, of course he would.

"When does Arthur arrive?" she asked.

"The day after tomorrow," I believe," Lady Thetford said. "You know that he is coming down in the royal train with the Prince and Princess of Wales?"

"Yes, he wrote to me just before I left to say he expected to travel with them."

"My husband was a Lord-in-Waiting to Her Majesty for many years," Lady Thetford said. "Service to royalty is in Arthur's blood and he never lets one forget it."

There was something in the tone of Lady Thetford's voice that surprised Sabina; then she thought she must have been mistaken.

"You must be very proud of your son," she said.

"Proud?" There was laughter in Lady Thetford's voice as she asked the question, and she looked at Sabina and added quietly:

"Yes, of course Arthur's done extremely well for himself. He is a very able and intelligent young man."

41

Sabina looked at herself in the mirror and then turned away.

"I am so afraid of failing him," she said, and her voice trembled.

CHAPTER THREE

SABINA stood on the balcony outside her bedroom window and looked up at the sky. It was after three o'clock in the morning and yet she did not feel tired. The excitement and thrill of the day and all she had done that evening made her feel tinglingly alive, as if she wanted to dance rather than go to sleep.

Never in all her life had she expected Monte Carlo to be so wonderful as it had proved to be. It was not only the beauty of it all—the white villas surrounded by their colourful gardens or the orange and lemon groves interspersed with every kind of exotic vegetation; it was not the music and the chatter of thousands of well-bred voices; or the Casino, with its silver-grey silk walls, dazzling chandeliers, gilt chairs and green tables. It was more than all this.

It was the welcome that she herself had received in this enchanting fairyland, where all the nobility of Europe came to play.

When she had appeared that evening at Lady Thetford's side, wearing the turquoise gown, her hair arranged by the skilful fingers of Marie, she had had what, even in her greatest modesty she could not deny, was an almost overwhelming success.

Lady Thetford had taken her to a party at which every man, young and old, had paid her court, and the women, all influential and distinguished, had smiled kindly upon her and said the most commendatory and flattering things about her to her hostess.

Sabina had felt it go to her head like wine. She had been afraid before they left the Villa Mimosa that evening, afraid that even her fine dress and beautifully arranged hair were not enough to carry her through a

42

social evening, when she knew Lady Thetford must inevitably judge her by the standard of whether or not she was good enough to be Arthur's bride.

She had been trembling as Marie finished dressing her.

"You look as if you are ready to swoon, child," Lady Thetford said, coming into the room, and Sabina had jumped guiltily, thinking there was an accusation in the older woman's voice.

"I am afraid I am always very pale," she said, in a voice that quivered.

"We are going to remedy that," Lady Thetford smiled. "The rouge, Marie, and the powder that came from Paris last week. It is so fine that it might be made of silk."

"But what would Papa say?" Sabina cried. "Suppose someone should tell him!"

Lady Thetford laughed.

"Shall I tell you a secret?" she asked. "Once, when your mother was just seventeen, I went into her room before a party and found her rubbing geranium leaves on her cheeks."

"You found Mamma doing that?" Sabina said incredulously.

"But, of course! I had done the same myself in my own girlhood, but as I was ten years older than your mother I had learned greater wisdom. I lent her a little of my rouge and not her father, her mother or any of the people that night had the slightest idea why Evelyn, who had always seemed so pale and fragile looking, should have such a lovely colour."

"I cannot believe it of Mamma," Sabina exclaimed.

"I will tell you another secret. She borrowed my rouge on many occasions after that, especially after she had fallen in love with your father."

"Papa would have been horrified if he had known."

"Ignorance keeps many a man's heart from grieving unnecessarily," Lady Thetford said dryly. "Now, let Marie see what she can do to your face, and I promise you no one will be able to tell."

The colour certainly did look natural, Sabina thought as she looked at herself a little later. It was the same face she saw reflected, yet the faint blush on her cheeks and on her lips and the invisible film of powder over her small nose made all the difference to the appearance.

"Now you look lovely," Lady Thetford approved.

43

"When you have grown as old as I am, you will realize that though people say what a pity it is to gild the lily, there is never a lily that isn't improved by a little gilding."

Sabina laughed before she said:

"Thank you for being so kind to me. And for my dress. I only hope that I shall not do anything foolish or wrong at this party. I have not been to very many, you know."

"But surely you had a season in London?" Lady Thetford questioned. "I vaguely remember reading about your being presented."

"Yes, I went to stay with Mamma's sister in Onslow Square," Sabina answered. A shadow passed over her face as she spoke, and Lady Thetford saw it and forebore to question her further.

"Come along child," she said, picking up her long cape of priceless chinchilla.

Marie brought a cloak for Sabina. Of pale blue velvet, it was lined with the softest white swansdown and she gave a little exclamation of delight as she snuggled into it.

"It is the very latest fashion from Paris," Lady Thetford explained.

"How kind you are to me, how very, very kind!" Sabina said a little breathlessly.

Lady Thetford looked down at the excited little face turned up to hers.

"I used to long to have a daughter," she answered. "And now, perhaps, I have one."

Sabina felt the quick tears come into her eyes. There was a sadness and a loneliness in Lady Thetford's voice which moved her even while she did not understand it. Impulsively she put out her hands towards the older woman, but Lady Thetford had already turned towards the door, the diamonds shining in her dyed hair and the frills of her skirt frothing out behind her as she descended the stairs.

Sabina had wanted to thank her hostess even more eloquently when they returned home that night, but somehow it was so difficult to find words to say all she felt and thought, and besides, Lady Thetford herself could talk of nothing but how she had won at roulette that evening.

"I knew my system must come right some time," she said, not once but several times. "I have lost for a week, but tonight everything I did was right."

44

"It was exciting to see the numbers you backed come up time after time," Sabina told her.

"Exciting!" Lady Thetford repeated with a little laugh. "There is no thrill like it in the whole world; but you won't believe that now. You will have to wait until you come to my age before you know that I am speaking the truth."

Her eyes were glittering as she spoke, and Sabina, looking at her, felt that she was somehow a very different person from what she had been earlier in the evening. There was a feverish excitement about her, a tension, a kind of almost fanatical concentration that had made her, as she sat at the tables, seem utterly oblivious of everything but the rolling of the little ball in the roulette wheel.

She had not wanted to come away—in fact Sabina had been surprised when, with the money stacked high in front of her, a liveried attendant had come up and bent his powdered head to whisper in her ear. Sabina had been standing near enough to hear what he said:

"It is three o'clock, *madame*."

For a moment Lady Thetford had not moved, but had sat with her eyes on the table, seemingly oblivious of the man's words. And then, almost without moving her lips, she had said:

"You must be mistaken. It cannot be as late as that."

"Positively three o'clock, *madame*," the man said inexorably.

With an obvious reluctance Lady Thetford rose. She picked up her money almost mechanically, still watching the roll of the wheel, and then at last, as though some light was extinguished in her face, she turned her back on the table.

"We must go home, Sabina."

They had moved through the brilliantly lit rooms, Lady Thetford smiling almost mechanically at the women who bade her good night, at the men who bowed courteously as she passed. Then, as they reached the carriage, she began to talk of her play that evening and the animation came back to her.

"I was sure my system was not at fault. I have made over £2,000 tonight."

"As much as all that?" Sabina asked in awe.

"I am still down on the month," Lady Thetford replied.

"I had begun to feel. . . . But no, the system must be right, and tomorrow I shall win again."

"Do you go every night?" Sabina asked.

"But, of course! Why else would one be in Monte Carlo?" Lady Thetford inquired impatiently.

Sabina was silent for a moment, then, because she was still curious, she dared to ask:

"Do you always come away at three o'clock?"

Lady Thetford gave a little sigh.

"Always. I instruct them to tell me when the hour is reached. But tonight it was difficult to come away, to force myself to stop playing. If I could have stayed another hour, I might have doubled my winnings—but I gave my promise."

There was a long silence and then, when Sabina felt that she had almost forgotten her presence, Lady Thetford finished:

"It was to someone who cared for me, who always knew what was best for me, someone whom I loved very much."

There was no time to say more before they arrived at the villa. The horses drew up with a flourish and the servants, who to Sabina's surprise were still waiting up, ran down the steps to open the carriage door.

"We are going straight up to bed, Bates," Lady Thetford said to the butler.

"Very good, m'lady. You will not be requiring anything?"

"No, nothing except some sleep."

"I hope your ladyship had a pleasant evening."

"Very pleasant, Bates. I won tonight."

"That is good, your ladyship."

Lady Thetford moved slowly up the stairs.

"Come along, Sabina," she said. "You need your beauty sleep, as I do. Besides, I want tomorrow to come quickly so that I can go back to the tables and continue my run of luck."

She bent to kiss Sabina at the door of the bedroom, then passed down the passage slowly and yet with a grace which gave every movement, every gesture, an elegance which was somehow indescribable.

Sabina went into her own room. The candles were lit on the dressing-table and by the bed, for she had learned that Lady Thetford had refused to have the new and much-vaunted gas lighting in any of the best rooms of the villa.

"It is garish and unbecoming," she said. "All women look their best by candlelight."

But the candles were insignificant in comparison with the silver moonlight coming through the window. Sabina drew aside the curtains and went out on to the balcony. How lovely the garden looked with its mysterious shadows and the tall palm trees silhouetted against the sky! Lower down the hill she could see the lights of the Casino and far out to sea there were the green and red lights of a ship coming in towards the harbour.

It was all very beautiful and at the same time mysterious. A world that she did not yet know; a world so very different from the quiet, humdrum existence she had lived at home. She felt, too, as though she was on the threshold of discovering something even more wonderful than just that which lay about her. There was excitement in the air; excitement in the quick beating of her heart; in everything she felt.

There was a sweet fragrance rising from the garden—from the flowers, from the orange trees. It was exotic and in its very perfume exciting.

And then, as Sabina stood there, she was suddenly aware of a stange, wild melody which seemed to come from the shadows beneath the trees. It was so soft that one moment she was not aware of it and the next moment it had crept into her thoughts, so that it was there for a long time before she was really consciously aware of it.

And then, as it continued, insidious, haunting and somehow strangely compelling, she suddenly became aware that she knew the tune, that she had heard it before and that it was Tzigany music. She leant over the balcony, looking into the shadows of the garden. The music came nearer and then suddenly the gipsy king stepped into the moonlight, his white shirt gleaming against the darkness, the violin under his chin.

He brought the tune to a close with a sudden crescendo of rippling notes, then put down his bow and threw back his head to look up at Sabina.

"I salute you, *mademoiselle*."

His voice was quiet, hardly above a whisper, yet she could hear every word.

47

"How did you know I was here?"

It was the first question that came to her mind and she saw him smile in response.

"You told me."

"Oh, but . . ." she started to expostulate, but he put his finger to his lips.

"Come down," he said. "I want to see you."

"How can I? Everybody has gone to bed. Besides. . . ."

"I have something to give you," he insisted.

"Something to give me?" Sabina questioned.

He put his hand in his pocket and then held out something so that she could see it flashing in the light of the moon.

"My brooch!"

The exclamation was one of sheer joy, and even as she said the words, she knew not only relief that her mother's treasured possession was returned to her but also something else—an unquenchable feeling of gladness that he had not stolen it after all. She had never believed that gipsies were like that. Or had she? She had a wild impulse to make amends, to apologize, to make up to him for some sin he did not even know she had committed.

She looked around her and then remembered that at the far end of the balcony there was a small, rather steep wooden staircase which led down to the garden. She had noticed it that morning when she had breakfasted outside in the sunshine and she had realized at the same time that there was no one sleeping in the room beyond hers.

Hastily she ran towards the staircase and started slowly, with her hand on the balustrade, to climb down the steps. It was dark because, owing to the trees, the moonlight did not reach this side of the house, and as she reached carefully with her foot for the bottom step she felt his hand come out to guide her down.

"Be careful," he said, and drew her away from the staircase and through the gateway in a hedge of flowering fuchsia into a part of the garden where she had never been before. There was a narrow path running between shrubs and flowers to where, against a blossom-covered wall, there was a pagoda of honeysuckle and roses.

Sabina saw where the gipsy king was leading her, but she said nothing until they reached the pagoda. At their feet was a small lily-pond in the centre of which a fountain played. Here he stopped and holding out her brooch offered it to her on the palm of his hand.

"Where did you find it?" Sabina asked.

"You must have dropped it as you stepped from the coach," he answered. "One of my men discovered it in the dust this morning."

"And you knew it was mine?"

"I was sure of it."

"I am so very glad to have it back," Sabina said, taking it from his hand.

"When did you discover that you had lost it?" he inquired.

"Last night," Sabina answered. "I had gone to bed and I suddenly remembered that I had not taken it off when I undressed."

"And what did you think?" he asked.

She felt the colour come into her face.

"What do you mean?"

"Did you think then that the gipsies had stolen it from you?"

The moonlight revealed the colour flooding her cheeks; her eyes flickered and fell before his.

"That is what I expected you to think," he said quietly. "That is why I brought it back myself. But there was another reason too."

"What was that?" Sabina inquired.

"I wanted to see you again. I wanted to make sure you were as lovely as I remembered you to be."

She stood holding the little diamond star in her hand, looking down at it, ashamed of the blush that had betrayed her into revealing how she had doubted his integrity; ashamed, too, of the sudden delight she felt in knowing that he still admired her, still thought her beautiful.

"And . . . now . . . are you . . . disappointed?"

She could not check the question. It came, almost in a whisper, from between her lips.

"Look at me!"

It was a command given in the voice of one who was accustomed to giving orders, and almost instinctively she obeyed him. She looked into his face. She had forgotten how tall he was, how handsome, in a strange, foreign manner to which she was unaccustomed. The moonlight was on both their faces and she could see again in his eyes the admiration that had been so unmistakable in the firelight.

"Don't you know," he asked in a low voice, "that you are the loveliest person that I have ever seen in my life? After you had gone the other night I felt that you could not be real, that you must be, as I thought at the time, a nymph or a sprite, visiting this mundane, mortal world, then disappearing again into some secret heaven where I could not follow. But now I see I was mistaken. You are real—and lovelier by far because of it."

"You should not say such things to me," Sabina said quickly. "I think perhaps they do not sound so wrong because you are speaking in French, but even so I should not listen."

"Shall I say them in your own language then?" the gipsy asked in English.

Sabina gave a little cry of astonishment.

"You speak English!"

"A little. Not as well as you speak French."

"It is not true. You speak exceedingly well."

"Thank you. Now it is you who pay me compliments."

Sabina laughed.

"Perhaps that makes it better. But I have not yet thanked you for bringing back my brooch."

"I have already told you I was glad of the excuse. Not that I really needed one. I should have come to see you anyway."

Sabina glanced hastily over her shoulder. Hidden by the trees and the fuchsia hedge, the villa was almost out of sight. The gipsy king watched her.

"You are ashamed to be seen speaking to me?"

"No, of course not!" Sabina's answer was quick and indignant. "Not ashamed; how could I be? It is just that my hostess might think it strange, and perhaps wrong, of me to come out into the garden tonight. You know as well as I do that if I was seen speaking to a man ... any man, it would be ... well ... misunderstood."

"Do you always do the correct thing?"

Sabina dimpled at him.

"I am afraid not. Sometimes Papa is very angry with me. Like the time when Harriet, my sister, and I went to the circus in the next village. Someone saw us and told Papa, and he was very incensed indeed, and hurt too, that we should have done such a thing without asking his permission."

The gipsy king smiled.

"At the circus you saw gipsies?"

"Oh yes, there were gipsies at the circus, and we have seen lots of gipsies at home—but they are not a bit like you."

"In what way are they different?"

"Well, English gipsies are ragged and poor and. . . ."

"And dirty?"

"Er—yes. But please do not think I am comparing them in any way. You are different, so very different."

"So, once again you are paying me compliments. It is charming of you, because I feel sure that, if you told the people here that gipsies helped you the other night, they had some very unkind things to say about my race."

Sabina looked embarrassed.

"They were mostly English people, so they were judging you by the wrong standards."

"That is generous, but you will find the French, too, have no affection for the Bohemians—as they call us. In Hungary it is different. We are accepted. Gipsies have a special place in my country. They can, if they wish, enter any profession and rise to any heights."

"And their music is very beautiful, I am told," Sabina said. "But how silly of me—I know it is! I heard your people playing last night—and now tonight I have heard you!"

"Thank you again," he said. "If you knew what it means to me to hear someone say those kind things, when so often we are regaled with abuse and every form of vice and wickedness is laid at our doors."

"Perhaps it is because people are afraid of you," Sabina suggested.

"Afraid?" he questioned.

"Yes. You seem free and happy. You go where you like and are not cluttered up with possessions and restrictions. Besides this, they think you have magical powers."

He smiled.

"Would you like me to read your fortune?"

"No," Sabina said quickly. "I do not want to know the future. The present is so . . . wonderful."

"You are enjoying Monte Carlo?"

51

"It is marvellous! I can't begin to tell you how exciting everything has been today."

"You look happy," he said quietly.

"But I am," Sabina said. "Who wouldn't be happy in this beautiful place? And this evening everyone was so kind to me. I forgot to be shy, forgot to worry in case I was doing the wrong thing." She gave a little sigh. "I expect my dress had something to do with it, if the truth be known."

"Your dress?" the gipsy inquired.

Sabina nodded.

"You see, I have never had a wonderful dress like this before. Oh, you would not understand, but I know that it is not me of whom people are making a fuss, to whom they pay compliments, but . . . my dress."

"I think perhaps I do not understand as clearly as I might," the gipsy said. "Will you not explain?"

Sabina made a little gesture with her hands.

"I should not be talking about myself. It cannot possibly be of any interest to you."

"On the contrary, it interests me very much. You must explain or I shall be consumed with curiosity."

"Well, it was like this," Sabina began. "When I went to London, soon after I was seventeen, I stayed with my aunt and she presented me at Court and took me to several balls, and I thought everything was going to be wonderful, just like it has been tonight, but . . . it wasn't."

Sabina sighed—a wistful, hopeless little sound.

"Mamma had taken a lot of trouble over my clothes. We could not afford grand ones. But the seamstress in the village, who always makes our things, came to us every day for three weeks and the gowns she made for me looked very fashionable and smart when we tried them on at home. But when I got to London, I realized how hopelessly dowdy they were. The girls laughed about me amongst themselves, and the men . . . well . . . they did not ask me to dance."

Sabina had no idea, as she spoke, of the pain in her voice or how revealing the words were of the inner hurt she had suffered at that time, and she did not say how much deeper the hurt had been than just at having no partners at the dances.

There had been that moment just before she left by

52

coach for London when her mother had drawn her aside and said:

"Try and have a good time, Sabina darling. I know Aunt Edith is old-fashioned and difficult at times, but it is so kind of her to have you stay with her for the season and to offer to present you at Court. I only wish I could do it myself, but, darling, we just haven't got the money, and it means everything for you to have the opportunity now—before the others grow up."

Mother and daughter's eyes had met, and Sabina knew all too well what was left unspoken. Four other daughters to follow her; four other girls all wanting clothes and the chance to go to London; five girls in all for whom to find husbands—and this was her big opportunity.

If only one person, one man, however unacceptable, however ineligible, had fallen in love with her, Sabina thought afterwards, it would have alleviated that sense of failure, of being a hopeless misfit in the world of fashion.

She was so deep in her thoughts that the gipsy's voice surprised her.

"How old were you?" he asked.

"When I went to London?" Sabina inquired. "I was just seventeen."

"Have you ever seen a foal?" he asked.

She was surpised at his question, but she answered:

"Yes, of course. We have several horses at home. A foal was born just before I came away—a dear little creature with a star on its forehead."

"When the foals get older," the gipsy said, "have you noticed how they go through a stage of long, nobbly legs, a head that seems too small for their bodies, of being clumsy and shy and starting away when anyone tries to approach them?"

"Yes, of course, I have noticed that," Sabina replied, puzzled.

"And then suddenly," he continued, "almost overnight as it were, the foal gets a little older and becomes perfectly proportioned and very beautiful."

"Why, now I understand," Sabina exclaimed. "You are trying to tell me that when I went to London I was clumsy, like a foal. Yet I do not feel as if I have altered very much in these last three years."

"But you have. You have grown older and lovelier, and perhaps a little wiser."

53

"I think you are laughing at me," Sabina said. "I do not know why I have told you this. I have never told anybody before."

"Not even the man you are going to marry?" the gipsy inquired.

"How could I tell Lord Thetford something like that?" Sabina asked. "He would not understand. But you do see how wonderful it is that I am engaged to be married, that I have been invited to stay in Monte Carlo, that I have wonderful dresses and ... and that people seem to like me."

"And it is all due to Lord Thetford," the gipsy said and it was a statement not a question.

Sabina nodded. Then suddenly, as though she awoke to the realization of what Arthur would say if he could see her at the moment, she said hastily:

"I must go, I really must! I cannot think how it has happened that I have stood here talking for so long. You have been kind, exceedingly kind, to bring back my brooch. Thank you so very, very much ... and good night."

She put out her hand and the gipsy took it in his.

"It has delighted me that you have talked to me," he said. "That you do not, like so many other people, think the gipsies are only knaves and robbers."

She gave a little start at his words. They were exactly what Lady Thetford's friends had said and she told herself that they sounded so much worse in English.

"Please, please forget such things," she pleaded. "You are different and I am sure that no one who knew you would be suspicious of you, even for a moment."

He raised her fingers to his lips.

"Thank you," he said softly. "And may I come and see you again?"

"No, no, of course not," Sabina replied. "Arthur ... I mean Lord Thetford, is arriving tomorrow. He would be shocked, terribly shocked, if he knew I had come here like this at night, or, indeed, that I have talked to you as I have. I should not have done it. . . ."

"Don't be afraid," the gipsy said quietly. "I will not tell anyone."

"No, of course not. I am being silly. It is just that it has been so nice to have someone to talk to ... someone who seemed to understand."

"Even though I am only a gipsy?"

"Perhaps it is because you are a gipsy that you have understood. I have told you that people think that you have magical powers."

"If I have magical powers, I am going to use them now," the gipsy said. "I am going to tell you that one day you will find real happiness, not just the sort that comes from a pretty dress or being a success at a party, or even finding that you are engaged to an English lord. You will find instead the happiness which comes from loving and being loved."

His voice was very quiet and yet it seemed to have some resonant quality in it which made Sabina feel as if her whole body vibrated to his words.

"We have a gipsy song which speaks of love, he went on. "I will try and translate the words into English. They begin 'Love is like a rough sea, you must surrender to its strength and majesty. It may devour you, but you can never understand it."

Sabina took her hand suddenly from his.

"I think I should be afraid of that sort of love," she said, and turned away.

"Wait one moment," the gipsy pleaded. "I want to remember you as you are now; in fact, I know I could never forget. Oh, my dear, so many men will tell you that they love you, because you have that within you which wakens a man's heart and makes him reach out towards you."

"I must not listen to you," Sabina whispered, but she did not move.

Poets always talk of an English girl being like a rose," the gipsy said. "But you are not like a rose, you are like a star—the little star that I have just given back to you—twinkling high in the sky above a man, which will guide him, inspire him and draw him ever onwards, and yet remain inaccessible. A star that is out of reach, Sabina, to a gipsy."

"Why should you be ashamed of being a gipsy?" Sabina asked. "You should be proud ... proud of your people who are honest and brave and kind when somebody is in trouble. Besides, you are a king."

"What use is there in being a king if all that one wants is still out of reach?" the gipsy asked.

"How can I answer a question like that?" Sabina inquired. "Besides, you are not really serious in what you say. You make things sound romantic and exciting whether you say them in French or in English. But perhaps it is because it is night and because this is a very romantic place."

The gipsy laughed softly.

"Are you trying to exonerate your conscience, little Sabina? What I am saying to you I mean in all seriousness. But I won't tease you any more tonight."

Once again he took her hand in his, but this time he turned it face upwards and his lips sought her palm. She felt his kiss, warm, hard and passionate against the softness of her skin. She felt herself quiver and a sudden thrill ran through her. Her breath suddenly was still, as though this one moment became fixed for all eternity.

Then, in a sudden panic, she had gone from him, running back across the garden, through the hedge and up the narrow wooden staircase on to the balcony. Without looking back she ran blindly into her bedroom, pulling the curtains to blot out the moonlight and then, only then, did she stand listening, both hands against the throbbing of her heart which seemed almost ready to burst the soft satin of her bodice.

Far away, faintly as a sigh upon the wind, came the sound of a violin!

It was dawn before Sabina fell asleep. She watched the last faint silver of the moon disappear in the gap between her curtains. She saw the first pale gleam of the morning sun supplant it and sweep away the shadows before, at last, sleep came to her. Then she dropped into a restless slumber. She dreamed at first—wild dreams in which a gipsy seemed to be saving her from deep, dark waters, from strange terrors that never fully materialized and yet were even more frightening because she could not identify them.

It was dawn before, at last, she slept deeply, and dreamlessly and awoke to find the day was far advanced and the sunshine was invading her room with a golden radiance. She awoke with a feeling of intense happiness and thought that everything that had happened the night before must have been a dream. Then slowly the events came back to her to convince her that she had not been asleep but awake.

She wondered now how she could have been so ill-behaved and so crazy as to act in such a reprehensible manner. To talk of love with a gipsy, a vagabond, a man who roamed over the face of Europe calling himself a Hungarian but who was, in fact, of no nationality for the nomad Romany tribes owed allegiance to no one except their own people. A king he called himself, and yet he was king of what? A tribe of wandering gipsies!

She felt herself blush as she remembered how intimate their talk had been, how much she had told him about herself. She thought now that she must have been intoxicated, but she had taken nothing to drink save a glass of wine at dinner and by no possible explanation could that have kept her bemused until four o'clock in the morning.

But even as she scolded herself she remembered how tall and handsome he was in the moonlight with his dark hair swept back from his square forehead and his golden brown skin. He looked strange if one compared him with the fair-haired pink and white Englishmen she had met at home and in London. And yet there was a kind of nobility about him which could not be denied, and he spoke English well. He had an accent, of course, but he spoke as if a thorough grasp of the language was by no means difficult to him.

Because he was who he was, because he was understanding and because he could never, at any time, mean anything serious in her life, it could not matter that she had talked to him as she would never have dared to talk to a man of her own class.

How impossible it was to think of speaking so frankly to Arthur, to whom she was betrothed! Sabina remembered, with a sudden sinking of her heart, that Arthur was arriving today. She ought, she thought, to be excited at the thought of seeing him, and yet she knew she was afraid. Arthur always made her feel *gauche* and insignificant, and yet he had singled her out and paid her the supreme honour of asking her to become his wife. She should feel elated at the thought that soon she would no longer be an unwanted spinster but a married woman. Arthur had changed everything for her—how grateful she should be!

She remembered now the first time she had seen him, that evening when the Squire had sent a note to the Vicarage to say that a member of his house party at the

57

Hall had been taken ill and would Lady Evelyn send one of her daughters up for dinner to take her place.

"It is kind of Sir George to think of us," Lady Evelyn said, as she read the note, but Sabina had known by the way her mother's lips tightened a little that her words belied her thoughts.

"Kind!" Harriet had snorted, who always spoke her mind. "I don't call that kind, Mamma; I call it jolly cheeky of them to ask us at the very last moment, as if we were servants to run to their beck and call. They never think of asking any of us to a party in the ordinary way of things. I believe it is because Laura and Dorothy are so plain and unattractive that they are frightened to let us near any of their precious young men!"

"Harriet! Harriet!" Lady Evelyn expostulated. "What would Papa say if he could hear you?"

"It is all very well for Papa," grumbled Harriet. "I know the living is in the Squire's hands, but he thinks in consequence he can say and do what he likes with us. But we are not chattels to be moved about to suit the convenience of the Bartrams, whatever they may think."

"Harriet, if you say one more word I shall speak to Papa," Lady Evelyn said severely. "I do agree with you that it would be nice if Sir George and Lady Bartram occasionally sent you girls an invitation that was not to fill a gap or to take the place of some unexpected cancellation, but at the same time we must remember not to be proud."

"I see no reason why we shouldn't be," Harriet argued. "The Squire only got knighted for political reasons. You have said yourself, Mamma, that your ancestry goes back to William the Conqueror, and the Wantages are quite a decent family. I have heard Uncle Herbert say that, and he is a snob if anyone is."

"Harriet, you are not to talk in such an unladylike manner," Lady Evelyn commanded. "And anyway, no one is expecting you to go to the party. Sabina will accept the invitation."

"Oh no, Mamma," Sabina protested. "You know how unhappy Laura and Dorothy always make me; I never can think of a thing to say to them. They always seem to be looking down their noses at us."

"Let me go, Mamma," Harriet pleaded. "I'll show them I am not afraid of anything they can say or do."

"Certainly not, Harriet. You are not yet out. Next year it will be different. Sabina will go. Fortunately your white dress, Sabina, is clean and we can add a blue sash to make it look a little gayer."

Sabina's protestations had been ignored and miserably apprehensive at the thought of an evening with the Bartrams she set off for the Hall in a hired carriage from the village. She had expected to feel like a fish out of water amongst the smart, rather raffish crowd of folk who were the usual type of visitors to the Hall, but she had been agreeably surprised to find herself at dinner seated next to a young man who wished to talk rather pompously about books and to dilate at some length on the political situation in Europe.

Sabina had not understood half of what he talked about, but she had listened attentively and was gratified to find that after dinner, when the gentlemen joined the ladies, he sought her out. The evening passed quite pleasantly and when she came to say good-bye, Lady Bartram asked if she would come over the following day to play croquet.

"We shall be odd numbers if you don't," she said. "So tell your Mamma that I shall be expecting you at two-thirty."

Lady Evelyn had pursed her lips again when she received the somewhat peremptory message unaccompanied by a written invitation, but Sabina had gone surprisingly willingly. Although she had not excelled herself at croquet—a game which she heartily detested—she was quite at ease with the young man who had been her dinner partner, and he came to her side as soon as she appeared.

It was the following day before she discovered his name and when she learned that he was Lord Thetford she had been quite overcome at having treated him in a rather casual manner.

"I believe your mother knows several members of my family," Lord Thetford said that afternoon. "I would like to pay my respects to her and to your father. Will they be at home if I call at the Vicarage tomorrow afternoon?"

"I will . . . tell Mamma," Sabina stammered, astounded and yet rather pleased that he should make the effort to call.

'That will teach the Bartrams,' she thought. The Squire and his family gave themselves such airs that they never accepted any invitations from the Vicarage although Lady Evelyn punctiliously asked them to tea at least once a year because she thought it was her duty.

"I am sure Mamma and Papa would be very pleased to see you," Sabina added, and was not at all surprised that Lady Evelyn was delighted to hear of the proposed visit.

She had no idea there was any deeper significance in it or in the fact that Lord Thetford, who was staying at the Hall for a week, called every day to see them. She took him for walks round the Vicarage gardens, and showed him the stables, by both of which he was singularly unimpressed. His visits passed quicker and more pleasantly when he sat in the verandah outside the drawing-room and talked to the whole family—with the exception of Papa—about himself and his life at Court.

Lady Evelyn, who had fond memories and a deep reverance for Her Majesty the Queen, was entranced, and Harriet and Melloney plied him with questions about London and the fashionable resorts whenever he paused for breath. Sabina thought secretly that most of his stories were rather dull, but she and Harriet agreed that it was a definite score over the stuck-up Bartram girls that he wished to spend so much time away from the Hall.

When Arthur Thetford proposed to Sabina at the end of the week she was dumbfounded.

"I have obtained permission from your father," he said, "to approach you on a very delicate matter. I want you, Sabina, to be my wife. You are the only person I have ever met who I feel would grace the position that I hold at Court."

"You have spoken to Papa?" Sabina gasped.

"Your father has given me permission to speak to you."

Some time later Sabina, dazed and astonished found that she had accepted him. She was not certain she had actually said so in so many words, but Arthur had undoubtedly assumed that there could be only one answer to the offer of his hand and heart.

"Darling, it is all I ever hoped for you," Lady Evelyn cried. "Think how wonderful it will be. Lord Thetford is Equerry to the Prince of Wales! You will be actually in Court circles; and think, darling, what you can do for the girls when they come out."

Harriet made it even more clear.

"I will come and stay with you, Sabina. You will give a dance for me, won't you? And the Prince and Princess of Wales will certainly be there, won't they? I shall be able to cut a real dash in London, Sabina, not have to be dragged around the dead bores as you were with Aunt Edith. He is rich and frightfully important. Oh, Sabina, you are lucky!"

Of course, she was lucky Sabina told herself, the luckiest girl in the whole world. Lucky to have the chance of a position where she could do so much for Harriet, Melloney, Angelina and Clare; lucky to be going to London, to meet the Prince and Princess of Wales and perhaps the Queen; lucky to have come to Monte Carlo; to be lying here in this golden room, knowing that today, in a few hours, she would be seeing ... Arthur.

CHAPTER FOUR

SABINA came into the drawing-room where Lady Thetford was waiting for her.

"That dress is quite perfect!" the latter exclaimed, as Sabina came through the door and stood for a moment in the full light of the windows which opened into the garden.

"It is the loveliest dress I have ever had," Sabina replied. "Except, perhaps, my evening gowns; they are even more beautiful. Oh, how can I ever thank you?"

Lady Thetford smiled.

"You pay for dressing—as the old English maid whom I had before Marie used to say. You look very different from the night you arrived. I am wondering if Arthur will recognize you."

"I have wondered the same thing myself. When I look in the glass after Marie has finished dressing me, I really believe that I see a stranger. It certainly isn't poor little Sabina Wantage, whose clothes always looked wrong somehow."

"One of the reasons was that you always chose them in the wrong colour," Lady Thetford said severely. "Why,

why do Englishwomen care so much for fawn and grey and all those nauseating washed-out shades they call pastel which always contrive to make them look sallow?"

"You are funny," Sabina laughed. "But it is so true. Everyone does wear a lot of pastel colours in England. It must be something to do with the climate."

"With your skin," Lady Thetford said, "you can wear almost anything but an indeterminate colour. I expected you to have the same golden hair as your mother, but her skin was never as fine as yours nor her eyes so blue."

"You are making me vain!" Sabina smiled; and then suddenly, with an impulsive little gesture, she ran forward to kneel at the older woman's side, and looking up, her little heart-shaped face very sweet and lovely, she said:

"Thank you, thank you. I cannot begin to tell you what a difference these lovely clothes have made to me."

Lady Thetford touched her cheek gently.

"Ridiculous child! You have thanked me quite enough. It has given me more pleasure than I have had for many years—and now we will see what Arthur says about it."

Sabina rose from her knees and looked at the clock on the mantelpiece.

"Did he say that he would come at four o'clock?" she asked.

"Oh no. Arthur would not commit himself to anything so precise," Lady Thetford replied. "He said he would come as soon as their Royal Highnesses could dispense with his services. As I have learned that the Royal *entourage* was due at luncheon time, I assumed that Arthur would call to see us some time about now."

"It is taking him a long time to get them settled," Sabina remarked.

There was just a touch of pique in her voice. She would have liked to think that Arthur was so eager to see her that he would feel compelled to rush round to the Villa Mimosa the very instant the train arrived at the station. Of course, he had to do his duty, she was well aware of that, but she could not help feeling there was somehow a lack of urgency about this arrangement which left him free to come at any hour which suited him.

As her eyes left the clock she caught a glimpse of herself in the gilt mirror over the mantelshelf. There was no doubt that her dress of leaf green bengaline trimmed with velvet ribbon and frills of pleated chiffon gave her an almost ethereal, spring-like appearance; and as she preened herself a little, she remembered a voice, deep and curiously moving, say, 'You look like a nymph'.

She had a sudden wish that the gipsy king could see her now; and then, almost before the wish was formed, she severely repressed it. The sooner such things were forgotten the better. She had no doubt in her mind what Arthur would think, not only of her adventure on the Upper Corniche Road, but of her long talk with the gipsy in the garden when he came to return her diamond brooch.

She should have taken the jewel and thanked him and dismissed him instantly, but instead she had lingered, telling him about herself in that reprehensibly frank manner for which she had been rebuked much too often. And then, worst of all, she had let him kiss her hand.

All through the night she had been conscious of that kiss burning in her palm. She had tried to forget it, tried to think of other things, to dismiss the action as one of familiarity and impudence on the part of the gipsy; and yet her mind returned to it, remembering his grace as he bent his head, feeling again that strange feeling, almost like a flame, which had run through her body at the touch of his lips.

Abruptly Sabina switched her thoughts, and turning away from the contemplation of her reflection in the mirror, she moved restlessly across the room to the window.

"Are you nervous?"

She had forgotten that Lady Thetford was watching her, and now she turned sharply at the question.

"Of Arthur?" she inquired. "Why should I be?"

Lady Thetford smiled.

"No reason, of course, my dear. I only wondered."

Sabina walked back across the room and standing by her hostess smiled disarmingly.

"I am a little," she admitted. "Arthur is rather a frightening person, I think."

Lady Thetford sighed, and then suddenly she looked up at Sabina and asked quietly:

"You love him, child?"

The question was unexpected.

"Yes ... yes, of course," Sabina replied quickly, stumbling over her words. "I am so grateful to him ... so very, very grateful."

Lady Thetford raised her eyebrows.

"For having asked you to marry him?"

Sabina nodded.

"It was so unexpected. I never for a moment thought that he even liked me. He talked to me at a dinner party at the Hall and when we played croquet together, but I imagined it was only because I was the choice of two evils. If he hadn't been talking to me he would have had to listen to Laura and Dorothy Bartram, and he would have found them both excruciatingly boring. Even Papa, good and sweet though he is, finds it hard to be attentive to them when they drone away in a nonsensical manner about things of which they know nothing."

"The choice of two evils," Lady Thetford repeated with a smile. "Did you really think that? My child, you must have a very modest opinion of your attractions."

"Have I any?" Sabina inquired.

Lady Thetford laughed.

"You have just been looking at yourself in the mirror. What did you see there?"

"I saw a very lovely dress," Sabina answered, "and an elegant *coiffure* arranged by very skilful fingers. If clothes can make the woman, then at the moment I am something of which to be proud."

"There is more to it than that," Lady Thetford insisted. "You are far too humble. Do you not realize that you are beautiful? If you had heard what my friends have been saying to me since you arrived in Monte Carlo, your head would be turned on your pretty little shoulders. Do not under-estimate yourself, Sabina. You are lovely, as lots of other men besides Arthur will be prepared to tell you before you leave here."

"Oh, I wish I could believe you," Sabina cried.

She wheeled round suddenly to stare at her reflection again and as she did so she heard the sound of horses' hoofs and wheels outside the front door.

"Arthur!"

She said the word almost breathlessly and Lady Thetford smiled as she rose from her chair.

"Yes, Arthur at last! And now he will be able to confirm what I have been telling you—that you look very beautiful, Sabina."

The two women stood in silence. They heard footsteps,

the low murmur of Bates's voice, and then the drawing-room door was opened.

"His Lordship, m'lady."

Arthur came slowly into the room. He was of medium height with fair hair, a clear, rather pale complexion and a small moustache. His features were sharp cut and his cold-grey eyes were set deep in his face under straight uncompromising eyebrows. His lips, which were a little thin and set in rather a harsh line, except when he was smiling, betrayed the unusual severity of his character and a lamentable lack of generosity.

But the first impression of the third Lord Thetford was that he was a good-looking, well-dressed young man with a proud carriage, and as he came into the drawing-room Sabina felt her heart give a little leap of excitement.

"Good afternoon, Arthur. We began to think that perhaps you had forgotten us or your train had been delayed," Lady Thetford said as she moved forward to greet her son.

"On the contrary, the Royal Train arrived at the exact moment it was expected. We had an excellent journey, Mother, and I came here as soon as it was possible for me to do so."

He did not kiss his mother, Sabina noticed, but took her outstretched hand for a moment in his and then turned towards Sabina.

He was smiling when he first looked at her, and then the smile faded.

"What have you done to yourself?" he asked.

The words of welcome which had been hovering a little shyly on Sabina's lips were silenced.

"I . . . I do not know," she stammered. "Do you mean that I . . . look different?"

"Of course that is what I mean," Arthur replied. "Your hair, your clothes!"

"Do you like them?" Sabina asked eagerly. "Please say you do. Your mother has been so kind to me. The gowns she has given me are the most wonderful things I have ever had in my life."

Arthur turned towards his mother.

"You have given Sabina some clothes?" he inquired.

Lady Thetford, who had been watching her son, answered quietly:

"Yes. I wrote to Evelyn and told her that my wedding

65

present to Sabina would be her trousseau and that it was best that she should use some of the dresses during her visit here."

"I should have thought such a gesture was quite unnecessary," Arthur said irritably.

"Oh, but Mamma was so pleased and thankful," Sabina interposed. "You see, she could not really afford to give me many things, especially the sort of clothes that would be wanted in Monte Carlo; and even if she had bought what she could, they would not have been at all suitable— not like the things Lady Thetford has been so kind enough to give me. Please, Arthur, say you like them."

Sabina's plea was almost pitiable. She knew without words, by the expression on his face, that Arthur was not pleased, and yet she could not understand why. Surely he did not want to see her in the dowdy, cheap clothes, that she had worn when they first met? Even in contrast with the dresses worn by Laura and Dorothy Bartram they had been shabby and out of date, but it was really terrifying to think what she would have looked like out here in fashionable, luxurious Monte Carlo if it had not been for Lady Thetford's kindness.

"I am sure you must admire this gown," she cried urgently. "And I have others even lovelier."

There was a long silence and then, as though the tension of it was more than she could bear, Lady Thetford said sharply:

"Don't be ridiculous, Arthur. The child cannot walk about Monte Carlo looking like a kitchen-maid. You know that as well as I do; you are only being difficult and making us all feel uncomfortable."

Arthur looked at his mother, and his eyes hardened and his lips tightened before he said grudgingly:

"Very well, have it your own way; but I shall have something to say, you know, in the way she looks."

"Sabina has already been very much admired," Lady Thetford retorted.

"Indeed! And by whom?" Arthur inquired.

"My friends," his mother replied.

There was a smile on his lips, but it was not a pleasant one as he replied:

"Exactly."

Sabina looked from one to the other in bewilderment; and then, because there was an antagonism and unpleasantness in the atmosphere which she could not understand, she moved forward impulsively and put her hand on Arthur's arm.

"It is all to please you," she said softly. "And now won't you say that you are glad to see me?"

He looked down at her and then, for the first time since he arrived, he put his hand on hers.

"I am glad to see you. But I liked you as you were at Cobbleford."

"I am just the same really," Sabina whispered shyly.

He looked down at her and she felt as though his tension relaxed, and then suddenly, with an exclamation, he took his hand from hers.

"Come here," he said.

He seized her by the arm and drew her towards the window, and there he looked down into her face for a long moment before drawing from his breast pocket a spotless white handkerchief. Then, before Sabina was aware of what he was about to do, he rubbed it against her cheeks, first one and then the other. She gave a little cry at his roughness, but before she could move he had released her and was staring down grimly at the handkerchief, soiled with the faint tell-tale smudges of rouge.

"This is your doing," he exclaimed looking across the room at Lady Thetford as she stood watching.

The accusation was almost shouted in a voice of such thunderous anger that instinctively Sabina shrank back against the windowsill, her hands rising towards her thumping heart.

"My dear Arthur! Must you frighten the child by such an exhibition?" Lady Thetford asked.

"Exhibition indeed!" her son replied. "Haven't you done enough by decking her out like some fashionable doll, without painting her like any harlot in the Casino?"

"A little rouge will not affect her morals!"

"That is what you may think," Arthur said rudely. "But I know exactly what such actions mean coming from you. You wish to make her like yourself. You wish to corrupt her, to spoil and defame her innocence so that you can prove to me that all women are the same and none of them are any better than you."

His voice seemed to vibrate in its fury around the room, but Lady Thetford faced him calmly.

"There is no need to lose your temper, Arthur, or to be

ruder to me than you usually are. Sabina has not been spoilt or ruined in any way because I have added a touch of rouge to her pale cheeks and put a speck of powder on her nose. She is as sweet and gentle as she has always been, but God knows how long she will remain so if she has to listen to your jaundiced outlook on life and learn that you always expect the worst in every woman."

"If your example has made me cynical, you have only yourself to blame," Arthur answered bitterly. "It was much against my will that I let Sabina come here and I see how right I was to be apprehensive."

"You let her come because you had to," Lady Thetford replied. "Don't let us have any illusions on that score."

"Very well then. But understand, I will not have her corrupted or spoilt. She will go upstairs now and wash her face; and if I ever see her rouged and powdered again, I shall send her home by the next train. Is that clear?"

He turned round as he spoke to face Sabina.

"Oh, Arthur, please . . . please do not be . . . angry."

Sabina's eyes were full of tears and her voice was almost strangled in her throat.

"You heard what I said," he replied sharply. "Go upstairs and wash; and the next time you use cosmetics, you will find that my threat is not an empty one."

Sabina ran towards the door. She pulled it open and it closed behind her with what was almost a slam as she ran up the stairs to her bedroom. It was only when she reached the privacy of her own room and had wiped away her tears with a clean handkerchief that she realized she was trembling all over.

How could he speak to his mother like that she wondered? How could such a small thing make him so angry that his voice seemed almost raw with the fury of his emotions?

She wiped her eyes again and stared at herself in the mirror on the dressing-table. Then she ran to the washstand and pouring some water from the flowered china jug into the basin, began to wash her face with her sponge. There was so little rouge and such a mere touch of powder that it was washed away in a second, and when she dried her face the towel showed no traces of the shaming cosmetics, as Arthur's handkerchief had done.

She went back again to the dressing-table. There was no doubt that she had looked prettier with colour in her cheeks and now that she had done as Arthur commanded she felt suddenly incensed at the manner in which he had demanded it.

Why should he be so rude to his mother? And why, indeed, should he take it upon himself to order her about until she was actually and in fact his wife? But even as she asked herself the questions Sabina felt her defiance ebb away. She wanted Arthur to be pleased with her, not angry. She wanted him to approve of her changed looks, not to find fault with them.

Last night the gipsy king had told her she was beautiful. She had seen the admiration in his eyes. She had known, as every woman knows, there was no pretence about the manner in which he regarded her. It had been the same at the Casino. All Lady Thetford's men friends had paid her compliments and other men whom she had not known had looked at her in a manner which could not be mistaken.

Arthur should be proud, not angry; and Sabina felt a sudden hard resentment against him grow in her breast— and then common sense came to her aid. He was right; of course he was right. Papa would not have approved, or Mamma for that matter. If anyone could see that she was painted, then Arthur was right in saying she must wash it away. She might look prettier, but that was not the point. It was unladylike and fast to be rouged, and she had only let herself be persuaded by Lady Thetford because she had thought it would be entirely imperceptible.

'I must apologize to him,' she thought, and forced herself to admit that it was necessary.

Slowly and with a reluctance which seemed to drag her back as though she was weighted down with heavy stones, she went step by step down the stairs and into the hall. She felt suddenly homesick as her hand reached out towards the drawing-room door.

There were never scenes like this at home. Papa, however upset he was by what any of them had done, never lost his temper. He rebuked them and yet it always seemed he was more hurt by their misbehaviour than angry. Mamma would sometimes be impatient, but like their own childish quarrels it was all over in a few minutes and then they would all kiss and love each other again and be even happier because a faint cloud of disagreement had shown up in its right proportion the sunshine of their happiness.

With her hand on the door, Sabina suddenly discovered something she had not known before.

'I am afraid of Arthur,' she told herself. Yes, afraid of him! In some ways such a discovery was astonishing. How often had she told her sisters that she was afraid of nothing—not even of ghosts or of growing old or of dying. But now she was afraid of a man—the man she was going to marry.

'He must not be angry with me, he must not,' she told herself, and then felt ashamed because she was such a coward.

He loved her! If she had done wrong, if she apologized he would understand.

She opened the door and went in, already rehearsing in her mind the words of apology she must say. She thought for a moment the room was empty, then she saw that Arthur was not there but Lady Thetford was lying on a sofa in the window.

Sabina advanced slowly across the room; for a moment she thought that Lady Thetford was asleep, and then she realized that she was staring across the garden, her eyes fixed sightlessly on the tall cypress trees.

"Has Arthur gone?" Sabina asked the question in a low voice.

"Yes. He is coming back to dinner."

"Oh!" Sabina could think of nothing else to say.

Then Lady Thetford, with what seemed to be an effort, turned her head.

"Come here, child; I want to talk to you."

Sabina went towards her obediently. She stood beside the sofa looking down at the older woman. She thought that Lady Thetford looked very tired. Her face seemed suddenly drawn, as though she was suffering.

Lady Thetford took a cushion from the sofa and put it on the floor beside her.

"Sit down, Sabina," she said.

Sabina did as she was told, her green skirts billowing out around her, her back resting against the sofa, her eyes fixed on Lady Thetford.

"I am sorry for what happened just now," Lady Thetford said. "It was my fault. I ought to have realized that Arthur would be angry—not only with me but with you."

70

"Is he still very angry?" Sabina asked.

"He will recover."

"I did not think he would notice."

"Nobody else would have," Lady Thetford replied. "He was looking for it. Suspicious as he always is of me, he suspected you just because you were with me."

"Why?" Sabina asked, puzzled. "Why should he be suspicious of you?"

"Because he hates me," Lady Thetford answered.

"Hates you?" Sabina repeated. "Oh, no, he couldn't. Why should he?"

"Has nobody ever told you anything about me?" Lady Thetford inquired.

"Nothing in particular. Mamma said how kind and sweet you had always been to her and how sad it was that she had not seen you for so many years. She was so pleased that Arthur was your son. That was one of the reasons, she said, why she and Papa were so pleased to give their consent to our marriage."

"I suppose that was why Arthur did not dare revile me to them," Lady Thetford said, ruminatively, as if to herself.

"Revile you?" Sabina questioned. "But why should he? How could he dare?"

"He would dare if it suited his purpose or if he had anything to gain by it," Lady Thetford answered. "But I see you still don't believe me. You, who have been brought up, in a happy home, loving your parents, cannot begin to realize what it is like to be hated by one's only child."

"Why? Why?" Sabina inquired.

"I will tell you," Lady Thetford said. "I would like to tell you about it myself. I had not credited Arthur with the delicacy of not having already given you his own version of my story."

She put her lace handkerchief to her lips, then continued:

"Arthur is very like his father, my husband. He was a strong character but very narrow and bigoted in his outlook. Once he had made up his mind on a course of action believing it to be right, he would stick to it whatever the arguments against it. Nothing would change him; nothing would swerve him from his chosen course. Arthur is the same. There is nothing I can say nor

71

anything that anyone else could say that would change his mind about me."

"But what have you done?" Sabina asked, bewildered.

"Let me tell you in my own way," Lady Thetford replied. "I was eighteen when I was married to Arthur's father and he was over forty. He was a widower; a man who had been married to a neurotic, difficult woman who had played no part in his life but had been in ill-health for nearly fifteen years. He had therefore grown used to being without women and making his life amongst men. He had no tenderness and very little sympathy for what has been called the gentler sex.

"We were married and Arthur was born. It was soon after that that I began to be actively unhappy. I had not really been in love with my husband when I married him. I admired him very much. I thought him a handsome and romantic figure. Because I was young and foolish I had no idea what living with a man of his temperament might mean. From being unhappy I became actively miserable. Because there was nothing else for me to do, I managed to force myself into making the world believe that our marriage was, to all intents and purposes, a success.

"I accepted a position at Court, which gave me other interests outside that of my home. I lived as social a life as it was possible to do and I filled my days with charitable works—anything to stop myself from thinking, from being alone with my husband.

"Arthur was a tremendous joy to me until he was sent away to school and afterwards to a university. He was very like his father in temperament as well as in looks, and perhaps the only person to whom my husband was in any way kind or understanding was his son. Arthur adored his father.

"The years went by and finally my husband died. I can't begin to tell you what it meant to be free—free of what had seemed like a cloud over my whole life for so long that I had grown used to living in the dark. The rows and disagreeableness, the jealousies, the injustices that had made my life unbearable, all ceased overnight. I was free, as I hadn't been free since I was a girl.

"It was then that I fell in love for the first time in my life, with someone whom I had known for a long time— a man who had loved me long before I was aware that his affection was anything but one of friendship. Unfortu-

72

nately he was married to a wife who had been in a lunatic asylum for nearly twenty years. There was nothing he could do about it; no chance of a divorce, for the law does not permit it."

"If your wife or your husband is mad is there no chance of ever being free?" Sabina asked.

"None," Lady Thetford replied. "And Guy was a man who longed for children, a man who would have made a perfect and very understanding father. It was perhaps that more than anything else that made me love him so much. He was growing old in years but he was young in heart. He had such an affection for young people. He seemed to understand them and they adored him—all except Arthur, of course. Arthur never liked him."

"What could you do?" Sabina asked.

"That was the question we asked ourselves over and over again," Lady Thetford replied. "What could we do? We loved each other—two people who had been lonely and unhappy for many years. He had no children to consider. I had only Arthur, who was grown up and who had never seemed to care for me.

"And so . . . yes, Sabina, we . . . we went away together. There was no scandal. I just gave up my position at Court and said I wished to live abroad owing to my health. Guy shut up his estates in Dorset and we went to a tiny place in Italy where nobody knew us. I don't think anyone had the least idea that we were together, except, of course, Arthur."

"You told him?" Sabina asked.

"Yes. I told him quite frankly and honestly what I was going to do," Lady Thetford replied. "I shall never forget the things he said to me then."

She shut her eyes for a moment as though what had happened was still too horrible to contemplate.

"Was he very angry?" Sabina asked in a low voice.

"He said everything that anyone could say under the circumstances," Lady Thetford said. "He told me, too, how he had always distrusted me, had thought that I was not good enough for his father, that I had not made him as happy as I might have done. He blamed me for everything. I was in the wrong; he and his father were always right.

"I told him that he would be well rid of me. I would not disgrace him because no one would know what had happened to me. He had only to keep silent and the secret would be as safe as anything could be.

"I left England with his curses echoing in my ears. I went to Italy and forgot everything in the first real happiness I have ever known."

"No one found out?" Sabina asked.

"No one that I know of," Lady Thetford answered. "But because of the free, untrammelled life I lived—six years with the man I loved—I found it impossible ever to contemplate living again in England in the dull, smug, conventional society that I had known when I was married to Arthur's father."

"What happened after six years?" Sabina asked.

"Guy died," Lady Thetford said. "He died bravely of an agonizing illness which lasted, thank God, only a very short while. His wife is still alive, but he is dead!"

"You never regretted going away with him?" Sabina asked.

"Regretted it? My dear, it was the only good thing I have ever done; the only worthwhile action of my life. We were divinely happy, and when Guy was dying he thanked me—thanked me, when through him I had known heaven for six short years!"

"What did you do after that?" Sabina asked.

"Ever since then I have been trying to kill time," Lady Thetford sighed. "I wandered about Europe and then I built this villa here, because the only thing which really makes me forget my loneliness is being able to gamble. I went to Homburg for a little while; but I like the sun, it reminds me of those happy years that Guy and I spent together in a little fishing village by the sea. Two people forgotten by the world; two people who had everything that a man and woman can ever wish for."

"Did Arthur ever come to see you?" Sabina asked.

"No, of course not," Lady Thetford replied. "Only once did he write and ask to see me, and that was because of certain legal difficulties which affected his estate. You see, Sabina, life is a strange thing with strange twists in it. My husband, who always reviled me, always told me I was hopelessly incompetent and stupid, when he died left a very strange will. The vast proportion of his money was, of course, left to his son, but he was not to inherit it until he was forty or unless he married with my consent and approval.

74

"It was strange, wasn't it, that he should have put it like that? When I had thought that my opinion was of no consequence to him and he so frequently found fault with my taste. Yet that was what he wrote in his will; so Arthur, for all that he disapproves of me, finds himself in the uncomfortable position of having to seek my consent to his marriage."

"So that was why I came out here," Sabina said.

"That was why," Lady Thetford answered. "Arthur wrote formally asking me to approve his marriage and I would agree to nothing until I saw you."

"Oh, I am glad you said that," Sabina exclaimed.

"Are you?" Lady Thetford inquired. "I am doubtful now if it was wise."

"I will tell Arthur I am sorry about my face and he will forget it."

Lady Thetford put out her hand and drew Sabina close to her.

"You have a very sweet nature," she said. "It is my fault that Arthur is angry with you; and I, only, am to blame. Perhaps subconsciously I wanted to taunt him a little. I paint my own face more vividly when he is here because it annoys him so much. He does not understand foreign ways and foreign customs. He judges everything in an insular manner just as his father did. If they had the chance, they would keep women in medieval servitude— the inferior sex, brought into the world only so that they may bear children and minister to the needs of the all-conquering man."

"Does Arthur really think like that?" Sabina asked.

"Perhaps I am being unkind to him," Lady Thetford said quickly. "Arthur has many good qualities, of that I am sure, and you may be the saving of him."

"In what way?"

"You may make him more human; you may even teach him that women should be loved and appreciated."

Sabina looked doubtful.

"I never thought that I might have to teach Arthur anything. I have only thought that he might teach me."

"Arthur has a great deal to learn," Lady Thetford retorted. "But if he loves you enough, then anything is possible. That is one thing I am as sure of as I am of my hope of heaven—that love can change and alter the most surprising person. Perhaps my greatest fault, my worst

75

sin, was that I married Arthur's father without loving him. You see, I didn't know much about love in those days; I didn't know how wonderful, glorious and overpowering it can be."

"Like a rough sea," Sabina said softly, remembering the gipsy's words.

"Yes, that is true," Lady Thetford said. "It is like a rough sea, or perhaps more like a fire. A fire can both purify and burn, it can create and destroy."

"Do you think that Arthur loves me like that?" Sabina asked, in a very low voice.

Lady Thetford hesitated for a moment before she answered:

"I don't think I am qualified to answer that question. Only you can answer it to yourself."

Sabina put up her face and kissed Lady Thetford's cheek.

"Thank you for telling me about yourself," she said. "And I am so glad that you found happiness, even for such a short while."

Lady Thetford gave a little sigh.

"The years go so slowly since then, but I have my perfect memories and that should be sufficient for any woman."

She kissed Sabina gently and then rose to her feet.

"Come, let us go and choose the dress you are to wear this evening. You must look lovely, and yet perhaps a little subdued."

There was a hint of mischief in her voice and in her eyes as she said the last words, and suddenly Sabina began to laugh.

"What is amusing you?" Lady Thetford inquired.

"It is just the idea of trying to look subdued in all those lovely frocks that you have bought me from Paris," Sabina answered. "Besides, I do not want to look subdued; I want to look lovely and exciting. I want Arthur to admire me."

"We must try to make him," Lady Thetford smiled.

"Yes, we must try to make him," Sabina repeated.

She was thinking of those same words when she came downstairs three hours later, wearing a dress of white mousseline trimmed with narrow bands of black velvet ribbon. It was the plainest gown she had and yet it had

76

the elegance and grace which only Paris could achieve, and she knew that it gave her both presence and an extremely beautiful figure.

She had heard Arthur arrive a few minutes earlier, and Marie had come from Lady Thetford's room to tell her to go down as her ladyship might be a few minutes late. With a beating heart Sabina entered the drawing-room and saw Arthur standing with his back to the fireplace. He looked extremely smart in his evening clothes and he wore a white gardenia in his buttonhole.

Sabina walked very slowly across the room towards him. He said nothing and made no movement and by the time she had reached him she was gripping her fingers together in a sudden agony of nervousness. It seemed to her that she had forgotten how tall he was or how reserved and aloof. It was as if he was hardly aware of her existence and she felt small and helpless.

"Please, Arthur . . . I am . . . sorry."

The words came faltering from her lips, and then, at last, he turned to scrutinize her cheeks to see that they owed nothing to artificiality and that the soft, pale bloom of her complexion was entirely natural.

"That's better."

He spoke with the condescending approval of a schoolmaster rather than as a lover.

"You are not . . . angry any more?"

It was the question of a child who has been frightened.

"I was very angry this afternoon, I can tell you that."

"I know, and I am . . . sorry. I did not think you would . . . notice or I would not have . . . done it."

"Naturally I notice everything about you," Arthur replied.

As if he suddenly recovered from his ill-humour, he put his arm round her and drew her closer to him.

"You have got to learn what is right and what is wrong, you know. You haven't been about much and have lived a very simple life, so I cannot entirely blame you for making a mistake. Besides, it was my mother's fault. But let me make this clear from the beginning. I like you as I first saw you. I don't want a dressed-up French doll for a wife; I want an ordinary English country girl—someone I can trust; someone who is content with being my wife and doesn't want to go about attracting attention."

77

"I understand," Sabina replied in a low voice. "But I do like my pretty clothes all the same. You could not really have liked that awful white frock I was wearing the first night I saw you. It did not fit me anywhere. Besides, I had worn it for over three years."

"It appeared to be quite nice to me," Arthur answered vaguely. You looked a lady; that's what I liked about you."

"Don't I look a lady at the moment?" Sabina asked, with a hint of mischief she could not entirely suppress.

"You look all right," Arthur said. "But I liked the old way you did your hair. It wasn't so fanciful."

"A Frenchman at the Casino last night kept on referring to *'La belle Anglais'*. I did not realize for a long time that he was talking about me."

"Damned cheek on his part," Arthur snapped. "Those frogs are all alike, can't trust them with a woman. You don't want compliments of that sort. You don't want any compliments at all, if it comes to that. It's un-English, you know."

"But I rather like compliments," Sabina said honestly. "You see . . . I have not had any before."

"And you don't want any now," Arthur said, a little roughly.

He looked down at her and then bent his head and kissed her cheek.

"You look very nice. Is that what you want to hear?"

"Yes, of course," Sabina smiled. "And thank you for saying it."

He drew her to him and again kissed her cheek.

"Then that's all right," he said. "Now you have got me here, you won't want to go listening to a lot of Frenchmen. My mother's friends, I suppose, and a collection of riff-raff, if I know anything about them."

"They seemed charming and they were very kind to me," Sabina murmured.

She could not help feeling disapproving that Arthur should criticize his mother to her. But Arthur did not appear to hear her.

"I dislike foreign countries—I always have," he said pompously. "But what I dislike more are the dagos who live in them."

CHAPTER FIVE

"Vingt-neuf, noir et impair."

Arthur put out his hand to pick up his winnings.

"You have won!" Sabina cried excitedly.

"It is of no great importance," he replied coldly. "I do not approve of people who take gambling seriously. It is only a pastime."

There was, however, a glint of excitement in his eyes when a few minutes later he won again. He had been standing at the table, but now he sat down in an empty seat and Sabina saw that for all his air of nonchalance he was intending to concentrate on the play.

She moved from behind his chair and he did not notice that she had gone. She walked across the room to where, seemingly oblivious of the noise and chatter around her and even of the friends who spoke to her in passing, Lady Thetford was playing *Chemin de fer*.

Sabina had learnt by now that Lady Thetford did not like to talk when she was gambling, so she stood for a while by her side and then moved away again. The Casino was getting crowded. Those who had dined late were beginning to arrive; the men, jovial and well wined, were smoking big cigars; the women, with their jewels glittering in the light of the chandeliers as they moved from table to table, looked like gay colourful peacocks—and sometimes like birds of prey.

Sabina felt lonely. It seemed that no one was particularly interested in her or had eyes for anything but the spin of the wheel or the turn of a card. Had she any money, she would like to have taken a chance and have staked a few francs at roulette. But Lady Thetford had never suggested that she should try her luck and she knew only too well that if she asked Arthur he would be shocked and surprised that she should wish to gamble.

She watched the people for a little while and listened to their tongues talking half-a-dozen different languages; and then, moving round the room, she found a door which

79

opened on to the terrace outside. A liveried attendant bowed her out, remarking in French:

"It is chilly tonight, *mademoiselle*. You will need a cloak if you wish to walk in the gardens."

"I am only going to get a breath of air," Sabina smiled.

She went down the steps and into the garden, which was lit near the Casino with fairy lights and then disappeared into the darkness under the shadow of the high palm trees.

The moon was on the sea. Sabina stood for a moment entranced by the beauty of it. She had a sudden longing to be with someone she could talk to, someone whom she could tell of the strange stirrings within herself as she looked on the beauty all around her.

She half-wondered if she would go back into the Casino and fetch Arthur. Would the moonlight have a magic for him as it had for her? And even as she asked herself the question she knew the answer. Arthur would merely think she was being imaginative and absurd.

She thought how last night she had talked to the gipsy king. Then resolutely she put the thought from her. She must not think of him. It was wrong, and she was a little ashamed that her thoughts should continually wander to a man who was only a vagabond and who had come into her life by the merest chance.

Almost as if she ran away from her thoughts Sabina moved across the terrace and passed a flower bed ablaze with flowers that were heavy and exotic on the night air. Then, as she turned a corner of the path, she saw ahead of her a seat and on it a man silhouetted against the lighter sky. His hand was raised and even as she saw him Sabina realized what he was about to do.

This was the 'Suicides' Garden'. She had heard of it often enough. Papa had told her that the Bishop of Gibraltar had written a letter to *The Times* deploring the spiritual dangers of Monte Carlo and the loss of life by those foolish and reckless men who forfeited all sense of decency when they squandered their fortunes at the gambling tables.

This was one of them! Sabina stared in horror—for the moment paralysed with fear so that she could not move. She felt every nerve in her body tense as she waited for the sound of a shot, and then, suddenly galvanized into action, she ran forward.

80

Small and fragile though she might appear, she had a certain amount of strength, and as she threw her whole weight upon the arm of the man in front of her she almost dragged him off the seat with the surprise of her attack.

He gave a sudden exclamation and then sprang to his feet, with Sabina still holding on to his arm.

"The devil take it! What's the meaning of this?" he inquired in English, as Sabina, panting and breathless, cried:

"You mustn't do it; you mustn't."

Then, as she stood clutching his arm, she looked down to his hand and saw that he was holding, not as she had imagined, a pistol, but a long, narrow cigar case, which, held in one hand towards his temple, had in the darkness resembled most closely the lethal weapon with which she had thought he was about to blow out his brains.

Slowly Sabina released her hold on him and then, the blood slowly rising in her face, she began to stammer:

"I am so terribly sorry ... but I thought ... thought. . . ."

"What did you think?" the Englishman inquired.

"That ... that you had a pistol in your hand," Sabina faltered. "Please forgive me."

There was no mistaking now her embarrassment, and for a moment the Englishman stared from her to his cigar case, and then suddenly threw back his head and began to laugh.

"Strap me, if that isn't a good joke!" he exclaimed.

"I am ... sorry," Sabina stammered. "But I have heard so many stories of ... what happens here in the garden, and when I saw you pointing something to your head, I imagined. . . ."

"That I was about to blow out the brains that no one has given me the credit of possessing," the Englishman laughed.

"I do not know what you must think of me," Sabina said. "I can only apologize, sir, and hope you will forget it."

She turned as if to go away, but the Englishman stopped her.

"Don't leave me," he pleaded. "Indeed, I should be mightily obliged to you for trying to save my life. There are not many people who would be interested enough.

Besides, you are English and I should like you to stay and talk to me. I am heartily sick of my own company."

"I think I should return to the Casino," Sabina said uncomfortably. "My *fiancé* will be wondering what has happened to me."

"May I ask his name?" the Englishman inquired. "I might be acquainted with him."

"He is Lord Thetford," Sabina replied.

"Thetford!" the young man exclaimed. "Don't mean Arthur, do you? At Eton with me. Used to call him 'Prosy Ponsonby' in those days."

"My *fiancé's* Christian name is Arthur," Sabina said, a little primly.

"Good Lord! Fancy old 'Prosy' getting married!" the young man ejaculated. "Must congratulate him on having chosen someone so quick-witted. Had I been doing what you suspected, would have been a dead man at this moment."

"Oh, please do not tell Arthur that I did anything so stupid," Sabina pleaded. "He would not understand. He would—indeed—think it most forward of me."

"Forward indeed!" the Englishman snorted. "Couldn't expect you to walk by and leave a fellow lying in his blood. Not the sort of thing a kind-hearted woman would do! But say nothing if you would rather I didn't."

"Please let us forget my stupidity," Sabina begged.

"I will if you tell me your name."

"Sabina Wantage."

"Shan't forget that. But why should we stand when we might be sitting?"

"I think I ought to go back," Sabina said hesitatingly.

"Beg you to stay for a few minutes. Introduce myself. My name is Sheringham."

"The Viscount Sheringham!" Sabina exclaimed. "But, of course, I remember you now. I met you at a ball I was taken to in London two years ago. We were introduced to each other but you did not ask me to dance."

"I didn't! Why not?"

"I do not know," Sabina smiled. "Except, perhaps, you did not like the look of me."

"Stuff and nonsense! I ... I mean to say, even in this light I can see that you are jolly pretty! Shouldn't have been such a numb-skull as to have missed dancing with you if we had met."

"But we did, really and truly," Sabina insisted. "I remember it quite distinctly. But I looked very different then. I did not have any pretty clothes and what I had were all the wrong shape. I looked a dowd, and that is what you must have thought me."

"Good Lord! Can't believe it," Lord Sheringham ejaculated. "Anyway, not going to deny we met. Makes us old friends, doesn't it? Friends of two years' standing. 'Prosy' can't object to us being acquainted."

"I am sure you ought not to call him 'Prosy'," Sabina said. "He would not like it."

Without really thinking about the matter she had sat down on the seat. The Viscount seated himself beside her. He was a very elegant young man, with an extremely high collar in the latest fashion, and his evening clothes seemed to fit him so closely that it was almost as if he had been poured into them.

"Shouldn't know who I was talking about if I called him Arthur," he replied to Sabina's rebuke. "Called 'Prosy' at Eaton because he was always prosing over one thing and another. Bit of a prig, too, I shouldn't wonder."

"You are not to say such things," Sabina cried.

At the same time she couldn't help smiling. The young Englishman had such an amusing way of speaking. He raised his eyebrows now and answered:

"Can't expect me to lie. Besides, chaps can't help their nicknames. Know a chap—colonel in the Army—who was called 'Pimples' at school. It still sticks to him. Can't live a thing like that down."

"What were you called?" Sabina inquired.

"Everyone calls me 'Sherry'," was the cheerful reply. "Too lazy to think of anything ruder, I suspect. Hope you, too, will call me 'Sherry'."

"I think that sounds much too familiar," Sabina replied. "Now, really I must be going."

She got to her feet and Lord Sheringham rose too.

"I'll escort you," he said. "Oughtn't to be walking about a place like this alone, you know, far too pretty."

"Everyone is much too busy gambling to pay much attention to me," Sabina smiled.

"Must be blind!" said Lord Sheringham. "Glad of it, all the same. You wouldn't have come out alone and met me if Prosy had been doing his duty."

"Do you gamble?" Sabina inquired.

83

"Don't care much for these foreign games of chance," he replied. "Prefer gaming at White's. Know where I am with my own friends. Besides, my French is so jolly bad I never know what the croupier is blabbering about. Damn difficult to follow, if you ask me."

Sabina gave a gurgle of laughter.

"Then why are you here?" she inquired.

"Brought my mother down for a holiday. Been ill and my father's too busy in the House of Lords to get away. Never been to Monte Carlo before. Thought I might as well look the place over—rather disappointing sort of spot, if you ask me."

"Oh, no, you cannot say that!"

Sabina stood still and looked up at the viscount in sheer astonishment. They had walked from the shadow of the trees out into the moonlight and she looked very lovely as she stood there, a faint wind blowing in from the sea stirring the curls of her fair hair.

"It is a wonderful place," she insisted. "Does not it seem to you full of magic? I feel there might be an adventure round every corner; that nothing could ever be boring, humdrum or commonplace. It is like a wonderful fairy story that has come alive so suddenly that one is a part of it."

"Sounds jolly fine when you crack it up," Lord Sheringham said. "Perhaps the adventure you're talking about is you and I meeting each other. What do you think?"

"I suppose in a way it was quite an adventure," Sabina said seriously. "In fact, it would have been a very big one if you had, in reality, been trying to commit suicide. But as it was. . . ."

She turned her face away and blushed.

"I do feel so foolish," she said.

"Mustn't do that," Lord Sheringham retorted. "Besides, no reason for it. No one will know. It's a secret—yours and mine."

"Yes, of course, a secret," Sabina agreed.

They walked together into the Casino. The heat, after the cool night air outside seemed for a moment overpowering, and then, as the crowd closed around them, Sabina looked at her new-found friend to find him staring at her with an expression of undisguised admiration.

"By jove, you are right! It is an adventure," he said. "As for having met you before and not dancing with you, that's a lie if there ever was one. Wouldn't be likely to forget anyone who looked like you."

"It is true, nevertheless," Sabina answered. "I ... I suppose I have changed a little."

"Two years ago, was it? Can't believe that two years would make all that difference to you, whatever it did to anyone else. Whatever made you get engaged to Prosy? Dull as a headache, poor chap. With looks like yours you could marry anyone."

He spoke so ingenuously that Sabina could not be angry.

"You are not to say such things," she admonished him severely; but all the time she admitted to herself that she found him amusing.

Arthur was at the table where she had left him; but now his luck had changed and the pile of money he had had in front of him had dwindled down to a few gold *louis*.

"Arthur, I have met an old friend of yours," Sabina said.

He rose to his feet, pocketing what money he had left and turned slowly towards her.

"Have you had bad luck?" Sabina inquired.

"I have lost the little money I gained," Arthur replied. "At the same time, as I think I pointed out to you before, it is of no consequence. It is only a foolish and extremely expensive way of passing time, because, by all the laws of average, a gambler cannot eventually be the gainer."

"There you are, Prosy, prosing on just as you used to do," Lord Sheringham said, slapping him on the back and holding out his hand.

"Hello, Sherry! What are you doing here?" Arthur inquired.

"Escorting my mother. Never expected to find you in such a den of iniquity."

"I am here with their Royal Highnesses," Arthur said, a trifle pompously, Sabina thought.

"Lord! Better you than me," Lord Sheringham ejaculated. "If there's one thing I can't stomach its royalty. Too stiff for my liking."

"You always were a feckless sort of a chap," Arthur said coolly. "I find His Royal Highness extremely congenial and I have, let me say, both a respect and an admiration for him."

"By jove, Prosy! You're just the same," Sherry said. "Used to talk in much the same strain when you were at Eton and we used to kick your backside for it."

"And you, Sherry, seem to be just as foolish and inconsequent as you were as a boy," Arthur replied crushingly. "Isn't it about time you grew up?"

"Now, Prosy, don't try and quarrel with me. Not going to have it. Matter of fact I want to congratulate you on your engagement. Your *fiancée* has just told me all about it."

"You have met Sabina, have you?"

"Met her? Known her for years," Lord Sheringham answered. "Two years, to be exact. Met at a ball in London."

"Indeed!" Arthur said coolly.

"Must both come and dine. My mother at the Hotel de Paris. Quite a comfortable place and the food's eatable."

"We shall doubtless be seeing you," Arthur remarked.

He bowed and deliberately moved away, taking Sabina with him.

"Where did you meet that young fool?" he asked, when they were out of earshot.

"Outside in the garden," Sabina answered.

"A very irresponsible young man—I never cared for him," Arthur said.

"Oh, but I like him," Sabina said. "He is very amusing."

"Then your sense of humour must be very different from mine."

"But, Arthur, it is nice to meet all sorts of different people. As Papa always says, it takes all kinds to make a world."

"There are some kinds who are quite unnecessarily tiring," Arthur said. "I am hoping, just hoping, Sabina, that their Royal Highnesses will ask that you should be presented to them. I have, of course, already spoken of our engagement and asked for their permission to make it public. I think, when they know you are here, they are certain to send for you. It would be a great honour."

"Yes, of course," Sabina said. "But I shall be very nervous."

"There is no need," Arthur answered. "I will tell you exactly what to do and if you follow my instructions everything will go off well."

"Will they ask to see your mother, too?" Sabina asked.

"Most certainly not!"

The reply was sharp and Sabina realized that she had been very tactless. She had been thinking of her own nervousness if she was to be presented, and now, uncomfortably, she remembered how much Arthur disapproved of his mother.

She should have let the conversation lapse, but some instinct for fair play made her say:

"Your mother has been very kind to me."

"My mother is a very difficult woman," Arthur replied. "I shall hope that you will not have to stay here long."

"Oh, but Arthur, I do not want to go back—not for a long time at any rate," Sabina cried.

"You must allow me to be the judge of what is best for you," Arthur retorted. "There are many things that you do not understand, my dear Sabina."

"About your mother?" Sabina inquired. "I think I do understand. She has told me about her life and why you disapprove of her."

"Then she had no right to do anything of the sort," Arthur said sharply.

"But can you not understand that she could not help what she did?"

"I refused to discuss it," Arthur interrupted. "It is disgraceful of my mother to have spoken of such a reprehensible indiscretion. If it had been necessary, I would have informed you of the circumstances myself. As it is, you will please forget it. You will speak of it to no one—least of all to your parents. I am ashamed, bitterly ashamed, that you should have been told of this ... shame which rests upon my family."

"Oh, but Arthur, there is no shame and no disgrace," Sabina argued. "The man whom your mother loved is dead."

"Will you be quiet?"

Arthur's face was almost distorted with anger.

"It is most unseemly that you should know of such things and worse still that you should speak of them. If you say any more, I shall send you home to your parents."

There was a long silence.

"I ... I do not like being threatened," Sabina said at length in a very small voice.

"Then learn to be discreet," Arthur snapped. "We will not speak of this again. You are here as my mother's guest, but it is to me that you must turn for advice and it is to me that you must look for instructions as to your behaviour."

Sabina felt a wave of resentment rise within her which made her want to defy Arthur, to argue with him, to say things which she knew, if they once passed her lips, she would regret.

And then, fortunately, they were interrupted. An elderly man came up to speak to Arthur and introduced his wife and daughter—a young, exceedingly pretty girl, with dark hair and dressed in the very height of fashion.

"Cecille is enjoying her visit," Sabina heard the elderly man say.

Sabina liked the vivacious little brunette at first sight, and after they had all had supper together she and Cecille went together to the cloakroom to collect their wraps.

"Is there any chance of our meeting each other tomorrow?" Cecille inquired.

"I am sure there is," Sabina answered. "I will ask Lady Thetford if I can invite you to tea. I am sure she would be delighted for you to visit us!"

"I would like that," Cecille said. "If I don't get a chance to talk to someone of my own age, I shall go mad."

"Why? What is the matter?" Sabina inquired.

"I can't tell you here," Cecille answered. "I doubt if you can help me—I don't think anyone can. But it will be a relief to confide in someone sympathetic."

There was so much suppressed emotion in the girl's voice that instinctively Sabina put out her hands as if to comfort her.

"You sound unhappy," she said. "Are you?"

Cecille nodded.

"Desperately," she said. "But I will tell you all about it tomorrow. Invite me to tea if you can arrange it; if not, let me come and see you during the afternoon. I would ask you to visit us, but we are staying at the hotel and Mamma would sit with us, which would be hopeless. We could talk about nothing that matters."

"I will do what I can," Sabina promised; and they parted at the door of the Casino, Cecille and her parents crossing the road to the Hotel de Paris while Arthur drove her home to the Villa Mimosa.

"Tell me about those people," Sabina asked, when they were alone in the carriage.

"Sir Edward Mason is a clever financier," Arthur replied. "He married late in life and Cecille is his only child. He is devoted to her, I believe."

"I would like her to come to tea with me tomorrow if it were possible," Sabina said.

"It is a good idea," Arthur approved. "Sir Edward has been useful to me at various times. I am sure he would be delighted for Cecille to be your friend."

They reached the villa and as they drove up to the door Sabina said:

"I wonder you do not prefer to stay here with your mother rather than at the hotel."

"I have no desire to stay under my mother's roof," Arthur said sharply, and Sabina realized that once again she had made a mistake.

"I ... am sorry," she stammered. "Good night, Arthur."

He kissed her cheek, then stepping out, helped her from the carriage.

"Good night, Sabina."

He did not touch her again in front of the servants, and without looking back she walked into the villa.

Upstairs in her room she saw that it was not yet two o'clock. She was alone in the villa, for Lady Thetford would not return until her appointed hour of three o'clock.

Sabina went to the window and drew back the curtains. It was very quiet in the garden. She waited for a little while, half-hoping that she would hear the music of a violin. But there was only silence and a sudden emptiness in her heart.

At length she drew the curtains again and began to undress, but all the time she knew she was listening— listening for a tune which never came. She wondered if he was sitting round the fire with his people, perhaps watching the dancer as she twisted and turned with her long black hair streaming out towards the flames. He would find her beautiful, with her golden skin, dark smouldering eyes and high cheek-bones.

Sabina looked at her own reflection in the mirror.

How pale she was! Her skin was almost transparent and her hair, in the candlelight, seemed only a faint replica of the gold in the gipsy dancer's ear-rings.

She gave a little sigh and blew out the light. What was the use of thinking about it? The gipsy king was far away and her thoughts should be on Arthur. But as her eyes closed she was hearing again a deep voice say, 'What the gipsies do they do for friendship or—for love.'

Morning brought a letter on her breakfast tray. For a moment Sabina only stared at it, wondering who could have written to her; and then when she had opened it and turned quickly to the signature, she saw it was from Cecille.

Please don't forget that you have promised to see me today. I am desperate or I would not ask this of you.

"What can be worrying her?" Sabina asked herself aloud. And then, as soon as Lady Thetford had been called, she went along to her room.

"Can I ask a Miss Cecille Mason to tea today?" she inquired, after she had greeted her hostess affectionately.

"But of course, child. Who is she?"

"Her father is a friend of Arthur's and I think she is unhappy. She said that she would like to talk to me."

"Ask her here at four o'clock and you can be alone," Lady Thetford said. "I have promised to visit the Comtesse Etienne d'Abrante—an old ladies' tea party which would bore you. It will be far more fun for you to have your young friend to yourself."

"How kind of you! I will write to her at once," Sabina said.

"Now we have to decide what you are to wear tonight," Lady Thetford remarked.

"Tonight?"

"Yes, didn't Arthur tell you? There is a fancy dress ball at the palace. The Prince of Monaco asked me a month ago if I would give a dinner party for it. I hoped that Arthur would come with us, but I think he will go with the royal party. It is a nuisance because it means we shall be a man short, unless I can think of someone nice and young."

Sabina hesitated a moment.

90

"Could we ask Lord Sheringham?" she said. "I met him last night at the Casino and we were introduced to each other two years ago when I was in London."

"Of course we will ask him," Lady Thetford exclaimed. "I know his mother, Lady Cheveron, well; she is an old friend of mine. I heard that she had arrived in Monte Carlo, but I did not know that her boy was with her."

"He was at Eton with Arthur."

"Yes, I know," Lady Thetford answered. "I am afraid they never got on very well together."

Sabina smiled.

"He said that Arthur was always called 'Prosy Ponsonby' and he still calls him 'Prosy'. I do not think Arthur likes it."

"I am quite certain he doesn't," Lady Thetford laughed. "But never mind, we will ask Lord Sheringham for dinner tonight and that will make us even numbers. And now run away, child, and write a note to Miss Mason. Bates can send one of the footmen with both invitations at the same time."

"Thank you so much," Sabina cried.

She ran to her room, wrote to Cecille, and an hour later a footman returned with the answer. It was very brief:

You are an angel!—Cecille.

Sabina spent the morning with Marie fitting on a fancy dress which Lady Thetford had ordered from Paris, but which, unfortunately, needed quite a lot of alteration. She was to go as Persephone. But the costume Worth had designed for the Goddess of Spring was so diaphanous that both Lady Thetford and Sabina knew that Arthur would have a fit at the sight of it.

"It is beautiful, but . . ." Sabina began, doubtfully, and Lady Thetford finished:

"But far, far too indecent! Marie will have to add several yards of chiffon to the skirt and cover up one shoulder. You look lovely, child, but if you appear like that you will evoke a storm of protest from my very particular son."

Marie left the room to get some material, and Sabina, holding a spray of spring flowers to her breast, asked:

"Why did you let him grow up to be so dictatorial?"

"It isn't my fault," Lady Thetford replied. "He is exactly like his father. Sometimes when I shut my eyes I

91

can hear my husband speaking, laying down the law, sweeping other people's opinions aside, allowing no one to have any ideas but himself. Most children take after their parents, and Arthur is no exception."

"Could you not have altered him? Made him more understanding?" Sabina asked.

"I tried and I failed," Lady Thetford answered. "Now it is your job my dear. There is nothing that a clever woman cannot do with a man she loves and who loves her. I blame myself that I did not love my husband enough to be able to soften his very harsh and prejudiced outlook on life. You will succeed with Arthur—love can conquer all things."

Sabina said no more because Marie returned. As the dress was pinned and arranged around her, she stood pensively looking out into the garden, a feeling of depression making her unusually serious.

"There, *mademoiselle*, I have finished," Marie said at last, taking several pins from her mouth and sticking them into a small, heart-shaped pin cushion which she wore suspended from her waist-band.

"Oh, it's pretty, Marie," Sabina exclaimed looking at the roses, violets, daffodils and forget-me-nots which were scattered over the bodice and skirt of soft green gauze and which trailed around her feet as if they were growing on the very ground on which she stood.

"Mademoiselle est ravissante!" Marie enthused.

"I do hope everyone will think so. I have never been to a fancy dress ball before," Sabina told her.

"And here is the mask," Marie said. "See, it is of green velvet and I am sewing roses at the corner of it and we will tie it with silver ribbons behind your head."

"What fun not to be recognized," Sabina said. "And can one dance with anyone regardless of whether one has been introduced or not?"

"Mais oui, mademoiselle. That is the real reason for a masked ball. Only at twelve o'clock must you unmask and see with whom you have been flirting all the evening."

"Marie, you are making it sound much more exciting than it really is," Sabina said. "I expect we shall just stick to our own parties and of course they will know who one is. Lord Thetford is going in eighteenth-century costume. He will look very grand."

"Eh bien! And it will suit mi-Lord!"

There was a sharpness in Marie's voice which did not escape Sabina. She was well aware that Marie did not like Arthur. And perhaps it was understandable. She loved her mistress and resented anything which brought her unhappiness.

But delight in her dress for the evening chased away from Sabina's mind the thoughts of Arthur and the gulf between him and his mother. She even forgot that Cecille was bringing her troubles to tea so that when she arrived Sabina's first words were:

"Are you going to the ball tonight? What are you going to wear?"

"I have a shepherdess costume," Cecille replied. "But it doesn't interest me because I don't want to go to the ball. I would rather go to bed alone, if Papa would permit it."

"But why?" Sabina inquired.

"That is just what I have come to tell you," Cecille answered. "I do not know why, but the moment I saw you at the Casino last night I felt that you were the one person who could help me. I have not seen anyone of my own age since I left England a fortnight ago, and directly we were introduced, I knew that you were kind and gentle and understanding."

"Do tell me what it is all about," Sabina pleaded, and then, at a warning glance from Cecille, realized that the footman had entered the room with the tea things.

They talked clothes and the ball until, at last, the silver tray with its heavy embossed teapot, kettle and tea caddy were all arranged on a low table in front of the sofa. Then the cake-stand, with its three tiers of cakes and scones was placed near the table and the plates of rolled white and brown bread and butter, the tiny sandwiches, the biscuits, the jam and honey had all been brought in.

"Now," Sabina exclaimed with a sigh of relief. "Now begin from the very beginning."

She felt as if she were back at home again listening to one of her sisters. If ever they were parted from each other for even a few hours, there always seemed to be something to be related, something to be whispered about and talked over.

"You are sweet," Cecille cried. "I really don't know why I should inflict my troubles upon you."

"Why not?" Sabina inquired. "We should be glad to help each other."

At the same time, she knew that while Cecille could confide in her, she could not confide in Cecille. There was some pride, some inner reserve, that would not allow her to speak of Arthur to a stranger, even though she longed, as she had never longed for anything before, to ask someone's advice about him. If only Mamma was here or Harriet! But Cecille had begun to speak and Sabina forced her thoughts away from herself so that she could listen wholeheartedly to the other girl's confidences.

"I was eighteen last month," Cecilla began. "Yes, I can see you look surprised. I look older, I know, but it is because I have travelled about so much with Papa. He is an international banker and I have been all over Europe with him to Germany and Paris, to Amsterdam and to Madrid. It has made me feel older in lots of ways; it has made me see and do things that other girls of my age have not done. But that doesn't mean I feel any different. I want to fall in love and to get married and to have children, just as every other girl wants to do."

"Yes, of course."

"I thought you would understand. And that's why I want to ask your advice. You have got to tell me what to do. You see, Papa wishes me to marry a man I do not love."

"Why?" Sabina inquired.

"It is something to do with banking," Cecille replied. "A question of their joint concerns amalgamating; of their becoming partners in some big amalgamation! I do not really understand it, but this man is a friend of Papa's. He fell in love with me when he came to our house in London one day. He is twenty-five years older than I am—twenty-five years! I do not love him; I do not pretend to love him—but Papa says that I have got to marry him."

"Even if you do not love him?" Sabina exclaimed.

"Yes, because it is good for business. Papa is rich enough as it is, but I suppose everybody wants more. He says it will make me one of the richest women in the world. I don't want to be rich; I want to fall in love, to find a man who loves me for myself, not because of the advantages I can bring him. I want somebody young, somebody who will laugh with me, enjoy the same sort of things that I enjoy. Instead, I have got to marry a man old enough to be my father!"

"Surely they cannot make you," Sabina said.

"They are making me," Cecille answered. "Oh, can't you understand? It is all very well for you—you are marrying somebody young and handsome, somebody you love and who loves you. I have got to marry a man I do not care a fig about—a man I have seen only twice in my life. When he arrives here this evening, it will be the third time I have ever set eyes on him. Yet I have got to be his wife, I have got to let him touch me and kiss me. It . . . it makes me sick even to think of it."

There was a sudden silence as Cecille's voice, throbbing and agonized, ceased.

"I never thought of . . . marriage . . . like that," Sabina said at last, in a low voice.

"You have never thought of it because it is not going to happen to you!" Cecille went on. "Yet I think all the time of what it will mean to be utterly alone with somebody who possesses me, whose name I bear, who owns me because he is my husband—owns me, body and soul. It is all very well for my parents to talk of the advantages of marriage, of being rich, of having carriages, houses and jewels. What do all those matter beside the fact that a man I do not love, I do not even like, is able to do what he likes with me? To take me in his arms, to kiss me, to. . . ."

Cecille stopped suddenly and covered her face with her hands.

"I cannot even say it," she said. "And yet it is something that is going to happen to me. Can you imagine what it will be like? Can you bear to think of that moment when there is no escape? When because one is a woman one is caught, captured, a prisoner, shut up alone in a strange bedroom with a stranger! Can you bear to think of that?"

Sabina was very pale.

"No . . ." she whispered. "No . . . no. . . . I cannot bear . . . to think of . . . that."

CHAPTER SIX

LADY THETFORD came into the drawing-room pulling her sable stole with its dozens of swinging tails from her shoulders. Sabina was sitting by the window, a book in her hand. She was not reading; she was looking out on to the garden. But she did not see the hanging festoons of scarlet geraniums and blue heliotrope. In fact she saw nothing but the tumultuous questions in her own mind. She was so intent that she did not hear Lady Thetford's entrance. The older woman watched her for a few seconds before she spoke.

"You are very serious," she said quietly, at length.

Sabina started and then got to her feet.

"I am sorry, I did not hear you come in."

"It is all right, child. I am late but I expected to find your friend still with you."

"No, Cecille left nearly half an hour ago," Sabina replied.

"You were looking serious," Lady Thetford said. "Are you worried about anything?"

"No, no, of course not," Sabina said so quickly that Lady Thetford looked at her searchingly for a moment before she walked across the room to ring the bell by the fireplace.

"We will have a fire," she said. "It has been hot all day, but it seems always to get a little chilly in the evening. It is hard to realize that there is snow in England."

"Is there?" Sabina asked. "How do you know?"

"I read it in the papers this morning," Lady Thetford said. "Snow and frost. It seems strange to think of it here."

"It does indeed," Sabina said. "But then Monte Carlo is like living in another world."

She spoke quietly and there was none of the eager vivacity which usually rang in her voice, so that again Lady Thetford looked at her.

"Are you looking forward to tonight?" she asked, after a moment.

"Yes, of course I am," Sabina answered politely. "Marie has finished my dress and I hope you will like it when I put it on."

"I am sure I shall," Lady Thetford said. "I want you to be the Belle of the Ball."

"I do not suppose there is any chance of that," Sabina replied. "But it will be enough to be there, to see the Palace and the guests. I wonder...."

What she was about to say was lost, for suddenly the door opened and Arthur came into the room. He was carrying in his hand a newspaper, and walking across the room towards his mother without even so much as a glance at Sabina, he held the paper out to her and pointed with his finger to a paragraph.

"Have you read this?" he asked, his voice hard and sharp so that Sabina knew that he was very angry.

Lady Thetford raised her eyebrows.

"Good evening, Arthur! I don't think that I heard you greet me as you came in, or Sabina either."

"Will you read that paragraph, Mother?"

"In a moment, dear. I must find my glasses. Oh, Bates," she added, raising her voice as the butler appeared in the doorway. "I rang for the fire to be lighted and ask Marie to bring me my spectacles. I am afraid I must have left them upstairs."

"Very good, my lady."

A footman hurried across the room and set a match to the fire, and nothing was said until Bates returned with Lady Thetford's spectacles case on a silver salver.

The butler and the footman withdrew and then, at last, Lady Thetford took her glasses from the case and put them on.

Arthur had stood all this time as if he were frozen into immobility. He had not moved or spoken, but the expression on his face proclaimed his feelings all too eloquently.

Sabina sat down again on the seat in the window which she had vacated on Lady Thetford's arrival. She tried to efface herself, feeling that whatever was about to occur concerned only mother and son and was no business of hers. And yet as she watched them, her eyes wide and troubled in her small, pale face, she found herself tense and fearful. She clasped her hands together in her lap and

97

in a few minutes her fingers, as she interlocked them, were white with the pressure.

"Now what is worrying you?" Lady Thetford said lightly to Arthur and picked up the newspaper. She looked at the paragraph that Arthur had indicated to her, but she did not read it, instead she took off her glasses and said:

"But I read this this morning. This newspaper is one which is delivered to the house every day."

"Do you know what it says?" Arthur asked.

"Yes, of course," Lady Thetford replied. "There is nothing new that can be said about the masked ball. We have been reading about it for weeks."

"It mentions your name as one of the dinner hostesses."

"Well?" Lady Thetford inquired, and now her eyes met her son's with the air of a deliberate challenge.

"It is impossible! You must see that," Arthur said, in a low voice. "Do you realize that the Prince and Princess of Wales are to be there?"

"I understood that the ball was being given for them," Lady Thetford replied.

"So it is," Arthur retorted. "That is why you must see that under the circumstances you cannot be present."

Lady Thetford gave a little laugh, and setting down the newspaper arranged herself comfortably in an armchair.

"My dear Arthur," she said. "Your coming here with the newspaper in your hand does not surprise me. I was half-expecting it when you did not mention the ball either to me or Sabina. You must be very foolish if you think that by keeping silent you could prevent us from knowing that both you and their Royal Highnesses were to be present at the palace tonight. Monte Carlo has talked over every detail—which of course included the names of the guests."

"All the more reason for you to understand the delicacy of your own position," Arthur said sharply.

"What position?" Lady Thetford said tantalizingly.

Arthur made a gesture which somehow bespoke the violence of his feelings.

"Don't play with me," he asked savagely. "I am not a child. Do you suppose that people at home really believe you went abroad for your health? The Queen may do so, she is out of touch with society, and after all, no one would dare to talk scandal to her. But our friends are not so obtuse. You have been seen in Paris. People have met you here. They must wonder why you have never come back to England; why you left so hurriedly; why you stayed away so long."

"Have they questioned you?" Lady Thetford inquired.

"No, not questioned me exactly," Arthur replied. "They have asked me how you were, of course, and I have always told them that the doctors considered it essential that you should remain in a warm climate."

"And we are in a warm climate now," Lady Thetford smiled.

Arthur looked embarrassed.

"I have perhaps given the impression that you were not as well as you are."

Lady Thetford laughed.

"A semi-invalid!" she exclaimed. "Or did you make me entirely bed-ridden?"

"There is nothing to laugh at," Arthur said gruffly.

"Why not, for it is, in its way, exquisitely humorous!" Lady Thetford replied. "But because you are a bad liar and a very stupid one, you cannot expect me to inconvenience myself to the point of putting my feet up on the sofa and going into a decline. No, Arthur! You must take the consequence of being so ill-judged as to make me out something that I am not."

"I forbid you to go to the ball tonight," Arthur said violently.

"Forbid me!" Lady Thetford raised her eyebrows. "Let me make this very clear—I have no intention of obeying such a command from anyone, least of all from my own son. Besides, even if I did concede to your quite unreasonable and outrageous wish, what excuse would you give to the Prince?"

"The Prince?" Arthur asked. "What Prince?"

"Your host tonight," Lady Thetford answered. "Prince Charles requested me nearly two months ago to give a dinner party for his ball."

"He requested you! Do you know him?" Arthur asked.

Lady Thetford put back her head and laughed—a laugh which seemed to Sabina to be quite genuine and spontaneous.

"Oh, Arthur! Arthur! How ridiculous you are!" she exclaimed. "Of course I know him. He is a very dear friend of mine. As a matter of fact he dined here only three or four days ago and we talked over all the ar-

99

rangements he has made for this ball which is causing you so much concern."

"I . . . I had no idea," Arthur said.

"No, of course not," Lady Thetford answered. "You are so certain that your own attitude towards me, of a scarlet woman ostracized by society, must be right, that you cannot conceive that other people may have very different ideas."

Arthur suddenly walked across the room and back again, as though the action relieved some inner agitation.

"What am I to say to their Royal Highnesses," he asked, "if by any chance your name is brought to their notice? I have not said that my mother is living here."

"If they ask questions, you will just have to explain that you had forgotten the fact that you had a mother—or one who is still able to move about on her two feet. Poor Arthur, how awkward it is for you!"

"Damnably awkward," Arthur said explosively. "Why did you have to be here at the same time as their Royal Highnesses?"

"I really cannot see why, just to suit you, I should leave what is my home for a large part of the year," Lady Thetford retorted. "Besides, there is no reason why there should be any awkward moments. I cannot believe amongst the enormous number of guests Prince Charles has asked that their Royal Highnesses will notice my quite insignificant name. If they do, you must explain as best you can that much to your surprise there is life in the old dog yet!"

"You make a joke of everything," Arthur said surlily.

"I laugh so that I shall not cry when I remember that you were once my baby—of whom I was so proud," Lady Thetford said in a low voice.

There was a moment of silence and then Arthur, with what seemed to Sabina almost an air of apology, turned towards her.

"I did not realize, Sabina, that I was to have the pleasure of seeing you this evening," he said. "I hope you will keep me some dances."

"I am so looking forward to the ball," Sabina said simply.

She had felt almost unbelievably embarrassed by this violent exchange between mother and son; and now, as she rose to her feet, she saw with an air of detachment that her hands were trembling.

Lady Thetford had turned towards her writing-desk and taken from it a piece of crested paper on which, in her large flowing hand, she had written the names of the guests for dinner.

"This is my party as I arranged it with Prince Charles," she said. "You will see that we both expected that you would be dining here with me tonight, as Sabina is one of my guests. But as you had not spoken of the party before, I realized that you would not be present and I have asked Lord Sheringham to take your place."

For a moment Sabina wondered if Arthur would protest at the name. Instead, he read the list of guests, looking a little surprised at the distinction of several of them. And then he handed the paper back to his mother.

"Perhaps . . . I owe you an apology," he said.

The words seemed almost to be dragged from his lips, and Sabina, although she knew him so little, realized it was a tremendous effort for him to force himself to say the words.

"There is no need to apologize," Lady Thetford said, in a hard voice. "I am quite indifferent to any action you may take or anything you may say as far as I am concerned. You have made it all too clear these past ten years what you think of me."

She turned away as she spoke and though her voice was hard Sabina suspected that there were tears in her eyes.

"You cannot expect me . . ." Arthur began, and then he stopped. "It is surely unnecessary to go into all that again."

"Quite unnecessary," Lady Thetford agreed.

"Then I will see you tonight."

He seemed uncertain for a moment as to how he should take his leave, either of his mother with her averted face, or of Sabina, who was looking pale and shaken. And then he forced a smile to his lips.

"I am sorry, Sabina," he said, "that you should have had to listen to what must seem to you an intimate family affair. But you, yourself, are in fact now one of the family. It is best for you to know the worst of us."

"Yes, of course . . . I understand," Sabina murmured.

"Good-bye then, for the moment. And keep your programme free for me. I shall have a number of duty dances, of course, but I shall be with you as much as is possible."

"Thank you," Sabina answered.

He held her hand for a moment in his, and then he looked towards his mother. Lady Thetford was still standing with her back to them, seemingly intent on something lying on her writing-desk. Arthur waited for a second in what appeared to be a slightly embarrassed manner and then, without a word, he left the room.

As he shut the door behind him, Sabina had an absurd impulse to call after him; to tell him he could not go like that, leaving his mother unhappy, hurt and wounded. She might say she did not care, but Sabina knew only too well that every unkind word was like a sword-thrust in her heart.

How she must have suffered, she thought, these long years when Arthur had come to hate her because she had followed the dictates of her own heart. Sabina thought of how her father and mother relied on each other; how Lady Evelyn's face would light up when her husband came into the room; how his first words on entering the house were to call her name or ask one of the children: "Where is Mamma?"

That was love. The same sort of love that Lady Thetford must have felt for the man she had run away with, for Guy who had died. Now Arthur was all she had left. Sabina thought that if Harry had spoken to Mamma as Arthur spoke to his mother, everyone in the Vicarage would have thought that the whole world was coming to an end.

"Oh, Mamma, you don't know what it is like to be home," Harry had said when he had last been back on leave. "I miss you so much that sometimes I feel I cannot bear to be away from you all."

"But, Harry, you do like the Navy, don't you?" Lady Evelyn asked anxiously.

"It is all right when I don't think about being at home," Harry replied.

Sabina and her sisters had always known that Mamma loved Harry the best of all of them. Harriet was Papa's favourite, although Sabina sometimes fancied that since she had grown up he liked her the best. But there was no doubt where Mamma's affection lay.

"There's a tie between mothers and sons which is

102

deeper than any other affection," their old Nanny had said once, as Lady Evelyn had run upstairs to shut herself in her bedroom after Harry had gone back to school.

"Do you mean that Mamma loves Harry more than us?" Angelina asked. She was very young at the time and the tears began to gather in her big brown eyes.

"Of course she does," Nanny answered stoutly. "And it is no use you carrying on about it either. It is mothers and sons and fathers and daughters in the natural course of things, and you can't go against nature—nobody can."

Sabina had often thought of those words and believed them. You can't go against nature! And yet, now it seemed to her that Arthur and his mother were destroying all the lovely things she had believed in ever since she had been a child. Home had been such a sure, secure background in her own life that she had thought it must be the same for everyone.

For a long moment she stood looking at the closed door through which Arthur had gone, and then impulsively she ran across the room to Lady Thetford and slipped her hand in hers.

"I am sorry," she said softly.

"Do not pity me," Lady Thetford replied in a strangled voice. "It is the one thing I could not bear, to be pitied. He was such a dear little boy."

She disentangled her hand from Sabina's and went from the room. Sabina heard her walking very slowly up the stairs, and the rustle of her silk petticoats sounded like the softest of sighs which accompanied her wherever she went.

The scene with Arthur and Cecille's confidences during the afternoon left Sabina feeling low and depressed. She had a sudden longing for her home, for the arms and lips of her own family, the warmth of their love surrounding her and the feeling that they were all secure and immune from the world and its miseries.

Monte Carlo had seemed a fairy-like place when she had arrived, but now mortal sorrows, problems and difficulties were presenting themselves, it seemed, at every turn. And when she thought of Arthur she felt herself tremble a little because of his anger and the hard coldness of his voice when he spoke to his mother.

She knew now that she was frightened of him. She had, if she faced the truth, been frightened of him from the very beginning, but she had told herself at first that what she felt was only a natural reaction because he was older than herself. A man of thirty was not to be compared with the boys whom she met in the county, with whom she danced or rode out hunting. Besides, he lived in a world of which she knew so little.

All this could account for the fact that she felt awkward and shy in his presence. But now, for the first time, she faced the fact that it was so much more. She did not understand him as she had thought she understood other men with whom she came in contact: and alone in her own room, Sabina asked herself a question which had been lurking at the back of her mind for a long time.

Why did he want to marry her? He did not seem like a man in love, she thought, although perhaps he had a strange, indifferent way of showing it.

'I am so ignorant,' she thought. 'I know so little about men and their feelings. I thought that love showed itself. . . .' She stopped suddenly. She was thinking of someone whose dark eyes burned with admiration when they looked at her and a voice that seemed deep when he spoke of love, either in French or English.

She made a sudden gesture as though she threw the thought away from her.

"I am mad to think of such things," she said aloud; and then feverishly, because she dare not question herself further, she applied herself to getting dressed for the ball.

Long before she came downstairs to wait for the guests to the dinner party to assemble, long before she showed herself to Lady Thetford and heard her words of approval, she knew that her dress was a success.

The spring flowers sewn on to the soft, gauze-like material, were an entrancement in themselves. But with her long, pale gold hair hanging over her shoulders and held only by a wreath of snowdrops, with her neck and arms bare and unadorned, with the soft draperies falling from her shoulders to flutter ethereally around her, she knew that she looked lovely and very unlike her usual self. She almost believed, as her mood of depression left her and was succeeded by a light-hearted gaiety, that she had indeed come from the gloomy portals of the underworld up into the sunshine and laughter.

Lord Sheringham sat next to her at dinner and made

her laugh again and again at his droll way of saying things, with his funny remarks about people and things.

"Strap me, but I wouldn't believe fancy dress could be so becoming until I saw you tonight," he told Sabina. "Most people in fancy togs seem to have slipping wigs and costumes quite unsuitable to their personalities. What's Prosy wearing?"

"I shall not tell you," Sabina replied. "You are going to say something unkind about him and you will say it in such a way that I am certain to laugh and then I shall feel disloyal."

"If Prosy's got any sense he will come as Don Juan with a prize bun in his hand for having captured the prettiest girl in the room. What do you want to marry him for? Why didn't you wait for me?"

"I have already told you that you had your opportunity two years ago and you turned up your nose at me," Sabina laughed.

She had never believed that she could feel so at ease with a fashionable young man, but Lord Sheringham was as easy to talk to as Harry might have been and they alternately teased and flirted with each other until it was time to drive to the Palace.

There were five carriages waiting outside the villa to transport Lady Thetford's guests, and Sabina found herself in one with her hostess, Lord Sheringham and the Duc de Guise, who was the most important guest at the party.

The Palace was on the other side of the harbour, beyond the Great Gorge which separated the sober ancient old town of Monaco from the frivolous, ephemeral elegance of Monte Carlo. Sabina forgot to talk or even to listen to the other occupants of the carriage as they drove past the deep ravine full of shadows and up the narrow, twisting road which climbed the massive rock on which was poised the ancient Palace.

Outside, the soldiers in their red, white and blue uniform presented arms. Inside, the beautiful *salons*, decorated with gold and lit by crystal chandeliers, sparkled and glittered with the vast company of guests who had gathered there at the invitation of the Prince.

Sabina felt almost dazzled with the splendour of the Palace until she forgot everything in the amusement of watching the dancers in their strange and varied costumes. There were toreadors and crusaders, clowns and kings, shepherdesses and harlequins, eastern potentates, slave girls and courtiers from every period of history, and also many strange and peculiar costumes to which it was hard to put a name save that they framed the beauty and bewitchery of their owners.

Everyone wore their masks except their host, Prince Charles III of Monaco, who received them when they arrived. He was an old man now and going a little blind, but he had a special word for all the guests whom he recognized, and when Lady Thetford presented Sabina he said:

"I am pleased to welcome you, Miss Wantage. Your future mother-in-law is a very dear friend of mine."

Sabina stammered a shy reply and then they passed on into the ball-room as other guests were received.

The band, in colourful Hussar uniform, was playing a waltz and Sabina was being whirled around by Lord Sheringham when she saw Arthur appear in the doorway. She had a sudden desire not to see him or speak to him. She could not explain it even to herself, but she felt that he would spoil the light-hearted enjoyment of the evening, the gaiety which seemed to bubble up around her as she danced.

"Let us explore the rest of the Palace," she said to Lord Sheringham, and slipping through a door on the opposite side of the ball-room, she was in a second out of sight of Arthur's searching eyes.

They found a staircase which led to an open courtyard and from there into the garden. Built on the side of the cliff, it was a place of secrecy and shadows, of great beds of rosemary and violets beneath mimosa and eucalyptus trees, flagged by bushes of jasmine and myrtle. Chinese lanterns hung from the trees to light the way to little alcoves arranged beneath pergolas of roses and honeysuckle.

The garden looked over the harbour and now Sabina could see the great sweep of mountainous rock on which Monte Carlo had been built. The lights were twinkling in every window of the white villas which in the daytime could be seen rising step by step up the mountainside, flanked by the orchards of orange and lemon trees, where the golden fruit hung like a million miniature lanterns on the dark green boughs.

"It is lovely!" Sabina exclaimed.

The words seemed to be wrenched from her very heart in their deep sincerity.

"And you are lovely, too," Lord Sheringham said. "Too lovely for most men's peace of mind. Damme, if I was Prosy I would snatch you up and take you away from here and shut you up in a castle where nobody would see you but me."

Sabina laughed.

"I had no idea you were so romantic," she teased.

"Right there. Not the sort of things I feel as a rule," Lord Sheringham replied. "Must be the sun that's gone to my head!"

They found a seat on the edge of the garden and sat down for a moment, looking at the harbour below them.

"Tell you what," Lord Sheringham said suddenly. "Could do with a drink! Bet you could, too. Wait here a moment while I go and see if I can find a waiter to bring us some champagne. Nothing like having a talk with a drink in your hand and a pretty girl to listen to you. There was a poem about it I read once. Something about a jug of wine and thou."

"That is in 'Omar Khayyam'," Sabina giggled.

"Don't know who wrote the thing. Seemed to have a bit of sense in it," Lord Sheringham announced. "Will you wait? Can't keep jigging around all the night in these infernally uncomfortable clothes."

He was dressed as a Cavalier, and he put his plumed hat down by Sabina's side and walked off into the darkness. She looked across the moonlit water, her thoughts closing in on her now that she was alone. She heard a step beside her and thought that Lord Sheringham had returned.

"You have been very quick," she exclaimed, and then saw it was not whom she had thought it to be, but a man dressed in a full-sleeved white shirt embroidered in strange patterns, with a jewelled knife stuck in the wide red sash around his waist.

"Will you dance with me?" A voice she knew only too well asked in English.

She started to her feet.

"Why are you here?"

"There are so many people in fancy dress," he replied.

107

"Who would know that a gipsy was only wearing his ordinary clothes?"

"Suppose they caught you?"

"They won't. Like Cinderella I shall leave before midnight when the unmasking takes place. Will you dance with me?"

"No . . . I do not know. . . . How could we dare?"

"I never thought you would be afraid," he said. "You were not afraid to come alone and unescorted to seek for help when your carriage had broken down. You were not afraid to drive alone along the Upper Corniche Road. Are you afraid now?"

"No, of course not," Sabina said. "Not like that. I was thinking of you."

"And not of yourself? Not what would happen if you should be discovered with a gipsy, a vagabond?"

"No, of course not," Sabina said hotly. "I am not that sort of snob."

There was so much anger in her voice that he smiled, and taking her hand raised it to his lips.

"You have not yet said you are glad to see me."

"I was so surprised and . . . afraid, too. How did you get in?"

He pointed to where far away in the shadows a high wall bordered the end of the garden."

"I climbed."

"But why?"

"To see you."

"You knew I was coming here?"

"Of course. All Monte Carlo is here tonight."

"And why, particularly, did you want to see me?"

"I wondered what you would wear. I ought to have told you—I am incurably curious. Most of my race are the same, that is why we travel, seeking different places, different people, different ideas."

Sabina suddenly put out her hand as if to stop him.

"Listen," she said. "Lord Sheringham will be returning any moment. If we are to dance together, we ought to go to the ball-room now by a different way."

"Come then."

The gipsy king held out his hand, she put hers into it. He led her down a path which ran in another direction from the one by which she and Lord Sheringham had come from the Palace. The Chinese lanterns lit the way

108

and passing a fountain, the water iridescent and sparkling in the light, they came again to the courtyard and climbed the stairway to the ball-room.

Only then did Sabina turn to look at her companion. His mask was heavier than hers, hiding half his face, but she felt she could read the expression in his eyes as he looked down at her. She was trembling as he placed his arm about her waist and swung her into the crowd of dancers, and then, almost at once, she was no longer afraid.

It was not only because he looked like everyone else—his dress more fancy than some and more becoming than most—it was because of the firmness of his hand, the touch of his fingers which made her feel, as she had felt once before, secure and safe in his keeping.

They swung round the room, Sabina's hair flying out a little as they turned. He was a beautiful dancer and Sabina felt as if she floated rather than danced, her whole body in tune to his.

"Are you still frightened?" he asked her.

"Not now," she answered truthfully.

"I wonder what the punishment would be if I were discovered," he said ruminatively. "A year in prison, perhaps. Helas, I am told that the prisons of Monaco are very comfortable!"

"Oh, do be careful," Sabina begged, but he only laughed at her and swung her round again.

Womanlike she had to ask the question which was uppermost in her mind.

"Do you like my dress?"

"I haven't had time to look at anything but your hair," he replied. "That first night when you sat in the firelight I thought it was the most beautiful thing I had ever seen. But now, when I look at it hanging over your shoulders, I want. . . ." He hesitated for a moment and Sabina looked up at him and asked a little breathlessly:

"What do you want?"

"To kiss it," he answered. "To bury my face in it, to feel the silk of it beneath my fingers."

Sabina felt suddenly as if she could hardly breathe. There was a constriction in her throat, a feeling as if her mouth was warm and aching, and then her eyes flickered beneath his and she felt the blood rising in her cheeks. She knew that she ought not to listen, she ought to tell

109

him that he must not speak to her like that, and yet the words would not come. She was conscious only of his arm around her waist, of his hand holding hers so tightly that his clasp was almost painful.

And then the music came suddenly to an end. They stood looking at each other; people were moving and talking and laughing around them, but they were alone in a world of their own—a world that was empty save for themselves. A man and woman together on the edge of eternity!

"I think you have bewitched me," the gipsy king said hoarsely. "There is some magic about you which haunts my mind so that I can think of nothing else. I came here tonight because I had to see you, I could wait no longer."

His words seemed like little thrills quivering over Sabina's body. Still she could not speak, could only look, her eyes held by his as though she were mesmerized.

It was then, as if from a great distance away, a voice interrupted them.

"Here you are, Sabina. I have been looking for you everywhere. I can't think where you have been. Her Royal Highness has graciously informed me that she would like you to be presented."

Sabina drew a deep, deep breath. For a moment she could not understand what had been said or who was standing there, and then slowly she turned her head to look at Arthur.

"Her . . . Royal Highness," she repeated stupidly.

"Yes. Come at once. She is at the far end of the room on the dais. I cannot think where you have been hiding yourself."

"I have . . . been here . . ." Sabina faltered, and then she turned to look for the gipsy king; but he had gone, the crowd had swallowed him up and she and Arthur were standing alone in the centre of the ball-room.

"Don't forget to call her Ma'am and curtsy as low as possible," Arthur instructed her; and now they were walking towards the end of the room where the Prince and Princess of Wales were standing with their host on a raised platform surrounded by members of the royal party.

The Prince was not in fancy dress and wore the Order of the Garter over his evening clothes, the Princess was in her favourite shade of mauve, with a high tiara of amethysts and diamonds. She was exquisite and Sabina found herself gasping almost audibly at the lovely oval face and breathtaking beauty of the Danish-born princess whose loveliness had captured the admiration of all England.

And then, as she drew nearer, she saw that the Prince, gruff and jovial, was talking to a lady garbed as Mary Queen of Scots, who, easily recognizable to Sabina, was seen by Arthur only as they reached the outskirts of the Royal circle. She felt him stiffen.

"You have been away from England a long time, Lady Thetford," the Prince was saying, in his deep, slightly guttural voice.

"Ten years, sir. I spend the winter in Monte Carlo and the summer in Paris."

"Our loss is their gain," the Prince said. "But we miss you. The Queen was speaking of you only the other day. She regrets your absence from Court as indeed we all do."

"Thank you, sir."

Lady Thetford curtsied and as she did so Sabina looked up under her eyelashes and saw the expression on Arthur's face. It was so revealing that she felt herself begin to laugh. It was only because she heard his voice, pompous and impressive, presenting her to the Princess that she managed to control the sound.

CHAPTER SEVEN

THE Princess of Wales was even lovelier than Sabina had imagined, and the many descriptions of her, which filled every newspaper, did not even begin to do justice to her beauty and her grace. Her movements were so exquisite that she made every other woman in her vicinity look clumsy, and her smile could enchant and delight anyone who was favoured by it.

She smiled now as Sabina rose from her deep curtsy.

"So this is to be your bride, Lord Thetford," she said with her attractive broken accent. "You are very lucky. I can see that you do not need our good wishes for your happiness."

"Thank you, Ma'am," Arthur said.

"At the same time, the Prince and I are very angry with you," the Princess went on.

"Angry, Ma'am?" Arthur questioned in consternation.

"Yes, indeed. You did not tell us that your mother was living here in Monte Carlo. It was only tonight at dinner that we learned from our host, Prince Charles, that she not only is here but has the most exquisite garden on the whole coast. Why did you keep this a secret from us?"

"It is not a secret, Ma'am," Arthur stammered. "I did not think it would be of interest to your Royal Highness."

"But of course we are interested," the Princess retorted. "The Queen so often speaks of your mother and how much she misses her. The Prince and I must find time to see the garden and her villa, so that we can tell Her Majesty all about it when we get home."

"My mother would be very honoured, Ma'am."

"Then you must arrange it for us, Lord Thetford," the Princess commanded; and then turning to Sabina she said: "Tell me, Miss Wantage, when you are to be married."

"In June, Ma'am."

"Then I hope you will ask the Prince and me to the wedding," the Princess said graciously.

Sabina stammered her thanks and then curtsied again as the Princess turned away to speak to someone else. Sabina felt Arthur's hand on her arm and they moved through the crowd of dancers and out of the room on to the landing where the staircase led down to the garden.

"Their Royal Highnesses are exceedingly kind," Arthur said. "Shall we go into the garden for a little while? It is so hot here."

Sabina had a sudden reluctance to go back amongst the flowers and the Chinese lanterns in case the gipsy king should be waiting there. But she could think of no excuse to make to Arthur for her reluctance and so she followed him down the staircase and across the courtyard and back into the shadowy, scented garden.

Athur led the way to the nearest arbour. Sabina sat herself on a seat which was covered with soft cushions.

"That was well done," he said, with warm approval in his voice, and Sabina realized that he was excessively pleased both with himself and the kindness of the Princess.

"Will they really come to our wedding?" Sabina asked.

"I have always hoped that as I am a member of the Royal Household we should be honoured by their presence," Arthur replied. "But one can never be certain until their Royal Highnesses actually suggest that they should be invited."

"I ... I think it is rather terrifying really," Sabina murmured.

"There is no need to be nervous," Arthur said reassuringly.

But it will make such an important event of our marriage," Sabina protested. "It makes me shy even to think of it."

"I personally am delighted," Arthur said.

There was a moment's silence and then he continued:

"I feel that things have not been very happy for you, Sabina, these last few days."

Sabina was about to protest, but looking at his face in the light of a lantern, she realized, astonishingly, that he was embarrassed. And then she understood that he was trying to apologize to her.

"I did not wish you to be involved in rows between my mother and myself," he went on. "But perhaps it is best that you should not have been kept in the dark with regard to our relationship."

"Your mother has been very kind to me," Sabina said.

"Yes, of course. I hardly expected her to be anything else," Arthur replied. "After all, she insisted on your coming out here."

"But you see how wonderful that has been for me?" Sabina asked.

"I am glad it has amused you," Arthur said in a repressive tone of voice. "But you will not have to see anything of my mother after we are married."

"But I want to see her," Sabina protested. "She has been so kind, so sweet and so very ... very generous."

Arthur's lips tightened for a moment.

"I don't think you understand," he said. "It is impossible for my mother and me to enjoy the usual relationship of mother and son."

"But why, why?" Sabina asked. "It is all over now."

113

"I will never forgive her for what she did—never!" Arthur said bitterly.

"Surely it did not affect you very much?" Sabina said. "People cannot have known, because look how kind Her Royal Highness has been this evening."

"That is indeed a relief," Arthur agreed. "But can you not imagine what I have been through all these years? Wondering what people are saying, thinking that they were whispering behind my back and believing that any moment my career at Court might be terminated because my mother was making herself notorious with a man who was married—yes, married—to someone else."

There was so much passion and anger in his voice that Sabina was half afraid to speak. And then, with a courage she had not realized she possessed, she said in a gentle voice:

"She was happy. Surely that counted a little."

"Happy?" Arthur queried. "How can anyone be happy when they are doing what is wrong and wicked? When they are creating a scandal which might affect their nearest and dearest—in fact, in my mother's case, me?"

"But it didn't affect you," Sabina protested.

"Which was more by good luck than by good judgment," Arthur snapped.

"And now that the man is dead," Sabina said, "nobody need ever know what happened. Surely you can forgive her now and forget?"

"I am afraid it is impossible for me to do either," Arthur replied. "If I had my own way, I would never see her again, and it was only because she forced my hand that I was obliged to let you come here and to stay with her."

Absent-mindedly, without asking permission, as though his feelings made him forget even his usual good manners, Arthur took a cigar from his case and lit it. Sabina, watching his profile, knew that he was seething with anger and that even to speak of his mother incensed him to the point that his very fingers seemed to tremble with an inner rage.

She felt as if this emotion was all too big for her to combat, too hard for her to understand. She only knew that she felt afraid and distressed by the hatred in Arthur's voice and the hardness of his eyes when he spoke of his mother. And yet, some inborn perversity in her made

114

her continue the argument even though she knew it would be better to agree with him or to lapse into silence.

"Arthur," she asked after a moment. "Why are you marrying me?"

He turned to face her, putting his hand along the back of the seat behind her, a faint smile for the first time curving the grimness of his mouth.

"Because I love you, Sabina. Don't you know that?"

"You told me so when you first asked me to be your wife," Sabina answered. "But if, indeed, you do love me as you say you do, can you not understand what your mother felt for the man she could not marry?"

Arthur took his hand away from behind the chair and sat upright with a jerk.

"Listen, Sabina," he said sharply. "I don't know what stories my mother has been telling you. I myself have always avoided the disgusting details of an intrigue which did its best to wreck my entire life. But I can assure you that love such as that, if you can call it by the same word, has nothing in common with the affection I feel for you. And what is more, I must beg you once and for all never to speak of my mother's sordid intrigue or of the man who was cad enough to inveigle her away from her home and her friends, and from the Court itself. As you say, it is now over and, by the grace of God, there have not been far worse results from her selfish and improper behaviour. Anyway, she need not concern us. Once we are married I shall not, under any circumstances, invite her to my house, and I will certainly not be a guest in hers."

Sabina gave a little sigh.

"I cannot understand you," she said.

"Then do not try so far as this is concerned," Arthur retorted. "Let us talk of something more pleasant. You are looking very pretty tonight, Sabina."

"You like my dress?" Sabina inquired.

"It is charming. The role of Persephone suits you. I must say I expected to find a fancy dress ball a bore, but tonight I have enjoyed myself."

"Do you like being with me?" Sabina inquired.

"My dear girl, what a strange question!" Arthur smiled. "Would I have asked you to marry me if I did not wish to be with you? To tell the truth, I fell in love with you that first night I saw you. You looked so different from the

115

other girls at that extremely dull party. If I must be truthful, I must say I liked you better then in your plain, simple dress than in those elaborate and quite unnecessarily extravagant gowns that my mother has bought you from Paris. I want simplicity in my life, Sabina. I want a wife who is prepared to devote herself to me, not to spend her time rivalling other women in the wearing of clothes and bonnets and making herself nothing but a fashionable clothes peg on which to show off her clothes."

"But, Arthur, will you not want me to be well dressed and to look smart for you?" Sabina inquired.

"Smartness, like too many clothes and jewels, generally betokens a frivolous character, Sabina," Arthur replied. "I want you just to be yourself, just as you were those first days we met. You looked charming, if I remember, that afternoon you came over to play croquet."

"But, Arthur . . ." Sabina began, with a little cry, and then the words died away on her lips. What was the use of arguing? How could she explain that the dress she had worn that afternoon at the Hall was an old, faded summer frock that had once been her mother's and which the village seamstress had altered for her? It was dowdy and out-of-date and she had known it, but she had nothing else to wear that afternoon, having spilt some coffee on her only decent dress the previous Sunday.

She felt a little throb of anger that Arthur should prefer her in those dowdy clothes rather than in the lovely things which had come from Paris; and then suddenly, with a perception that was often hers when she was studying other people, she understood.

Arthur wanted a wife who was in every way the exact opposite to his mother, whom he hated. In some twisted way the natural love of a son had become a fierce, undying hatred which criticized and condemned everything, both big and small, that Lady Thetford did. If she was well dressed, his wife must be the opposite. If she wore jewels, his wife must go unadorned.

Sabina understood, at last, why Arthur had chosen her, unknown and insignificant, the daughter of a country parson, rather than one of the many well-bred, aristocratic girls that he met in Court circles. She felt suddenly humbled and at the same time a little resentful. There was something impersonal in Arthur's affection for her.

She was a symbol, not so much of what he liked but the opposite to what he disliked.

Arthur suddenly threw away his cigar and put his hand along the back of the seat again.

"Sabina, we are going to be very happy, you and I," he said. "I shall have a lot to teach you, but I know that you are willing to learn. You have only to trust me, to believe that what I am telling you is the right thing, and we shall have no disagreements, no quarrels."

He smiled then and added:

"I am not usually so bad tempered as I have been these last few days."

He had charm when he wished to use it and Sabina suddenly longed for something that she could not even explain to herself. Some reassurance, some understanding, some surety, perhaps, which would assuage and soothe the nagging questions which lay persistent and unanswered at the back of her brain.

"Shall we be happy? Are you quite sure we shall be happy?"

It was the cry of a child in need of comforting, and in response Arthur put his hand under her chin and lifted her face up to his.

"You will make me very happy," he said. "I am sure of that."

He kissed her gently and instinctively Sabina's arms went up towards his. She wanted him to hold her, she wanted to be assured that he was right, that he loved her and that she loved him and that they would live happily ever after.

Then even as she moved Arthur took his hand from her chin and moved away.

"We must not be seen courting like any Tom, Dick and Harry," he said repressively. "In fact I think we should return to the ball-room. We must not forget that I am in attendance on their Royal Highnesses tonight."

"Yes, let us go back, it is quite cold," Sabina said.

She shivered as she spoke. She felt suddenly defeated and intensely disappointed. She did not know why, she only knew it was as if her whole body ached for something that was out of reach, something so intangible that she could not even put it into words.

They went back to the ball-room in silence and the

moment Sabina entered the room Lord Sheringham appeared at her side saying reproachfully:

"Oh, here you are at last. Do you realize that you have already cut half my dances?"

"Have I, Sherry? I am so sorry," Sabina smiled.

Even as she called him by his nickname, which he had asked her to use, she realized by the start Arthur gave that he was annoyed by it and thought it familiar.

"Miss Wantage has been in the garden with me," he said, with an accent on the prefix.

"All right, Prosy," Lord Sheringham said cheerfully. "Not going to call you out for something I would do myself if I got the chance."

Arthur gave him a look which Sabina translated as being one of offended dignity, and walked away towards the dais where the royal couple were still greeting friends.

"What's upset him?" Sherry asked, as he put his arm round Sabina's waist and swept her into the throng of dancers.

"I do not think he liked my calling you Sherry."

"Good lord, Prosy's getting too big for his boots. Royalty must have gone to his head. Has called me Sherry since he was twelve years old. Can't expect his wife to stand on formality?"

"I think that is what he does expect," Sabina said, almost beneath her breath; and then, because she thought it was disloyal to be talking of Arthur behind his back, she began to tell Sherry about Cecille.

"I want you to meet her," she said. "She is so sweet, I know you will like her."

Sherry looked at her quizzically.

"Match-making already?" he asked. "Always the same. Moment a girl gets engaged thinks everyone else must do the same. Too late to introduce me to pretty girls. Know as well as I do that I'm in love with you."

"Oh, Sherry, what nonsense you talk!"

"Truth," he said. "Been thinking about you ever since we met. Can't sleep at nights."

"That is not because you are thinking about me," Sabina laughed. "It is because you stay at the Casino until the early hours."

"Well, can't sleep when I do go home. Keep thinking about you, wondering why I didn't get there first. Suppose we couldn't run away together?"

"No, Sherry, of course we couldn't. Arthur would be furious. Besides, I am not in love with you."

"And you are with Arthur, of course?"

It was a question which took Sabina unawares and there was a moment's pause before, blushing, she answered:

"Why else should I marry him?"

"Plenty of reasons for marriage besides love," Sherry remarked. "But if you ask me love is the best one."

"Of course it is," Sabina agreed.

She felt as she spoke a sudden yearning to be in love as Lady Thetford had been. To be ready to give up everything! To be in love as her father and mother still were, their faces lighting up at the sight of each other, their instinctive need of one another showing itself in every crisis, in every daily task however trivial.

Yes, of course, she told herself, she was in love with Arthur. Who wouldn't be? He was so good looking, so important, so attractive in his own way. And yet somehow something was missing. Was it the fire of which Lady Thetford spoke, or the type of love of which the gipsy talked so much and so often?

Her thoughts shied away from this. Was he still in the room? she wondered, and found herself forgetting Sherry as she searched amongst the dancers for the sight of a golden skin beneath the darkness of a black mask; of a dark head held high; for a lissom, graceful body which seemed to have been made to dance. But there was no sign of him. Once she thought she had a glimpse of an embroidered, full-sleeved, white shirt, and then, even as her heart seemed to leap into her mouth, she saw that she was mistaken. The man who wore it was smaller and had a long, dark moustache.

"What are you thinking about?" Sherry asked suddenly, and Sabina wondered how long she had been silent.

"The correct answer is, of course, that I was thinking of you," she replied, laughing. "But actually I was thinking of myself."

"Selfish!" he rebuked her. "Come on, let's get out of this scrum and find a glass of champagne. Really too hot to dance."

"It is growing colder outside," Sabina said, remembering how she had shivered when she had been with Arthur.

"Haven't got enough on, that's the matter," Sherry retorted. "Glass of wine will soon warm you up."

He led her to another room where there was a bar loaded with delicious things to eat and where waiters were hurrying between the guests, plying them with champagne.

Cecille was looking very pretty and was talking to a man dressed as a Venetian Doge. He was tall, thin and aristocratic looking; at the same time it was obvious that he was not a young man, and Sabina guessed that this was the suitor whom Cecille's parents favoured and whom she was being forced to marry.

Cecille introduced him as Mr. Rochdale, and then Sabina presented Sherry.

"Sabina been speaking of your charms all day," he told Cecille. "Extolled them to such an extent thought she must be exaggerating! Now I've met you find they were an understatement."

"What a lovely speech!" Cecille smiled.

Sabina found herself talking to Mr. Rochdale.

"Is this your first visit to the Palace, Miss Wantage?"

"Yes. The first, as it happens, to any palace."

"Then you have chosen an excellent one on which to start," Mr. Rochdale said. "I always think when I come here what a delightful contrast this is. The Great Rock, the Palace and the Fortress, all three so grey and very, very old, as they have stood for nearly six hundred years. And then on the other side of the Ravine that gaudily tinted fungus, which we call Monte Carlo, splashed like a jester's coat and ephemeral as a rainbow."

"How exciting you make it sound!" Sabina cried.

"But not half as exciting as the tale really is," Mr. Rochdale replied. "One day people will write a story of Francois Blanc's gigantic venture and make it more thrilling than any novel. Do you realize that already there have been one hundred thousand visitors to Monte Carlo this year, where only a few years ago the croupiers used to stand outside the Casino and scan the road with telescopes to see if there was a diligence on its way carrying a few precious gamblers?"

"Did you ever come here then?"

"As a matter of fact I did," Mr. Rochdale replied. "Prince Charles is an old friend of mine and I was able to advise him on some of the difficulties which cropped up, both as regards the Casino itself and when there was a rebellion amongst the inhabitants of Monaco."

"A rebellion?" Sabina questioned. "Did they not like the Casino?"

"They didn't think they were getting sufficient benefits from it quickly enough. Like the rest of the world they were greedy."

"You sound as though you think we are all tainted with that vice," Sabina accused him.

"Isn't it true that most of us are?" Mr. Rochdale parried. "None of us have enough—power, money or affection. We always want more."

"I suppose that is true," Sabina agreed thoughtfully.

"Instead of using the word affection shall I say love?" Mr. Rochdale asked. "We all want love—rich and poor, young and old. It is like the sunshine, and the people who are without it sit in darkness."

Sabina looked up at him. He was smiling and yet there was a hint of seriousness behind his grey eyes.

'I like him,' she thought to herself quickly. 'I like him and if he loves Cecille she will be a lucky girl.'

Cecille was laughing and flirting with Sherry, and now, turning to Sabina, she said:

"Have you had any supper yet? Let us all go down together, shall we?"

Sabina looked worried.

"I am wondering if Arthur will expect me to wait for him."

"No, he won't," Sherry interposed. "Be in the Royal procession. Certain I saw the whole crowd, Prosy amongst them, moving out of the ball-room nearly twenty minutes ago."

"Oh, that is all right, then," Sabina smiled.

"Come along, I am ravenous," Cecille said.

She took Sabina by the hand and they led the way down a long corridor decorated with a fine collection of pictures, towards the great banqueting hall. Moving quickly, the two girls got separated from their supper partners for a few moments, and Sabina said in a low voice:

"I do hope you like Lord Sheringham."

"He seemed charming," Cecille answered. "But very young."

121

"Young?" Sabina inquired. "He is the same age as Arthur."

"Indeed! But I think an older man has so much more distinction, and young men are often so tiring with their enthusiasms and their predilection for talking about themselves."

Sabina looked at her in astonishment, then she smiled.

"I too thought Mr. Rochdale charming," she said.

Supper was a gay and hilarious meal, with Sherry and Mr. Rochdale capping each other's stories and Sabina and Cecille laughing until they both declared their sides ached. In contrast, at the other end of the banqueting hall, the Royal party, with Arthur amongst them, was subdued and decorous, and Sabina, glancing towards them once or twice, felt thankful that she was not grand enough to be one of the women guests.

Even as she thought of it she remembered that the day would soon come when she, like Arthur, would be hovering around their Royal Highnesses. Sabina had a sudden vision of evening upon evening when she must make conversation with people with whom she had little in common, when there would be that formal stiffness and depressing lack of vitality over everything that was said or done.

She had heard stories of how bored the members of the Court were at Windsor; and although the Prince of Wales was fond of gaiety, on more public occasions he, too, could be formal and extremely regal.

Sabina found herself envying Cecille and Mr. Rochdale. The latter was telling stories of people he had met on his travels, making them laugh with his descriptions of the economies in a German castle and, in contrast, the lavish entertainment one received in Russia.

How different Cecille's life would be from hers! Yet, only that very afternoon, Cecille had cried out against having to marry Mr. Rochdale and made Sabina quite unhappy with the idea of the miseries she must endure on becoming his wife. He was, indeed, much older, and at the same time Sabina could see his attraction and how fascinating his knowledge, wisdom and experience could be to a young girl.

Mr. Rochdale continued to talk of foreign countries until Sabina asked:

"Have you ever been to Hungary?"

"But of course," he said. "I have very many friends amongst the Hungarians. They are a charming, kind, warm-hearted people. They love good wine, beautiful music and lovely women."

"I can believe that," Sabina said. "I ... I met a Hungarian once. He said some very charming and delightful things, but I wondered if one could believe him and if he were speaking the truth."

"If he was saying charming things to you, then you can believe every word of them," Mr. Rochdale said gallantly.

Sabina blushed.

"I was not meaning that exactly. I just wondered if. . . ."

"If they had a blarney like the Irishmen?" Mr. Rochdale finished for her. "It is a difficult question for me to answer. Shall I put it this way? Hungarians have strong, deep emotions. Everything they do is a combination of heart and mind. If they hate it is with force and passion. If they love, they love to distraction. Is that what you want to know?"

"Who is this Hungarian?" Sherry inquired, who had been listening to the conversation. "Damme I'm exceeding jealous."

"Oh, it's not anyone of any importance," Sabina answered; but she could not help the colour coming into her face, and Cecille gave a little laugh and asked:

"Does Arthur know about him? He is the one to be jealous, not Lord Sheringham."

"You are making a mountain out of a molehill," Sabina protested. "I was only asking Mr. Rochdale, as a matter of interest, about the character of the people as a whole."

"Nonsense!" Cecille told her. "But we won't tease you, dearest, because I hate being teased."

"Another thing I must remember," Mr. Rochdale said.

Cecille pouted at him, but she was smiling and there was a light in her eyes that Sabina had not seen there before.

'I need not have worried about her,' she thought to herself. 'She was just dramatizing a situation and making the most of it.'

They went on talking and laughing, not noticing that the Royal Party had left the room, and it was quite half an hour later when Sabina started as Arthur came behind her chair.

"My mother has gone home some time ago," he said stiffly. "She wanted to visit the Casino. I promised her that I would take you home when you were ready."

"Do you want to go now?" Sabina asked.

"It is getting late," Arthur replied, looking at the clock over the mantelpiece.

"Nonsense, Prosy. Being a spoil-sport," Sherry remarked. "Come, sit down, have a glass of wine. Mr. Rochdale telling us stories that'll split your sides open."

"I don't think you know Mr. Rochdale, Arthur," Sabina said quickly.

The two men shook hands and then, pressed once again by Sherry, Arthur sat down at their table. But with his coming the gaiety seemed to have fled from it. Where before the conversation had flowed without an effort, everyone eager to speak, hardly waiting for one pair of lips to become silent before another began, now there was a constriction and an effort.

Arthur had no idea that he was in any way a check on their joviality. He began to speak of the Royal plans for the following day and with a sense of embarrassment Sabina saw Sherry smother a little yawn.

"I think you are right, Arthur," she said. "It is time for me to be going home."

It was obvious that Arthur was only too eager to be gone. Sabina shook hands with Mr. Rochdale and Sherry, kissed Cecille and then, having collected her wrap, walked with Arthur through the fine marble entrance hall and out through the great doors to where the sentries marched up and down outside and where the heavy cannon pointed towards the sea.

Sabina stepped into the carriage and a powdered footman covered her knees with a fur rug.

"It was a lovely party," she said as they drove off.

"I am glad you enjoyed it," Arthur said. "Although I cannot help wishing you had found someone more interesting to dance with than that young wastrel, Sheringham."

"You are unkind about Sherry," Sabina replied reproachfully. "I thought you two were friends as you were at Eton together."

"We were at school together and I see a certain amount of him in London," Arthur admitted. "But Sheringham is a feckless young man who wastes his time to no good purpose."

"What would you have him do?" Sabina inquired.

"What other men of his age do. Take myself, for instance," Arthur replied.

"But you had, perhaps, exceptional opportunities," Sabina answered. "Your father was at Court. You stepped into his shoes."

"Yes, that is true to a certain extent," Arthur said. "But I pride myself I have made my own way in my career. My father had not the same position as I have at my age."

"Did you like Mr. Rochdale?" Sabina inquired, anxious to keep the conversation from becoming controversial.

"I hardly noticed him," Arthur replied. "Who is he? Do you know anything about him?"

"No, nothing very much," Sabina answered. "Except that he is to marry Cecille Mason and he is a banker, like her father."

"Good lord, do you mean to say that is Rochdale? *The* Rochdale?" Arthur said. "Why on earth didn't you tell me? The Prince was speaking of him only last night. I had no idea that he had arrived in Monte Carlo."

"Is he a friend of His Royal Highness?" Sabina inquired.

"He has a certain intimacy with the Prince," Arthur replied evasively. "And I must let H.R.H. know at once that he has arrived. Do you know where he is staying?"

"No, I am afraid not."

"It is sure to be the Hotel de Paris. This is good news. The Prince will be delighted. I only wish that you had made it clear to me so that I could have said something to him, prepared him for the Royal summons."

"I did say his name very distinctly," Sabina murmured.

"Yes, but Rochdale meant nothing. Besides, I didn't expect to find him with you."

"No, of course not!"

Sabina wished that Arthur didn't always make her feel deflated and of so little importance. She was somehow glad to realize that she and Sherry had spent several hours in the company of Mr. Rochdale and from the way he had exerted himself to amuse them and to make them laugh it was obvious that he, at any rate, considered them of some importance.

125

The horses were drawing up the hill to Monte Carlo when Sabina put out her hand and touched Arthur's.

"I do want to be a help to you," she said softly. "I want to do the right thing, to make you proud of me."

Arthur took her hand in his as he laughed.

"I don't think you will be able to help me, Sabina," he replied. "The boot will rather be on the other foot; but if you do what I want you to do and listen to what I tell you, I feel sure we shall get along admirably."

Sabina tried to repress a sigh. Somehow it was an unsatisfying answer.

At the door of the villa Arthur kissed her good night and then helped her from the carriage.

"Will you not come in?" she asked. She had a curious reluctance for him to leave her and find herself alone.

"My dear girl, at this hour of night?" Arthur inquired, scandalized. "We mustn't forget your reputation, must we?"

"No, of course not," Sabina said hastily.

She passed through the front door held open by a footman and Arthur got back into the carriage. She heard it drive away.

"Has her ladyship returned yet?" she asked the butler.

"No, Miss. It will be another half an hour before her ladyship will leave the tables."

"Good night, Bates."

"Good night, Miss."

Sabina went slowly up the stairs. She didn't know why, but she felt lonely. Perhaps she was tired, she thought. Perhaps it was just reaction from too much gaiety, too many late nights.

She opened the door of her bedroom. The lights were lit on her dressing-table and by the side of the bed. Yvonne had offered to wait up for her, but Sabina had refused. She wasn't used to being waited on by a maid and she hated to think of a girl who had worked all day sitting up hour after hour waiting for her to return.

She shut the door behind her. The candles were flickering in the draught from the window, which was open, and the soft satin curtains were billowing out. She would not look at the moonlight tonight, Sabina thought. Besides, instinctively she knew that there would be nobody there. The gipsy king would have gone back to his people after his dance with her. He had said that was the only reason why he had come to the Palace.

Mr. Rochdale had said that the Hungarians loved with great passion. She could believe it. When the gipsy spoke of love, his voice was deep; there was a tremulous undertone which made Sabina's heart beat in a strange manner and her breath come quickly.

She crossed the room and as she did so her eyes fell on her bed. Something was lying on the pillow. She moved swiftly towards it. It was a bunch of roses, red roses, only just in bud. Their fragrance seemed, as she lifted them to pervade the whole room. And then, as she took them in her hands, she saw there was a small card attached to them. There were only two words written on it; two words in a bold, rather arresting writing: 'For Persephone'.

For a long time Sabina stood staring at the card, and then she hid her face in the roses. He must have stolen into the garden and climbed up the wooden staircase to the balcony, crept along it and into her room, to lay the flowers on her pillow. She thought of the risks he ran. If he had been caught, he would have been arrested immediately for being a robber, for having gone into the house with intent to steal. No one would have understood or believed that he had any other reason for being there.

The thought of him in her bedroom made Sabina's heart beat quicker. As he had stood here, had he thought of her lying asleep? Had he thought what she would feel and think as she came back from the ball to find his gift and a card in his own writing? She shut her eyes and let herself remember the tone in his voice, the feeling, wild and almost frightening, that had surged through her veins when he had said he wished to bury his face in her hair.

She wondered if he guessed how tumultuous her feelings had been. Why, why, she asked herself, had he the power to make her feel as if she had wine rather than blood in her veins? To make her throb and feel and feel and feel?

Were all women the same who came in contact with him? Did they all react to his magnetism? To that strange vibration that was so disturbing and yet, in a way, so enchanting. She looked down at the roses. How lovely they were! And somehow she understood why he had chosen them.

Roses in bud! And red roses, which were the age-old symbol of love! Did he think that love was budding in her? And if so—for whom?

CHAPTER EIGHT

SABINA was sitting in the garden alone. She was shaded from the sun by the roof of the small summer-house which lay at the end of a picturesque path winding through rose bushes ablaze with colour, banks of sweet-scented rosemary and hedges of choisya. Behind her a high wall was covered with cascades of scarlet geranium, in vivid contrast to the almost blinding blue of the sky. The dazzling expanse of shimmering sea stretched away to a misty horizon.

Lady Thetford was lying down, but Sabina, feeling that she could not bear to waste even an hour of such beauty in sleep or confined within the four walls of her bedroom, had come out into the garden carrying the letters from home which had arrived by the morning post.

She had already read them once, but that had been rather hastily because she and Lady Thetford were going out in the carriage and she dare not keep the horses waiting. Now she had time to peruse them, to savour every word of Harriet's quick amusing effusion and her mother's loving, lengthy epistle, which told her all that they had been doing at the Vicarage since she left.

She had only to open out the closely written sheets of writing-paper to see them all so clearly. Mamma seated at her desk, her head bent a little as she struggled to find the right word to express herself. Harriet, dashing off a letter on scraps of foolscap which she had collected from the untidy drawer where they all kept their school books.

I am absolutely miserable without you, Harriet wrote; but, flattering though it was, Sabina knew that Harriet could never be miserable for long but would be bubbling over with excitement or enthusiasm for anything that happened during the day or for any anticipated treat in the future.

Sabina put down the letter and sighed. She missed Harriet too. It was such fun to be with someone whom one loved, to be able to tell them things, to share those small trifles of happiness and sorrow which occur every day and which, if one appreciates them sufficiently, make life a continual adventure.

If only Harriet were here, she thought. If only Harriet could see the beauty of Monte Carlo, could meet the interesting and amusing people with whom Lady Thetford surrounded herself, could go to the parties, the balls and the Casino. How she would love it, and what a success she would be!

Never mind, Sabina thought. When she was married she would see that Harriet had a good time. None of her sisters would have to make their début under Aunt Edith's chaperonage as she had done. She would have Harriet to stay, she would give her lovely clothes and she would find her an important and interesting husband. Not that Harriet would ever marry anyone she did not like— Sabina was sure of that. She was far too determined and self-willed to accept any offer however advantageous unless she was absolutely convinced that the man in question was someone she could love and respect.

Sabina's thoughts drifted away from Harriet to herself, and then, with a little start, she picked up her letters again. Even to touch them made her feel homesick. It was no use pretending that anything, however exciting or attractive, could replace the dear familiarity and lovingness of one's own home.

Sabina thought of the big, shabby drawing-room, of the girls grouped round the fireplace and Papa reading aloud; of her own bedroom which she shared with Harriet, their small, white-covered beds side by side, the window looking out over the paddock where Benjamin, their fat pony, grazed contentedly on the lush, green grass. She had only to think of it all to feel almost like crying.

How ridiculous she was! Sabina gave an exclamation of annoyance at her own stupidity and ingratitude and then raised her head to see that one of the footmen was coming across the garden to where she was sitting. She gathered her letters together and awaited his approach.

"What is it, James?" she asked when he was within earshot, expecting him to reply that Lady Thetford wanted her.

"There is a gentleman to see you, Miss."

"A gentleman!" Sabina exclaimed. "Did he give his name?"

"No, Miss. But he asked particularly for you and said I was not to disturb her ladyship."

Who could it be? Sabina wondered. Sherry would have given his name, for a certainty.

"The gentleman is in Naval uniform, Miss," James volunteered.

Naval uniform! Sabina stared at the footman with astonished eyes. It couldn't be—or could it?

She jumped to her feet.

"I will come back to the house at once, James," she said, and set off across the garden with feet that carried her so quickly that she almost broke into a run.

As she neared the house she turned to look back at James who was following.

"Is the gentleman in the drawing-room, James?"

"Yes, Miss."

Sabina took the short cut across the lawn and crossing the flagged terrace outside the drawing-room went in through the french windows. There was a tall figure in Naval uniform standing by the fireplace. Sabina took one look and then, with a cry of sheer delight, ran across the room with both hands outstretched.

"Harry! Harry! Why did you not tell me? Why did you not let me know you were coming?"

Harry put his arms round his sister and kissed her affectionately on both cheeks. Then he held her away from him and looked down at her, taking note of her sparkling eyes, her fashionably arranged hair, her dress of blue tarlatan with its frilled and laced trimmings. Finally he pursed his lips in the suspicion of a whistle.

"You've got yourself up to look fine and dandy!" he exclaimed.

"Do you think I look nice?" Sabina demanded.

"I should hardly have recognized you," he replied. "In fact you don't look like Sabina at all. Shall I bow or would you prefer me to kiss your hand?"

"Do not be ridiculous!" Sabina laughed. "I am just the same, really. It is just that Lady Thetford has made me a fashionable miss instead of a dowd! But do not let us talk about me. Tell me about yourself. Why are you here?"

"My ship is in the harbour," Harry replied.

"H.M.S. *Magnificent!*" Sabina exclaimed. "How wonderful! But why did you not let me know you were coming to Monte Carlo?"

"We didn't know ourselves until yesterday," Harry replied. "We came in about midday, but to tell the truth, Sis, I wasn't certain whether you would be pleased to see me or no."

"Harry, what do you mean?" Sabina asked.

"Well, you know what it is. Mamma wrote and told me how smart you were, staying with Lady Thetford, and Arthur with the Prince and Princess of Wales. I can't live up to that sort of thing, you know, and I didn't want to force myself on you."

"Force yourself! Really, Harry, I have never heard such a nonsensical notion in the whole of my life. As though I would not want to see you. As it happens, when the footman came to tell me you were here I was reading letters from Mamma and Harriet and wishing with all my heart that they were with me. I am having a wonderful time, of course, but it is not the same as being with one's own family."

"You are just the same, Sis," Harry smiled approvingly. "In spite of looking like a figure out of the *Ladies' Journal.*"

Harry took after his father. He was very tall and exceedingly handsome, with a straightforward, unpretentious manner, which made him all the more charming. There was something unaffectedly simple and honest about him which made him the recipient of a thousand confidences and the adored idol of small children and dogs. Sabina thought that in his Naval uniform he looked heart-breakingly attractive, but she was too well used to her brother to tell him so, knowing that it would only make him embarrassed and that he would tell her to shut up.

"What do you think of Monte Carlo?" she asked. "Have you ever been here before?"

"No, never," Harry replied.

Then, to Sabina's surprise, he walked across the room to see if the door was closed.

"As a matter of fact, Sis," he said in a low voice, "I'm in a spot of bother."

"Oh, Harry! What has happened?" Sabina asked.

He looked embarrassed, and tactfully she took him by the hand and led him towards the sofa by the window.

"Come and sit down and tell me all about it."

"It's pretty desperate," he confessed.

"Harry! What have you done?"

Harry swallowed and then told her.

"I've lost some money at the Casino."

"When?" Sabina inquired.

"Last night. I came ashore with a couple of other chaps. I thought of trying to see you and then I wasn't sure what sort of reception I'd have, so we had some dinner at a small restaurant and then went into the Casino. I never meant to gamble. I swear to you, Sis, I'd never given it a thought. Then I watched for a bit and saw how easy it was to make money! It sort of fascinated me."

"I can understand that," Sabina said. "Indeed most people are fascinated by it."

"But it's a dangerous sort of fascination, I know that now," Harry said ruefully.

"How much did you lose?" Sabina asked.

"I don't think I dare tell you."

"Do not be ridiculous, Harry. You could not help it."

"Well, it's rather a lot."

"How much?" Sabina inquired.

Harry took a deep breath.

"Nearly a hundred pounds."

For a moment Sabina could only stare at him, and then, when she got her breath, she repeated stupidly:

"A hundred pounds!"

"Yes, I know. Don't look at me like that, Sis. I've been a fool, a damned fool, and there is worse to it than that."

"Worse?" Sabina questioned.

"Yes, much worse. You see, I won a bit at first and then I started losing and I thought I was certain to get it back. I had about run out of money and so I cashed a cheque. The authorities let me do so because I am an officer of the Royal Navy."

"But, Harry, you have not got a hundred pounds in the bank," Sabina said.

"Yes, I know. Of course I haven't. I told you I thought I was certain to win it back, but I didn't."

Sabina clasped her hands together.

"So you mean they will cash the cheque and. . . ."

"And there will be nothing there," Harry said grimly.

He put his hands up to his head.

"I must have been mad. As a matter of fact I had had quite a lot to drink. I suppose being a bit foxed made me sure it would come all right, that I would win the money and get back the cheque. Now I shall lose my commission."

"Oh, Harry, not as bad as that."

"Of course. Officers in Her Majesty's Forces are not expected to give dud cheques. If they do, they face the consequences?"

"But . . . but what will Papa say?"

"Do you think I haven't been worrying about that?" Harry asked miserably.

"He will never get over it," Sabina exclaimed. "Nor Mamma either. They are so proud of you, Harry. Oh, I know you always wanted to go into the Cavalry and because you didn't make a fuss when Papa could not afford it, and because you have done so well, they are both quite vain about your prowess."

"Don't rub it in, Sis," Harry said hoarsely.

"We have got to prevent their knowing about this," Sabina said. "And there is no reason why they should if we can get the cheque back before the Casino authorities send it to the bank."

"But where can we get a hundred pounds?" Harry inquired.

"I shall have to ask . . . Arthur," Sabina said slowly.

"Do you think you could? No, I've got no right to ask you to do that. It isn't fair to make you feel embarrassed and ashamed of me. But—I don't know what else to do."

"Yes, of course I must ask Arthur," Sabina said firmly. "A hundred pounds is nothing to him. He is so rich, and besides he will not want a scandal just as he is about to marry me."

"I'll pay it back, I promise you I will pay it back," Harry said. "It'll take a bit of time out of my pay, but I'll manage it somehow."

"A hundred pounds," Sabina said, with a little sigh. "It might as well be a million as far as we are concerned. We cannot ask anyone except . . . Arthur!"

"Do you think he will mind very much?" Harry inquired.

"No, no, I am sure he will understand," Sabina replied,

a little doubtfully. "After all, he has never known what it is to be hard up, to be unable to do the things that other people can do . . . so easily."

Harry sighed.

"How well you understand!" he exclaimed. "It has always been the same. I always seem to be the poorest among my friends. I can never treat anyone to a meal, never do the things that the other fellows are doing. I'm not grumbling, honestly, I'm not grumbling, Sabina. I was a fool last night, but I could not believe that I should have such a run of rotten luck."

"The bank always wins in the end," Sabina said. "I have heard the people say so who live here and who go to the Casino every night."

"And yet some chaps are lucky," Harry replied. "There was a man at the tables last night who put the maximum on a number three times running and each time it turned up. I had a feeling I might do the same, but, as you know, it didn't come off."

"Poor Harry! I don't think somehow that as a family we shall any of us ever make much money."

"You will be rich."

"I suppose so," Sabina replied. "But oh, I do wish this had happened after I was married and not before. Perhaps then I would have been able to give you the money without asking Arthur."

Harry looked at her searchingly.

"Listen, Sis. If it's going to upset you too much, I'll manage somehow. I'll write to Papa and tell him exactly what has happened. I daresay he could raise the wind from somewhere."

"A hundred pounds! How could he? Unless he went to the Squire or someone like that, and he would rather die, you know he would. The only thing we have got of any value at home is the horses, and you couldn't expect him to sell those."

"Sell his horses!" Harry gasped. "Why, Papa would never do that."

"He would have to if it was a question of saving you," Sabina said practically. "But it is not going to come to that, Harry. Papa would be so hurt, not so much about the money but because you had been so foolish as to let yourself get led astray. You know that."

"Yes, I know, Sis. But a chap has to have a bit of fun

sometimes. I haven't been ashore for weeks and I haven't seen a pretty woman for six months. You know that we have been on a cruise down the coast of Africa—nothing but blacks and the mosquitoes raising a lump the size of a billiard ball every time they bite you."

"Oh, poor, poor Harry, and I understand exactly what you are feeling now. I will speak to Arthur, I know it will be all right."

"When are you going to see him?" Harry asked.

"He is coming here at four o'clock."

"Will you ask him then?"

"I will ask him as soon as he arrives."

"What do you think I had better do? Hang about until he has gone?"

Sabina thought for a moment.

"We will go and sit in the garden," she said at length, "and I will tell James that when Arthur comes he is to fetch me. You can wait. Arthur will give you the money right away; then if you pay the Casino authorities what you owe them, they can tear up the cheque."

"That sounds all right," Harry answered. "But we must wait and see what Arthur has to say about it."

"Let us go into the garden now," Sabina suggested. "And let us talk about something else instead of this beastly money. I wish you had not thrown it away on those horrible tables."

"Not half as much as I do!" Harry said, in heart-felt tones. "You're quite sure, Sabina, that you don't mind asking Arthur."

"I do not like it," Sabina answered, honestly. "But there is nothing else we can do, is there?"

"I have thought and thought," Harry said. "When I realized what I had done, I nearly dropped myself overboard."

"All our lives this bugbear of money has hung over our heads," Sabina sighed. "I do not think rich people realize how lucky they are not to lie awake all night wondering how they can pay for something."

"They say that money is a curse," Harry remarked. "But all the same I could do with a bit." He put his arm round Sabina and drew her close to him. "You're a brick, Sis—you always have been—and I hate saddling you with my troubles."

"I should have been furious if you had not told me,"

135

Sabina said. "That is what it means to be part of a family—to be there when things go wrong, to be able to help each other."

"As I said before, you're a brick," Harry repeated. "I must say I felt quite sick at the thought of having to tell Papa."

"Poor Papa, he would never understand," Sabina said. "Mamma is different. All her family were gamblers. Was it our grandfather or our great-grandfather who was the Regency buck who gambled away all the family fortunes?" Sabina stopped and put her fingers up to her mouth. "Harry, do you think it is in your blood?"

"I'm damned sure it isn't," Harry replied. "I tell you one thing, Sis. If you get me out of this hole, I'll never gamble again, I promise you that."

"Never?"

"Cross my heart and hope to die," he said, making the solemn vow they had always made when they were children.

"I believe you," Sabina smiled. "And now let us go into the garden."

She spent two happy hours talking to Harry, but it was a very white-faced and apprehensive Sabina who came walking back to the villa when James, the footman, informed her that Arthur had arrived.

It had seemed easy to tell Harry that she would appeal to Arthur for help, but it was a very, very difficult thing to face Arthur himself. She kept assuring herself that he would understand, that he would behave as any of her family would behave if one of the others were in trouble; but deep in her heart she knew she was afraid that Arthur's reaction would be very different.

She did not enter the drawing-room through the french windows as she had done when she had heard that Harry was there; but instead, because it took longer and because it seemed more formal, she went round by the path and into the villa through the garden door. She paused for a moment in the hall to arrange her hair in front of one of the mirrors, and then, feeling suddenly cold and with a very empty feeling in her inside, she entered the drawing-room.

"Good afternoon, Sabina."

Arthur was standing in the window looking out over the sunlit garden, and he turned at her entrance and held out his hand. She moved across to him and lifted her face to be kissed.

"I must apologize that I am a few minutes late," Arthur said. "His Royal Highness asked me to sit with him after luncheon and as we talked together of many interesting and important matters I completely lost track of the time."

There was no mistaking the satisfaction in Arthur's voice, and Sabina thought, with a raising of her spirits, that he was in a very good temper.

"Do tell me more," Sabina begged. "What did you discuss?"

"I am afraid I should be betraying His Royal Highness's confidence if I imparted that sort of information," Arthur answered. "No, you must not press me for secrets. Members of the Royal Household have to be exceptionally discreet, Sabina, and if, when we are married, I ever by any chance mention things which concern my position at Court, you must take the utmost pains to see that you never speak of what you hear from me to anyone else— not even to your family."

"Yes, of course I understand," Sabina said.

"You will be careful?" Arthur inquired.

"Yes, I promise."

"Good. Now tell me what your plans are for this evening."

"Before we talk of that," Sabina said in a very small voice, "there is something I want to ask you, Arthur."

"What is it?" he inquired.

"It is something of the greatest importance to me," Sabina said. "One . . . of my family is . . . in trouble."

"In trouble?" Arthur inquired sharply. "What sort of trouble?"

His voice was rather hard, she noticed, and she felt there was a wary look in his eyes which had not been there before.

"It is Harry," Sabina said.

"Harry! I thought your brother was at sea."

"His ship is here in harbour."

"Of course, the H.M.S. *Magnificent*! I saw this morning that she had come in. I think the authorities realized that, if His Royal Highness was in Monte Carlo, it was only right that a capital ship of Her Majesty's Navy should be

137

somewhere in the vicinity. I remember now that you told me that your brother was aboard the *Magnificent*."

"Yes, I did tell you that," Sabina answered. "And do you remember that I showed you his photograph one day and you said how nice-looking he was and how smart he looked in his uniform?"

"I am afraid I do not remember such details," Arthur retorted. "But never mind that. Tell me what has happened."

"Harry went to the Casino last night . . ." Sabina faltered.

"Well?"

"I am afraid . . . he lost some money. Quite a lot of money."

"Indeed! It will take him a long time to pay it back out of his salary. I understand that the services of sub-lieutenants are not rewarded over generously."

"Harry is quite prepared to pay back every penny," Sabina replied quickly. "In fact he knows he must do so. But, unfortunately, he cannot do so at once. It will take some time, perhaps years."

"Indeed!" Arthur replied. "I am afraid he will find that very monotonous."

"Please try and understand," Sabina said desperately. "You see, this money he has lost has got to be found at once."

"How much has he lost?" Arthur inquired.

"Nearly a hundred pounds," Sabina replied.

She could not look at Arthur as she said it. The sum seemed so gigantic, so much worse now than when she had first heard it from Harry. One hundred pounds! It was almost as much as they spent on food at the Vicarage in the whole year. It was more than Papa had paid for all his horses and they had naturally not been bought all at once but one at a time.

There was a long silence until at last Arthur said:

"Your brother has certainly been gambling pretty deep for a Naval commander. You must give him my commiserations on his misfortune, or should I say his stupidity?"

Sabina raised her eyes to Arthur's face.

"Please, Arthur. . . . Please help us."

"Help you?" he inquired. "What am I expected to do?"

"Harry gave a cheque at the Casino. He thought he was certain to win the money back . . . instead he . . . lost

138

it. He has not that much money in the bank, and if it is found out that he ... deliberately wrote a cheque that ... that would not be honoured, he will have to resign his commission. Oh, please Arthur ... do not let that happen!"

"Your brother should have thought of this sooner," Arthur replied in a cold voice.

"He got carried away. He has been sailing down the coast of Africa for six months. I can see so well how it happened. He had a good dinner, a little too much to drink, and roulette looked so easy, so simple, he thought perhaps he would win a lot of money—instead he lost."

"You have every sympathy with him, I can see that," Arthur said sourly.

"I know he has been very stupid," Sabina said. "But how could we tell Papa of the mess he is in now? It would almost kill him."

"I doubt it," Arthur answered coldly. "Parents seldom die because their children misbehave."

"But Papa has not got the money either," Sabina explained. "You know how poor we are; you know how simply we live. Please, Arthur, lend Harry the money. He will pay you back, I know he will."

"I made a rule many years ago never to lend money," Arthur replied. "My father was the same. 'If you lend money you lose a friend'—that is what he told me, and I have always proved it to be true."

"But Harry is not just an ordinary friend," Sabina cried. "He will be your brother-in-law."

"I realize that," Arthur said, "and that is one of the reasons why I am most reluctant to become involved in this very reprehensible affair. You must understand, Sabina, and I want to make it clear right away that I am marrying you, not your family."

"What do you mean?"

"Exactly what I say. I fell in love with you and I wish you to be my wife, but that does not indicate that I want Harriet, Melloney, Angelina and your other sister—I have forgotten her name—hanging around my neck for the rest of my life, any more than I intend to finance your brother."

Sabina had gone very white. For a moment she did not speak and then, at last, she said in a voice that was hardly audible:

"Are you suggesting that I should not see my family?"

"No, no, of course not," Arthur said testily. "Of course you will see your family at reasonable intervals and when it is convenient. But I do not wish them either to live with us or on us. Nor do I wish you to spend your time engrossed in your family's affairs to the exclusion of things that concern my comfort and my well-being."

"But, of course I should not do such a thing," Sabina protested.

"I do not know about that," Arthur said ponderously. "Your family obviously mean a lot to you. They have, until now, quite rightly been your first consideration and have held first place in your affections. Now that must be changed. You will be my wife and I want you to concern yourself with my interests, my home, my affairs. You will not have much time left over for anybody or anything else. Do you understand?"

"Y . . . Yes . . . Arthur."

"And now, as regards your brother, Harry. I quite appreciate that this is one of those awkward situations in which circumstances force my hand."

The shadow on Sabina's face was suddenly lightened.

"You mean," she asked breathlessly, "that you will . . . help him?"

"I mean I shall have to," Arthur said a little roughly. "As my future brother-in-law I cannot have the scandal of him being dismissed from Her Majesty's Navy. I shall be forced, and much against my will I may add, to lend him this money to pay off his debt. But he will pay me back. Because I consider it a salutary lesson which he must remember both now and in the future."

"But, of course he will pay you back," Sabina said. "Oh, Arthur! How can I ever thank you for being so kind?"

Arthur gave a short, rather disagreeable laugh.

"A kindness which is hardly voluntary," he said. "You have put me in a very uncomfortable position, Sabina, as I hope you realize."

"I can only realize that you are being kind and very generous to Harry," Sabina replied. "He has been almost desperate with worry, and we would not have asked you if there was anything else we could possibly have done to get the hundred pounds."

"I will tell the young fool exactly what I think of him," Arthur said. "Where is he?"

"In the garden," Sabina answered. "But please, Arthur, do not be too harsh with him. He is very sensible of how foolish he has been, and very sorry that he should have caused so much trouble and anxiety, and he will pay you back every penny, if you will only give him time."

"I shall make my own stipulations as to that," Arthur said. "Now promise me, Sabina, that you will remember what I said. I am marrying you, not your family."

"Yes, I heard you," Sabina said, in a low voice. She pressed her lips together as if she was keeping back the words of protest which sprang instinctively to her mind. "Shall I fetch Harry now?"

"In a moment," Arthur replied. "It will not do him any harm to cool his heels a bit, to be, I hope, a little apprehensive as to what my answer might be."

"I felt sure that you would not fail us," Sabina said confidently.

"On this occasion my hand is forced," Arthur answered. "But I assure you, Sabina, I shall not be so pliable or so generous on other occasions. In fact I shall make quite sure that your family is not continually coming to me begging with outstretched hands. I may be a rich man, but I am not a fool."

Sabina drew herself up a little proudly.

"My family have never thought that they were likely to get anything out of you, nor are they given to begging."

Arthur laughed.

"So that has hurt your pride, has it?" he asked. "I am sorry, Sabina, but I am afraid I have got a somewhat practical outlook on life. I am not so stupid as not to realize that your parents, with five daughters to settle in life and a son to support, are glad for their eldest daughter to have found a rich husband."

"I think both Mamma and Papa want us to be happy more than anything else," Sabina retorted.

"And if the happiness is well gilded that is all to the good," Arthur said cynically.

Sabina suddenly lost her temper and stamped her foot.

"I think you are hateful to speak like that," she cried. "If you only knew how gentle and unworldly Papa is. He never thinks of money and he gives away every farthing he ever possesses to people poorer than himself. If he heard what you are saying now, I really believe that he would command me to go home at once."

Arthur laughed again; and putting out his arms he drew Sabina close to him.

"I did not know you had a temper," he smiled. "Do you want me to apologize for having made you angry?"

"Those were ... cruel and ... unkind things to say," Sabina answered, her voice breaking a little and the tears coming into her eyes.

"Don't cry," Arthur said. He bent suddenly and pressed his lips to hers. For a long moment he held her prisoner; and when he released her, the blood came flooding into her cheeks.

"Send this young jackanapes in to me," he said.

Sabina's eyes would not meet his as she turned quickly away and ran through the window and into the garden. Harry, looking anxious and distressed, was pacing up and down the path behind the fuchsia hedge. He looked up in relief when he saw Sabina coming towards him.

"What did he say?" he asked.

"It will be all right," Sabina said, with a small sob. "But, oh, Harry, do not say anything to him however much he provokes you, however angry you may be."

"Is he being unpleasant about it?" Harry asked.

Sabina nodded.

"Dammit . . ." Harry began.

Sabina reached out and put her hand on his arm.

"Listen, Harry. Whatever he may say, you have got to keep silent, you have got to bear it. There is no other way that we can get a hundred pounds—no other way at all. Promise me you will say nothing except 'thank you'."

"But if he has upset you . . ." Harry began.

"Promise me," Sabina interrupted. "Do be sensible, Harry. If I can put up with it for your sake, you can put up with it for your own."

"All right, Sis."

He gave her hand a squeeze, and then, squaring his shoulders, walked towards the villa. Sabina looked round for the nearest seat and then sank down on it, her face in her hands. Her heart was thumping, both with anger and resentment, and yet she found it difficult to repress the tears that kept welling weakly into her eyes.

"I am a fool to mind," she told herself out loud. And then, as she fumbled for her handkerchief, she realized that she was in the little pagoda where on the second night she had been in Monte Carlo she had talked with the gipsy king.

She found herself remembering his words, and the low, resonant tone of his voice, as they talked together. How vividly she could recall the warm firmness of his hand and then the touch of his lips as he kissed her palm! She gave a little sigh and suddenly the tears were running unchecked down her cheeks. . . .

She was, however, calm and composed twenty minutes later when Harry came walking back into the garden. She knew, by the expression on his face and the squareness of his jaw, that he was feeling pugnacious, and almost before he was in hearing she cried out anxiously:

"Is it all right? Has he given you the money?"

Harry nodded, as if for a moment he could not bring himself to speak: and then, seating himself beside Sabina, he put his hands in his pockets and stretched out his legs in front of him.

"Phew!" he exclaimed. "I've been in many uncomfortable spots in my life, but never anything to equal that."

"You did not say anything?" Sabina asked.

"It's a good thing you made me promise to be silent," he answered. "Once or twice I contemplated hitting him, and then I remembered what you had said."

"Harry! You must be mad."

"Mad or not it would have given me the greatest satisfaction I have ever known."

"Have you got the money?"

"Yes. He gave me the hundred quid and I have got to pay him back within a year."

"Within a year!" Sabina exclaimed. "But will that not leave you. . . ."

"With practically nothing of my pay," Harry said. "But it will be a lesson to me! He made it very clear that what I wanted was a lesson."

"It is hard, terribly hard," Sabina said. "But at least you will not have to tell Papa."

"I kept thinking of that," Harry said. "I kept saying under my breath, 'Sabina, Papa, Papa, Sabina,' over and over again, otherwise——"

"Do not think about it," Sabina said, quickly. "Just forget. You have got the money, that is all that matters."

143

Harry suddenly sat up and turning towards Sabina put his hands on her shoulders.

"Listen, Sis," he said. "Do you love this man?"

The question took Sabina by surprise. For a moment blue eyes looked into brown ones, then, with a little cry she turned her face away and shook herself free.

"Stop worrying me, Harry; there has been emotion enough for one day. I do not want to talk about myself or about Arthur. You are safe, that is all that matters."

"I'm thinking about you," he said obstinately.

"Think about something else," Sabina begged him, and added in a deliberately light tone of voice: "I am perfectly all right and perfectly happy, Harry. I do not interfere with your life and you are not to interfere with mine."

"But, Sis, you have got to think."

"I have thought," Sabina answered. "I have thought a lot and talking is not going to make any difference one way or another."

Harry shrugged his shoulders.

"Very well, then. I'll be going now."

"Please stay and have some tea," Sabina said, then added quickly: "But I had forgotten ... is Arthur still here?"

"No, he left. He told me to tell you that he was sorry he could not stay longer but he had promised to go for a drive with Her Royal Highness."

Sabina felt the relief was almost overwhelming.

"Then you can stay for tea," she said weakly. "Lady Thetford always has afternoon tea about five o'clock. Do stay, Harry."

"If you will forgive me, Sabina, I won't. I feel a bit shaken as a matter of fact and I can do with something stronger than tea. Besides, I've promised to meet some chaps."

"All right, Harry, I understand."

Sabina could, indeed, understand that he wanted to get away. She raised herself on tiptoe, put her arms round his neck and drew his face down to hers.

"Take care of yourself, darling Harry."

"And take care of yourself," he answered.

"Shall I see you tomorrow?"

"I'll come along after luncheon, if you'll be alone," Harry promised. "That is if I can get shore leave."

"Yes, do," Sabina answered. "I am usually alone about the same time as you came today."

Harry kissed her and they walked together arm in arm towards the villa. Sabina said good-bye to him at the front door, then she ran upstairs to her room to bathe her eyes and wash away any traces of tears. Lady Thetford had keen eyes and somehow Sabina felt she could not bear to explain what had happened, least of all to Arthur's mother.

They dined quietly at home that night, with only two friends of Lady Thetford's for company. There had been plans, of course, for going on to the Casino later, but when the time came Lady Thetford had a headache and said she must go to bed.

"I think I have eaten something that has disagreed with me," she said. "One has to be so careful out here. I certainly do not feel well. Will you forgive me, Sabina, if we have an early night?"

"But, of course," Sabina answered. "As a matter of fact I should like to go to bed early myself. I am not used to such gaiety. At home we always go to bed about ten o'clock."

The other two guests laughed and paid Sabina compliments about her complexion, saying it was obvious that an hour before twelve was worth two afterwards. They soon took their leave and then, yawning a little, Lady Thetford led the way upstairs.

"I shall make Marie give me a little laudanum," she said. "I do not really approve of taking it, but if I have a really good night's sleep I shall be quite all right tomorrow."

"Then I hope you sleep really well," Sabina said, kissing her affectionately.

"Good night, child," Lady Thetford replied. She lingered for a moment with her hand on Sabina's shoulder. "I have not told you, yet," she went on, "how much I love having you here. It makes me realize, for the first time, how lonely I often am without knowing it."

She smiled at that and then walked away to her bedroom leaving Sabina looking after her a little wistfully. How sweet she was! How very gentle and understanding! If only Arthur would be the same. Men and women were very different from each other, Sabina thought, and it was

145

wrong of her to grumble or to complain when Arthur had been kind enough to give Harry the money he needed.

She went into her bedroom and shut the door, and then, taking off the pretty, elaborate dress she had worn for dinner, she put on a wrapper of pale blue muslin that had been made for her before she left home. She sat down at the dressing-table and was just about to take the combs out of her hair when there came a knock at the door.

"What is it?" she asked.

"Lieutenant Wantage to see you, Miss."

"At this hour!" Sabina exclaimed, and then remembered it was not yet eleven o'clock.

She rose to her feet and opened the door. Bates, the butler, was outside.

"The lieutenant is very anxious to see you, Miss. I told him that you had retired, but he said it was of the utmost importance."

"I will go down to him," Sabina replied. She pulled her wrap around her, tied the ribbon sash a little tighter and then ran downstairs to the drawing-room.

Harry was waiting, pacing up and down the carpet. He turned at Sabina's entrance and as she saw his face she uttered a cry of horror.

"What is the matter?"

In reply Harry walked across and took both her hands in his.

"I'm finished."

"Finished? What do you mean?"

"What I say. I'm writing to Papa tonight, but I thought I ought to tell you first."

"What is the matter? What has happened?" Sabina inquired. "Oh, Harry, do not look like that. Tell me quietly what has occurred."

"I can't."

"Cannot tell me? What do you mean, why not?"

Harry suddenly sat down in one of the chairs, and put his handsome young face in his hands. He groaned aloud.

"Why it had to happen to me I can't think," he muttered.

Sabina dropped down to her knees at his side.

"Harry, you have got to tell me at once what is upsetting you" she commanded.

Harry took his hands from a ravished, unhappy face.

146

"I have lost the money," he said abruptly.

"Lost . . . it?"

Sabina felt as though the words were strangled in her throat.

"Yes, lost it."

"But how could you? It is impossible! Tell me everything from the very beginning!"

Harry took a deep breath and swallowed what was suspiciously like a sob before he replied.

"As you know, Sis, I left here with the money. I was grateful to you for getting it, though I admit that I was mad as fire at what my future brother-in-law had chosen to say to me about my behaviour. I know I've been a fool—nobody knows it better than I do—but he insulted me almost past endurance. I thought I'd meet the chaps, have a drink and then go along to the Casino.

"Well, I met them, as arranged. We had a couple of drinks, and afterwards they wanted to go off and see some sort of entertainment down near the quay. It was pretty crude and coarse—not the sort of thing you would take a lady to—but there were two women of a sort there and we got into conversation with them. Eventually we asked them to spend the evening with us and we all went off to get some dinner.

"I had not forgotten about the money, of course, and I had not spent a penny of it, I promise you that. I had five shillings left before I came here and I gave that to the others and explained that I could not pay any more. But they were in funds, so they offered to treat me. It was all quite fun and above board, and there was nothing really wrong about it. The women were not the type that I could introduce to you or Mamma, but they seemed quite decent and were well dressed—really rather smart, for that matter."

"Go on," Sabina said breathlessly.

"We went to dinner at a little place they knew about—jolly good food and not too expensive—and then they said, 'What about the Casino?' So we all agreed to go there. They went to the ladies' room to tidy and we three men finished off the wine. They were gone rather a long time—in fact so long that we began to make jokes about it, wondering what they could be doing and if they were discussing us. 'I expect they're giving us time to toss for them,' one of my shipmates said. 'Bags I the blonde.' That made me realize what I had not thought about before. We were one man too many, and that was me, so I said, 'I won't be with you. I've got to go to the Casino and then I'll slip away.' As I spoke I put my hand in my pocket, and realized that the money Arthur had given me was gone."

"Gone!" Sabina ejaculated.

"Yes, gone," Harry repeated. "At first I could not believe it. I went through every pocket I had; I even took my coat off to be quite sure, but it had completely vanished—and so had the women."

"You mean they stole it?" Sabina asked.

"That is about it. We had taken a carriage to the restaurant. There were five of us so we had to sit rather close. You know what women of that sort are—or rather you don't—but they are always over-affectionate, clinging to one's arm, putting an arm round one's neck. They might have pinched it at any moment during the drive."

"Harry! Harry! What can you do?"

"There is nothing I can do," Harry replied. "You can't ask your Arthur again. And one thing is quite sure. I wouldn't let you. Besides, from what he said, I'm jolly certain he would not give it to me."

"But, Harry, there must be some solution. Can you go to the police?"

"Do you imagine they would take any notice of me? To begin with they are not likely to believe that I was carrying so much money; and secondly we do not even know the names of the women. One was fair and one was rather dark—she looked like a gipsy. No, there is nothing for it. I'll go and see the captain tonight and offer him my resignation, and then I'll write to Papa."

"Wait!" Sabina cried. "Did you say that one of the girls was a gipsy?"

"I did not say she was one," Harry answered testily. "She was dark and wore big ear-rings and had a sort of golden skin, you know the type. I prefer fair women myself."

"But what was her name?" Sabina asked. "Think, Harry. You must have heard her name."

"She called herself Katisha," Harry answered. "The other one was Mimi, and she was much the nicer of the two."

"It does not matter whether they were nice or nasty,"

Sabina said impatiently. "If this Katisha was a gipsy, I might, I just might, be able to do something."

"What do you mean?"

"Never mind," Sabina replied. "There is not time for explanations. But you are not to do anything, such as going to the captain or writing to Papa, until I tell you everything else is hopeless. Do you promise me?"

"What are you going to do?" Harry asked.

For a moment there was a touch of hope in his voice and in his eyes, and then it faded.

"Don't worry, Sabina," he continued. "It can't be helped. I'm the biggest fool that ever stepped God's earth—as the man you are going to marry pointed out, very clearly. Well, he was right, completely and absolutely right. I've mucked things up so badly that there is nothing I can do now except face the consequences. I'll be going. I only thought you ought to know the truth."

"Listen, Harry," Sabina said. "I have got an idea. I believe that I . . . I might be able to get that money back."

"How?" Harry inquired.

"I am not going to tell you that," Sabina answered. "Let me think." She was still for a moment, her fingers against her temples, and then she said: "Harry, you have got to get me a horse."

"A horse?" he inquired in astonishment.

"Yes. I think you will find quite a good one at the stables where Lady Thetford keeps her carriage. She spoke about my riding later on, and she has given me a habit from Paris because she said she knew that any child of Mamma's would want to ride."

"You want a horse now, at this hour of night?" Harry asked bewildered.

"Yes, now, just as quickly as you can get one," Sabina said. "But do not let them bring it to the front door. Wait at the far end of the garden where the wall goes down to the lower road. Do you know where I mean?"

"Yes, I think so," Harry said. "But, Sis. . . ."

"Please, Harry, do not argue or question me. Go and get hold of a horse, and mind it has a ladies' saddle on it. I will meet you on the road in about a quarter of an hour."

"One horse is not going to carry us both," Harry

protested. "Although the Lord knows where you are going."

"You are not coming, anyway," Sabina retorted. "You have just got to wait about, Harry, until I come back. It may take an hour, perhaps two, perhaps three; I do not know. Go and find your friends. Do anything you like, but do not spend any more money."

"You can be jolly sure I won't do that," Harry answered, "because I haven't got any. But look here, Sis, I can't let you go off on some wild goose chase."

"It is not as wild as all that," Sabina answered. "Oh, Harry, if I can get this money back, will you swear you will take it straight to the Casino?"

"Do you think I'm an idiot?" Harry asked. "Of course you do—because I am one. But I never dreamed of things like this happening to me! I suppose it's because I've never been in a place like this before."

There was something so young and bewildered about him that instinctively Sabina put out her hands and laid them on his shoulders.

"We are not going to be beaten by this, are we, Harry?"

"I don't know, Sis. There doesn't seem much hope of a miracle happening——"

"Go and get that horse," Sabina commanded. "And keep your fingers crossed." She kissed him, then turned towards the door. "Not a word to anyone," she whispered. "No one must know about this!"

"I should jolly well think not," Harry ejaculated. "As for that fellow you're going to marry, heaven knows what he will think of it."

"But of course Arthur must not know!" Sabina answered. She felt herself tremble at the thought, then she put up her chin with a pathetically brave gesture of defiance. "We will believe in that miracle until the last moment, Harry. It is a forlorn hope, but there is ... someone who I believe might be able to ... save you!"

CHAPTER NINE

SABINA tiptoed along the balcony keeping close to the shadows for fear she might be seen. The servants might be awake, or worse still, Lady Thetford might be standing at her window. However, she reached the narrow wooden staircase and started to descend finding it difficult to move quietly owing to the encumbrance of her riding skirt.

The habit, which Lady Thetford had bought for her from Paris, would have looked very strange in an English hunting field, but it was the fashionable riding costume worn by smart French women and if Sabina had had time to look into the mirror, she would have found it extremely becoming. She had, however, dressed in the greatest of haste, slipping on the soft, lace-trimmed shirt and the beautifully cut velvet coat, which gave her a tiny and very accentuated waist, and pulling down on her hair, without even a glance at her reflection, the tri-corn hat with its long, curled ostrich feather which, curving over the brim, just touched her cheek.

Picking up a pair of riding gloves, Sabina had glanced round her room and then blown out the candles. Now, as she descended the staircase, she remembered she had no riding whip and hoped that Harry would bring her such a spirited horse that she would not notice the lack of it.

It took her but a few seconds to find her way across the moonlit garden, to hurry down the stone steps and along the long paths between the scented flower beds until she came to the high wall which bordered the garden of the villa. It was darker here because of the shadows from the cypress and olive trees.

Sabina forced herself to go slower, picking her way with more care, until finally she found herself right against the wall. She looked around for a foothold, and finding a protruding stone levered herself up on it until she could look over the top. For a moment, with a sense of dismay, she thought no one was there, and then she saw Harry waiting a little further up the road. He had a horse with him; a groom was holding it by the bridle.

"Harry!"

Sabina called his name, but in such a soft voice that he did not hear her. And then, instead of repeating it, she gave the long, low whistle which they had always used as children to attract each other's attention.

Harry came hurrying down the road.

"Is that you, Sabina?"

"Yes, I am here. The difficulty now is how to get over this wall."

"Climb up," Harry commanded, "and then if you jump I can catch you."

"It is not as easy as that," Sabina retorted, half amused, half exasperated by her brother's cool assumption that she could spring up on the wall as easily as she had done when she was a child, unhampered by long skirts and elegant clothes which were far too tight to enable her to indulge in athletic feats.

However, she was not going to talk about her difficulties to Harry, it was too dangerous, and finally she managed to scramble on to the top of the wall, although not without hearing, with a sense of dismay, several stitches give in her coat.

"There you are!" Harry exclaimed. "I felt sure you could manage it. Now jump."

"I am going to do nothing of the sort," Sabina replied. "You will either miss me or we shall both land in a heap in the dust. Come near and lift me down very gradually."

Harry did as he was told, first taking a firm hold of her legs below the knees and then gradually easing her downwards until she stood on the ground.

"There, I have done it," she said, looking up at him and laughing, her face flushed with exertion, her eyes shining.

"It is not like you to make a fuss about climbing a wall, Sis," Harry reproached her. "I've seen you shin over them quickly enough before now and I could easily have caught you for you're as light as a feather."

"I am here, that is what matters," Sabina said. "But do not let us stand talking in case someone hears us. I see you have found me a horse."

"It's not a bad beast," Harry replied. "I had difficulty enough to get anything that wasn't as slow as an old cow or had a mouth like a mule. In the end I had to give the owner of the stable your name. He wouldn't trust me with a decent piece of horse-flesh otherwise."

Sabina gave a little sigh of dismay.

"Oh, Harry. I forgot that you would require credentials of some sort." Then she gave a little shrug of her shoulders. "Well, I suppose it does not matter. He cannot tell Lady Thetford until tomorrow that I have been out riding, and even then there is no reason why he should mention it."

"We can swear him to secrecy when you return," Harry said. "I didn't want to say anything, now it would have sounded so suspicious."

"Yes, of course it would," Sabina agreed.

"As a matter of fact," Harry went on, "there wasn't much I could say. You haven't told me where you are going or what you're doing. Let me come with you, Sis."

Sabina shook her head.

"No, Harry, I could not let you do that. You have just got to trust me and pray that I shall be able to help you."

"If you don't I'm finished."

Harry's face was suddenly quite haggard, and instinctively Sabina put out her hand and laid it protectingly on his arm.

"Do not think of that yet," she said. "I must be successful . . . I must!"

They reached the horse and Sabina looked it over appraisingly. She saw at once that it was a fine animal, well bred with a liveliness which kept it moving restlessly around and pawing the ground.

"The man at the stable said this wasn't at all the kind of animal he would recommend for a lady to ride," Harry said. "I expect he's used to mounting a lot of chicken-hearted French girls and doesn't know what a thruster you can be when the hounds find and you're well away ahead of the rest of the field."

Sabina smiled for a moment, then she gave a little sigh.

"You make me quite home-sick, Harry, and hunting was never the same when you were not there."

"If you only knew how much I miss it," Harry said. "If only. . . ." He stopped. The words died away to silence, but Sabina knew he had been going to add 'If only I had been in a cavalry regiment'.

That was where his heart lay, with horses and riding, not with the sea. But there was no point in talking about it now—or ever, for that matter. She had dreamed soon after she got engaged to Arthur of asking him one day if he would pay for Harry to transfer into the Army. But now, after what had happened today, she knew that such an idea was doomed from the very start.

"Help me on, Harry," she commanded, her voice sharp because of a sudden fear which she dare not question. Obediently he lifted her into the saddle. She arranged her skirt carefully and took up the reins.

"Where shall I meet you?" he asked.

"Wait for me here in two hours' time," she replied. "I may be longer, but if I am don't worry. I am not certain how long it will take me."

She was about to ride off, but Harry's hands were on the reins stopping her.

"Change your mind, Sis, and let me come with you. I oughtn't to allow you to do this. Think of what Papa would say."

"It is to save Papa from knowing anything that I am going," Sabina replied. And then, before Harry could say any more, she started off up the hill.

The horse was fresh and though inclined to be obstreperous he soon realized that the gentle fingers that held him had a masterful touch about them, and when once they were out of the town, he settled down into a quiet easy canter.

There were a few carriages to be met along the roads, filled with people going to the Casino or returning home from one of the many evening entertainments arranged in the principality. Sabina rode past them quickly, where possible keeping her face averted in case in the brightness of the moonlight she should be recognized; but when the last villa was passed, the roads became empty and she was moving away from civilization into the wild, uninhabited countryside.

She had been climbing all the way since she left Harry, but now, when at last she reached the Upper Corniche Road, she could let her mount go faster and feel the strong wind from the sea blowing in her face and tumbling her fair hair around her cheeks.

It was so pleasant to be on horseback again that had her mission not been so serious and had she not been so apprehensive as to the outcome of it, she would have enjoyed herself. She felt suddenly free and untrammelled.

There was a kind of buoyancy in being alone in this wild, beautiful countryside, with the sea far below her and the great, bare cliffs of rock rising above. It was easy to understand why the gipsies hated the confinement of walls and wished to sleep close to the earth beneath the star-strewn sky.

Sabina galloped on, and after a while she realized that almost unconsciously she had been praying. Words familiar since her childhood were moving her lips, but her mind was concentrated on praying that the gipsy king would help her and that the money would be returned so that Harry could be saved.

She did not dare think of what would happen if he refused or was unable to get back the money. She could still hardly allow herself to dwell, even for a second, on the thought of Arthur or on the things he had said to her that afternoon.

The expression on Harry's face as he had come to her across the garden was still vivid in her consciousness. Could either of them face throwing themselves on Arthur's mercy once again?

Rather than that, Sabina thought, she would do anything, go to any lengths or sink to any depths!

Only once did she wonder if she was really crazy to come on this long ride alone or to seek help from a man who, until a few days ago, had been a complete and utter stranger to her. The moon went behind a cloud and for a moment she had to rein in her horse and move more slowly. With a sudden sense of panic, she asked herself whether she was doing the right thing. There were other alternatives surely, and yet she could not think of them. It was then she remembered that first night when the gipsy king had risen from the fireside to come towards her as she stood, frightened and dismayed, conscious of the hostility in the dark eyes of the dancer and the question asked by a hundred suspicious faces turned towards her.

He had looked like a king as he walked proudly in the light of the fire, and she had known in that moment that she could trust him. Again when he led her back towards her carriage, his hand holding hers, guiding her over the rough ground, she had been conscious of his strength and of the force of his personality.

With a sudden leap of her heart Sabina thrust away her

doubts and misgivings. She had done right to come, she was sure of that.

There was a small rise ahead, and beyond it the country on the right-hand side of the road suddenly widened out. She had not yet arrived at the place where the wheel had fallen from her carriage that first night on her way to Monte Carlo, and to her surprise she saw only a short distance away the light of a fire, vivid and brilliant against the darkness, the sparks from the flames flying in the air almost like fireworks.

She reined in her horse. If these were the gipsies she sought they had moved nearer to Monte Carlo than they had been when she first encountered them. If it were not them, could it be another tribe, perhaps dangerous and by no means so trustworthy as those who had given her help when she needed it? Yet the fire was just as she had seen it before, and she could not pass on without finding out whether here unexpectedly soon were the gipsies she sought.

She felt she could dimly discern the roofs of wagons and more than once she saw the shadow of a man, or it might have been a woman, silhouetted against the flames. She turned her horse's head towards the fire moving quietly over the rough grass and drawing nearer to the light. Almost like an echo of what had happened before she heard the sound of music, the gay, wild melody of a guitar and a violin; and now, as she drew nearer still, she felt as if she must be re-dreaming an old dream. Once again there was a circle of wagons, the crowd of gipsies sitting around the flames, and again there was the dancer, twisting and turning and swirling—her dark hair flying out, the gold of her ornaments glittering and tinkling as she moved.

Sabina drew nearer still and now, just as she had done before, the dancer stopped suddenly to stare as she appeared from the darkness, her horse moving his head a little nervously from side to side as if he were afraid of the fire.

Tonight Sabina spoke first.

"Good evening," she said, in French. "I would speak with your king."

For just one moment there was silence and then the dancer replied. What she said Sabina had no idea, for she spoke in a strange tongue and her words resembled no

156

language Sabina had ever heard before, but there was no mistaking her meaning.

Moving forward until she was within a few feet of Sabina, she denounced her, insulted her and invited the other gipsies around her to a violence that was all too obviously betrayed by her waving arms, her flashing eyes and spitting lips. Why she was incensed or what she had done to deserve such an outburst Sabina had no idea, but it was evident that the men and women seated around the fire were excited by the dancer's fury, and rising to their feet they, too, came nearer until Sabina found that she and the horse were practically surrounded by them. And still the gipsy screamed on, pointing with her long, brown fingers, her whole face and body distorted with the eloquence of her hatred and her desire for Sabina to go away.

The music had ceased. It seemed that everyone there listened to the dancer and the only sound, beside her shrieking voice, was the deep, almost grunting murmurs of approval which came from the throats of the other gipsies.

"But I must speak to him, I must," Sabina tried to say above the tumult.

"Go! Go!"

She did not understand the words, but she knew that was what the gipsy was saying to her; and now it seemed that the dark-eyed men were drawing even nearer. Sabina saw one put out his hand to touch the bridle of her horse and with a sudden fear she thought, for the first time, that perhaps they might do her an injury.

It was then, as an arrow of fear pierced her and the blood was receding from her head, making her feel curiously faint, that the door of a wagon drawn up on the further side of the fire, was opened and the gipsy king came out on to the little platform above the steps which led down to the ground.

For a moment he just looked around him, disturbed perhaps by the noise and not as yet aware of what had caused it. And then one of the gipsies on the outside of the circle saw him, said something which caused the others in the close vicinity to him to turn their heads and, as a ripple of movement went over the whole throng, they relaxed their tension and their concentration on Sabina, and turned towards their king.

157

Only the dancer had no idea of what was happening, still yelling out in her fury, her voice high and shrill and yet infinitely menacing. But Sabina had seen whom she wanted to see and before those around her were aware of what she was about to do, she spurred forward her horse to pass through the throng of gipsies and rode up to the steps of the wagon. Seated on her horse, she was almost level with him.

"Sabina, what are you doing here?"

He spoke to her in English and she answered him in the same language.

"I had to come. I want your help."

He realized then what had been happening and for the first time Sabina saw an expression of anger on his face as he looked away from her towards his people. He spoke only a few short sentences, but the tone of his voice and the sharpness with which he spoke told Sabina only too clearly that he rebuked them. The men looked sheepish and uncomfortable and the women drooped their heads, their long eyelashes veiling their eyes.

Only the dancer stood unabashed, silent now but glaring, her enmity, her eyes seeming to smoulder in her face, her arms with their tinkling bracelets folded across her breast. Then the gipsy king spoke to her.

It was only one word, but Sabina, though with no knowledge of the Romany language, understood it as clearly as if he had spoken it in her own. It was the word of dismissal, and when he had said it the dancer's defiance left her and her dark hair fell forward to cover her face as turning, she walked from the light of the fire into the shadow of the wagons.

Two men sprang to the horse's head as Sabina dismounted and the gipsy king's hands helped her to the ground.

"I have got to talk to you," she said, her voice a little breathless.

"Will you honour me by coming into my wagon?" he asked.

"But of course," she replied.

He helped her up the steps and she went in through the elaborately painted door. The wagon was not large and yet she was astonished at its comfort. There were lanterns on either side to light it; the chairs held gay cushions; a divan at the far end was covered with a brilliantly

158

coloured rug embroidered with gold thread. There was a table of polished and inlaid wood at which she could see the king had been writing, and there were soft carpets on the floor.

Sabina glanced around her with fascinated eyes and then realized that the gipsy king was standing just inside the closed door watching her.

"I never dreamed that I would see you here," he said softly.

She flushed a little at his tone.

"Please do not think me too unconventional," she said. "I would not have come like this if it had not been of the utmost importance."

"I am sorry if my people frightened you."

"It . . . it was the dancer," Sabina said. "Why does she hate me?"

The innocence of the question brought a little smile to his lips.

"Are you not woman enough to answer that question for yourself?" he inquired.

Sabina looked at him inquiringly, and then she felt the blood rising in her cheeks.

"You mean that she . . . lo . . ." her voice died away. "I did not think of that," she added after a minute.

"Sit down," he said quietly, "and let me bring you some wine."

"I do not think I want any," Sabina answered. But he filled a goblet of cut crystal from a flagon of embossed gold and brought it to her.

"Drink a little," he commanded.

It seemed easier to obey him than to protest. Sabina sipped from the goblet and then, setting it down on the table she drew her hat from her head and put up her hands to her untidy hair.

"What must you think of me . . ." she began, but he interrupted her.

"I was thinking that you looked as lovely as you did that first night. Your hair had been caressed then by the wind and was blown around your cheeks, just as it is this evening."

Sabina smiled shyly for a moment at his words and then, forgetting everything but the reason why she had come, she said:

159

"Please do not let us talk about me. I have something to tell you."

"I am listening," the gipsy king said.

"I want your help," Sabina pleaded. "I want it more than I have ever wanted anything in my life before. Please ... please say that you will help me if you can."

"Do you really need me to tell you that?" he asked. "Don't you know that I am ready to serve you, that I am yours, utterly yours, to command?"

His voice seemed to vibrate round the walls of the wagon and now Sabina looked up into his face and for a moment was spellbound. She felt as if she were drifting through the darkness towards some great and blinding light. She felt as if great waves lifted her and carried her forward on a tide that was too strong to be resisted; and then, with an effort, she forced herself to continue.

"I have come ... I want help ... not for myself," she stammered, "but for my brother, Harry."

"Your brother?" the gipsy inquired. "I thought it was your sisters of whom you were always thinking. Of Harriet, Melloney, Angelina and Claire, all of whom, if I remember rightly, are to benefit by your marriage."

"They are all in England," Sabina answered. "But Harry is here in Monte Carlo. His ship came into the harbour last night and today he came to see me," she gave a little sigh. "Oh, please try to understand. He is young—only just twenty-one ... and now he has been at sea for a long time. He has been sailing down the coast of Africa, and he has not seen a white woman nor had any fun for months and months."

Sabina fell silent as if she suddenly found it hard to continue, and after a moment the gipsy king said gently.

"Won't you tell me what has happened?"

"I am trying to do so," Sabina replied. "But I want to make you understand as ... someone else did not understand, that Harry is not really bad or stupid. He is just young and because he has so little money—far less than most other officers on his ship—he does not often have a good time or get a chance to enjoy himself."

"I understand only too well," the gipsy king said quietly. "When a man is young, it is natural for him to be gay and carefree."

Sabina flashed him a grateful smile.

"I knew you would understand," she said.

160

"And what has your brother done that has caused you so much worry?" the gipsy king inquired. "Can he have lost money in the Casino?"

"How did you guess?" Sabina exclaimed.

"It is what so many people do when they come to Monte Carlo."

"And, Harry is no exception," Sabina sighed. "He lost ... you will be horrified ... nearly one hundred pounds!"

"You are asking me to give him the money?" the gipsy king inquired.

Sabina sat up suddenly with a little gesture of pride.

"No, no, of course not. I would not think of asking you to give or even lend Harry—whom you do not know—a huge sum of money like that. Oh, please do not think I came for that reason. Besides, I knew that you yourself, would not have so much money as that."

"All gipsies are not penniless."

"But a hundred pounds is a fortune! That was not why I came. When Harry told me he had lost the money and that he had given a cheque which would not be met when it was presented to his bank, I went to ... my *fiancé*— Lord Thetford."

"That was, of course, very sensible of you. And he gave your brother the money?"

"Yes .. he ... gave Harry ... the money," Sabina said, not realizing, in the reluctance of the words as they came between her lips or the sudden darkening of her expression, how much she revealed of the unpleasantness of that transaction.

"Then if your brother has the money," the gipsy said, "I do not understand how I can be of assistance."

"My *fiancé* gave Harry the money—in francs, of course—and he put them in his pocket. He intended to go straight to the Casino, pay his debt and ask them to return him the cheque he had given the night before. But he met some friends and they went off to a place of entertainment near the harbour. They met two women there and they asked them out to dinner. It was only when dinner was over and the women retired that Harry realized he had lost the money that he had had in his pocket. It had gone. All the francs that Arthur—I mean my *fiancé*—had given him."

"Gone? You mean that the women had stolen them?"

"They must have done. They went to the Ladies' Cloak-room and they did not come back."

"I see!"

"And that is where I feel you may be able to help us," Sabina went on. "Harry said that one of the girls was fair, but the other was dark, almost like a gipsy he said, and her name was Katisha. I thought ... I thought that perhaps you would know her and that you might . . . make her, if she is indeed a gipsy, give ... back the money she has ... stolen."

"I see, so that is why you came to me."

"But of course. Do you not understand that you are perhaps the only person in the world who can help us now. If you cannot get the money back, you do not know how awful it will be or what will happen."

"What will happen?" the gipsy inquired.

"Harry will have to write tonight to Papa and tell him what he has done. But because he knows he cannot ask Papa and Mamma to find such an immense sum of money—indeed they have not got it—he intends to resign his commission."

Sabina spoke simply and yet it was easy to see the tragedy in her eyes.

"You mean there is no one else who would give or lend you one hundred pounds?"

"There is no one else we could possibly ask to give it to us," Sabina answered. "And as for lending—well, that, too, is impossible. You see, Harry has promised to pay back the hundred pounds that he has already borrowed from my *fiancé* within a year. It means that he will be able to buy absolutely nothing for himself; it will take up almost his entire salary."

"I thought you said that Lord Thetford had given him the money."

"He gave him the actual francs," Sabina replied. "But, of course, Harry has to pay it back."

"In somewhat harsh circumstances, surely?"

"Arthur was very annoyed with Harry," Sabina said in a low voice. "He . . . he does not wish to do . . . very much for my family."

"And so you have come to me."

"Do you think you can help us," Sabina asked, clasping her hands together. "Please, please say that you can. I don't know what Papa and Mamma would do if they

162

hear that Harry has got into trouble. They are so proud of him. He is their only son and he has done well so far. He got promotion much younger than most men of his age. It would break their hearts if he had to leave the Navy in disgrace. Please help us."

The gipsy king bent forward and took Sabina's hands in his.

"Listen, Sabina," he said. "You have not got to plead with me. I want to help you; I will help you."

"You will? Oh, thank you, thank you," Sabina cried. "If you only knew what it means to hear you say that. I felt that somehow you would not fail me, and how right I was!"

"Why did you feel that?" the gipsy king inquired.

"I do not know," Sabina answered. "There is ... something about you ... there always has been ... that made me feel I could trust you and that you would understand."

"As other people have not understood, perhaps?" the gipsy king inquired.

Sabina looked away and took her hands from his.

"Some ... people are very ... intolerant of weakness or stupidity."

"Perhaps they don't understand other things as well," the gipsy said. "For instance, how beautiful you are when you smile, how exquisitely pathetic when you look sad. Did you know that your eyes darken when you are frightened, and when you are happy they seem to lighten and to shine so that your whole face seems transformed?"

Sabina drew in a little breath and got to her feet.

"I must ... go now," she said quickly. "Will you come too ... and find Katisha? Will you make her give up the money ... at once?"

"Are you going because you feel you ought to?" the gipsy asked, "or because you are afraid to listen to me?"

"Afraid?" Sabina asked in a low voice.

"Yes, afraid," he answered. "You are running away, Sabina. Running away because your heart tells you to stay."

Sabina stood very still. She did not answer him; her eyes were on her hands playing with her gloves which she had picked up from the table.

"Have you nothing to say to me?" he asked, his voice deep and caressing.

163

She turned then, suddenly; her face very pale in the light from the lanterns, her lips trembling a little.

"Yes ... I have something to say," she said. "Something else ... to ask you."

"What is it?" he inquired.

"Please ... please do not make me fall ... in love with ... you."

It was a cry that seemed to come right from her heart—the cry of a child who is frightened of the dark. He stood looking at her and for a moment neither of them moved. Then, very quietly he asked:

"Isn't it too late?"

Her eyes fell before his.

"Yes, too late, Sabina," he went on. "Too late now to draw back, to forget that we have ever met each other, to pretend that we have not stood together and talked, that our eyes have not met and said things which our lips were afraid to whisper. And I think, my darling, if you are honest with yourself, you already love me a little."

"No! no!" Sabina whispered.

"Then why," he asked, "are you trembling? Why is there a little pulse beating in your neck as if you were excited? Yes, excited, Sabina, at being near me."

"It isn't ... true!" she moaned. "It isn't true!"

"Will you swear to that?" he asked. "Swear it as you look me in the eyes. Will you tell me that from the moment we met I have meant nothing to you, that you have never thought about me, that you have never wanted to see me again? Say that firmly and without hesitating and I will go out of your life—never to return."

"I ... would not ask ... that of ... of you," Sabina murmured.

"But you have asked me not to make you love me," the gipsy continued. "And I am telling you, Sabina, that it is too late. See, I am not touching you and yet you are quivering as if I were holding you in my arms. Your heart is beating and your breath is coming quickly as if your lips were very close to mine. I am not touching you, Sabina, and yet I think, in your heart, you want me to."

She threw up her head as if to make one last effort of protest; but as she looked at him, her eyes very wide, a sudden light in them that could not be hidden, the expression on her face revealed the truth. For a moment she could only tremble and then she felt a sudden flame of ecstasy shoot through her. It was as wonderful and as thrilling as if, indeed, he held her in his arms.

Then the world stood still and they were, in that second, so close to each other in spirit that the confines of the body were utterly and completely forgotten. Until, as if human nature broke under the strain, he went down on his knees before her and lifted the hem of her skirt to his lips.

"I love you, Sabina," he said. "I vow myself to your service. I will not force myself upon you or take you in my arms here lest it should be against your will. Because I love you so deeply, because I know that we were meant for each other, you and I—I will not kiss you until you ask it of me, either by word or action. But I should be blind, deaf, dumb, and unworthy of my love and yours, if I did not know at this moment that you love me a little, however much you may wish to deny it."

"I . . . we cannot . . . we must not . . ." Sabina said wildly.

"You must not, you mean," the gipsy answered. "And yet, again, why not? I am a man. I love you. I cannot offer you the same life, the same position that Lord Thetford can do, but I can, perhaps, give you happiness."

"Oh . . . please," Sabina begged. "You do not . . . understand." She put her hands to her face and turning away from him, as he knelt there, sat in the chair, her head bowed.

"Darling, I have made you cry," the gipsy exclaimed. "Fool that I am, when I wish you nothing but happiness."

"I . . . I think I am crying for happiness," Sabina answered. "Because you are so kind, so good and so very sweet to me. If only we could have met a few months ago. But now . . . now it is too . . . late!"

The gipsy rose to his feet and stood looking down at her bowed head, a curious expression on his face.

"Why is it too late?" he asked.

"Because . . . of so many . . . things," Sabina answered brokenly. "Mamma . . . is so pleased and . . . and there are . . . the girls."

"Harriet, Melloney, Angelina and Claire," the gipsy said.

"Yes . . . all of . . . them," Sabina answered. "Oh, I know that Arthur has said he does not intend to do . . .

much for them when we are married, but perhaps I will be able to persuade him to change his mind. Anyway, they can have many things of mine ... clothes, any money I have ... and they will be able to come and stay. They ... and Mamma ... are counting on it!"

"And it wouldn't be the same if we could offer them the hospitality of a gipsy camp."

Sabina flushed at that and took her hands from her face.

"It is not that," she said hotly. "You are not to think it is because you are a gipsy or that I am ashamed of you. I would be proud, proud to be...." The words died away. The gipsy bent forward.

"Say it," he urged. "Say the words, my sweetheart, that I long to hear from your lips."

"But I must not," Sabina protested. "Do you not understand? We must not even ... think about it.... I am engaged to Arthur ... I have got to marry him. Besides, Harry owes him ... a hundred pounds."

"Oh, you darling, you baby," the gipsy said softly. "Do you think one hundred pounds matters, when something concerns your whole life. Come away with me. Let me teach you what happiness means. Let me teach you how to love, to come alive, to thrill, as no Englishman can teach you—as no other man in the world could do, because you and I were meant for each other."

"You are not ... to tempt me," Sabina whispered. "You are not to ask such ... things of me. I am not strong; I am not ... good; I am weak and ... bad where you are concerned. I want to do all the things I ought not to do. I want to be with ... you. I want to hear you talking. I want you to ... touch me."

The gipsy suddenly turned away from her.

"You must go now, Sabina," he said. "There are bounds beyond which a man may not be driven and behave as he should. I love you! Do you not think that I want to take you in my arms, to cover your face with kisses, to kiss your mouth, your eyes, your neck, to pull down your hair and kiss that too? I love you. Love is not the weak, anaemic thing that Englishmen make of it. Love, to me, is a force which will drive a man to do desperate things. It is something for which a man will hunger, steal and fight and, yes, be willing to die. That is love, Sabina. And now, you must go or I shall forget that you are my guest, accepting my hospitality, and because of it I may not touch you."

There was so much emotion, so much pulsating force in the gipsy's voice, that Sabina could only listen, spellbound, and then feel, in the thumping of her heart and the warmth of her lips, a wild impulse to respond. She loved him! She knew that now. This was love, rising like a leaping flame within her. And then, as she hesitated as she thought, that not all the will-power in the world could prevent her from flinging herself in his arms, raising her lips to his and inviting those kisses of which the very thought made her quiver and thrill, the gipsy pulled open the door roughly. The cool, night air came blowing into the wagon, making the lanterns flicker and blowing Sabina's hair away from her cheeks.

"Come!"

It was a command rather than an invitation as, without looking at her, the gipsy held out his hand to lead her through the doorway. Automatically Sabina picked up her hat and gloves and then, aware that her mind was in a turmoil so that she could hardly think or speak, she let him lead her down the steps of the wagon to where her horse was waiting.

He assisted her into the saddle with what seemed to her an almost disinterested efficiency, and then he gave a command and a few seconds later a gipsy returned leading a black stallion into the light of the fire. It was a magnificent animal with a touch of Arab in its arched neck. The saddle was ornamented with silver and the stirrups also were of polished silver.

The gipsy swung himself on to the back of the horse. He gave some orders to his men and then he and Sabina rode, together, through the camp into the darkness beyond. As they went, Sabina felt some of the wild elation ebb away from her, but her breath still came quietly between her parted lips and her body still throbbed with an almost intolerable delight. She was acutely conscious of him beside her, his head held proudly as he rode, seemingly a part of his horse, as a man rides who has been used to horses all his life.

What must he think of her? Sabina wondered. Not only for refusing him, but for clinging to her engagement to Arthur. Did he, in his heart, condemn her for being a snob? Did he think it was only because of her position as

Arthur's wife that she must refuse to marry a wandering gipsy, a man who had no settled home? Did he understand that, if she were free, if it were not for her family, she would stay with him tonight, she would never go back to Monte Carlo?

This was love, Sabina thought. A love which tore one in pieces, which seemed to burn one's whole body, mind and soul. And yet, how could she forget the pain she would give to her family and the benefits of which she would deprive them?

Harriet was counting on coming to London, and Mamma had seemed younger and prettier since her engagement to Arthur. It was because she was not worrying so much about the future and not struggling to hoard every farthing so that Harriet could have some pretty dresses in which to make her début.

Sabina thought suddenly of Arthur; of his cold, rather harsh voice, speaking to her as he had done that afternoon. She shivered, and instinctively moved her horse a little nearer towards the gipsy. As if he sensed what she was thinking and feeling, he turned suddenly and spoke to her for the first time since they had left the camp. She could see his face in the moonlight, his dark hair swept back from his square forehead, his face strangely foreign and yet strong and trustworthy, his mouth full and generous, his eyes dark and penetrating and yet seemingly almost afire with the burning passion within him.

"We are riding side by side," he said, in that low resonant voice which seemed to play on her emotions as if she were an instrument which responded to the master touch. "Side by side, Sabina. Does that mean anything to you? To me it means all I have dreamed of and all I hope for—tonight and for eternity."

CHAPTER TEN

SABINA stirred and woke, and instantly thoughts and memories like a crowd of importunate beggars, came flooding into her mind. There was so much to remember of last night, and yet her thoughts seemed to linger most on that ride through the darkness beside the gipsy king.

There had been no need for words. There was a closeness and understanding between them which made speech superfluous. There was for Sabina an utter contentment in just riding beside him, in feeling the strength of his personality vibrating towards her, in knowing that she had but to put out her hand and she could touch him.

Only as the lights of Monte Carlo gleamed ahead of them did she say:

"Surely your camp has moved since I first came to it?"

He turned his head to smile into her upturned face.

"I wanted to be as near to you as it was possible to be," he replied.

She had thought this must be the explanation, but there was an irrepressible joy in hearing him say the words. They rode on again and finally, as they came to a meeting of the roads where the first white villa nestled amongst its green trees, the gipsy reined in his horse.

"I am going to leave you now, my dear one," he said, "but I will meet you later. Where can I find you?"

"I have told Harry to wait for me in the road below the villa," Sabina answered.

"I will come to you there," he said. He reached out his hand and took hers. She was wearing her riding gloves and he turned down the broad cuff and kissed the bare skin of her wrist. She felt herself tremble, but before she could say anything or even ask him what he was about to do, he was gone, spurring his horse forward to ride away into the darkness of the twisting road which Sabina knew led down to the town.

She followed her own way more leisurely. There were still lights in many of the windows in the villas and far away in the distance she could see the garish illuminations of the Casino. People she thought, were gambling in the brilliant building, concentrating with every nerve tense and strained on the spin of the wheel or the turn of the card. It was like a will-o'-the-wisp which lured the unwary and the foolish, giving pleasure to many, yet inevitably proving a pitfall for the inexperienced and the unsophisticated.

But one could not protect people against themselves. Harry had learned his lesson. It had been a harsh one and through the long months ahead he would remember it bitterly. With a sudden start Sabina remembered that Harry was not yet safe. The gipsy king had to find Katisha; he had to persuade her to give up the money before Harry could be rescued from the pit of humiliation and degradation in which he now found himself. It was then that Sabina realized that she was absolutely certain that Harry would be saved. She could not help but trust the gipsy king, and she knew he would not fail her.

She was smiling as she reached the Villa Mimosa and passed the front door to ride lower down the hill. Harry was waiting for her in the shadow of the trees. As she came in sight, the groom ran forward to take the horse's head, and in an instant Harry was standing beside her.

"Is it all right?"

He hardly breathed the words, and she saw by the dark lines under his eyes how much he had been suffering.

"I think it will be," she answered in a low voice.

He helped her dismount and the groom led the horse away.

"You haven't got the money?" he inquired.

She shook her head.

"No. But someone I know will bring it to us. I am sure of that."

"Who is this person?"

"Someone I met when I first came here," Sabina replied evasively.

"It is a man, of course," Harry said.

Sabina did not answer. Something in her face and in the tenseness of her body made her brother, who was not usually perceptive, add:

"What does he mean to you?"

Sabina gave a little sigh.

"Why do you ask me that?"

"Because you are being secretive and strange about him," Harry replied. "Because he is ready to help you and—look here, Sis, you're not in any trouble are you?"

"Trouble! What sort of trouble?" Sabina asked with a kind of lilt in her voice.

Harry looked down into her face.

"If you ask me, you're in love with him," he said slowly.

"Whatever makes you think that?" Sabina asked, trying to speak lightly, but unable to help the tell-tale colour flooding into her face.

"You can't lie to me," Harry said. "And you never were a good liar anyway. Are you in a tangle, Sis? If you are, I'll help you if I can."

Sabina reached up her hand to touch his cheek.

"Dear Harry. We have always told each other things, have we not? But I cannot talk to you about this; you would not understand."

"How do you know I wouldn't? You don't trust me."

"It is not that," Sabina said. "It is just that I cannot, dare not, talk about it. He is my friend, that is all I can say. And when he comes, you must be nice to him—please, Harry, promise me that!"

She realized later that she need not have extracted his promise. Harry, after one startled look at the gipsy king, had not seemed to find him strange or, indeed, a peculiar friend for his sister. It was true that he was at first so overwhelmed at receiving the roll of notes which the gipsy handed him that he could only stammer his thanks and reiterate, over and over again, how grateful he was.

"So you got them back," Sabina exclaimed. "I felt sure that you would do so."

"Did you really procure these from Katisha, sir?" Harry inquired. "I thought after Sabina had gone to find you that I had made a mistake in suggesting that she was the culprit, I remembered that in the carriage it was the fair girl who sat next to me and who would therefore have been more likely to have taken the money than her friend."

The gipsy king smiled.

"Shall we ask no questions? The money is yours, that is what matters, is it not?"

"It is, indeed," Harry cried.

"And may I suggest, if you will not think it impertinent, that you take it to the Casino authorities immediately."

"I will go now. But how can I ever thank you, sir, for what you have done for me?"

"I require no thanks," the gipsy answered.

"But I feel I must tell you . . ." Harry began, only to be interrupted by the gipsy who said:

"You will only embarrass me. Hurry now, for fear that your cheque should already be on its way to England. Make it quite clear that they must cancel it, but try not to visit the tables before you have called on the cashier."

"I am not quite as bird-witted as that—not a second time," Harry said. "Good-bye, sir. Good-bye, Sis. I never thought the day would end as happily as this."

Sabina kissed him and he hurried away up the road. She watched him go and then turned to find the gipsy watching her.

"How can I thank you?" she asked, softly.

"I need no thanks," he replied. "I am only so proud that you came to me, that you trusted me to help you."

His voice made her quiver, and because she was shy Sabina looked at the wall beside which they were standing.

"I must go," she murmured. In answer the gipsy suddenly lifted her in his arms and swung her up so that she was sitting high above him on the smooth stones.

"Don't move until I can help you," he commanded her. He swung himself over the wall and into the garden. On the other side he put up his arms and lifted Sabina down. For a moment she was very close to him. She felt that she could hear his heart beating as his arms held her close against him. She felt her head swim, felt a sudden wild emotion which made her want to cling to him. She wanted, as she had never wanted anything in the whole of her life before, to feel his lips against hers. And then, suddenly, she was free and they were standing a little apart between the trunks of the trees, the moonlight making a strange pattern on the ground between them.

"I hate to tell you that you must go," the gipsy said quietly. "But you are tired. You have been anxious and upset; you have suffered enough emotions for one day, Now you must go to bed and sleep."

His consideration made Sabina feel like tears.

"But everything is all right now," she said.

"Everything?" he inquired, raising his eyebrows a little.

She knew that he was thinking of his love for her and the fact that she was engaged to Arthur. She turned her head away and he said:

"But I am determined not to trouble you with any more tonight. There comes a point in all our lives when we cannot think clearly and we are torn between our brain and our heart. And that, my little love, is the position I think you find yourself in at the moment. No, don't speak," he went on as she would have answered him. "But there is one thing I want to say before I go.

172

Never again must you risk coming in search of me, riding alone along dark and dangerous roads. If you need me, you have but to come on to your balcony carrying a candle in your hand. Tie this handkerchief, which I will give you, round the balustrade, and within an hour I will be at your side."

"You mean that someone will be watching?"

"Always. You will not see who watches; you need not be afraid; but somebody will be there, ready to come for me should you wish to see me."

As he spoke, he took a silk handkerchief from his neck and gave it into her hand. She felt her fingers close over the softness of it and she thought with a sudden pang that it was something of his, something that he had worn, something that she would be able to treasure for ever.

"And now good night," the gipsy said softly.

He took her free hand in his and peeled the glove from it. Then he stood looking down at the open palm.

"Shall I try to read the future for you?" he asked. "Or shall I tell you that you stand at the cross roads? There are two ways you can go, and only you, Sabina, can decide which one you will take."

She gave a little murmur as if she protested against the thought that she must decide, and then felt his lips— kissing first the palm, then each finger separately, and finally lingering, warm and compelling, against the soft blue veins at her wrist.

"I love you," he said very softly. "Remember nothing else tonight except that I love you."

She had gone to sleep with his words ringing in her ears and she awoke to find that she had slept all night with his silk handkerchief beneath her cheek.

It was daylight, the sun was coming into her window and she tried to tell herself that everything would seem different. Last night had been a dream, a wild, exciting dream, the thought of which could still make her blood pulsate through her veins. But surely today she must look at things from a different point of view?

How could she even for a moment contemplate marrying a gipsy, she asked herself. A man of whom she knew nothing; who might, if the truth were known, have half a dozen wives of his own tribe.

Sabina suddenly gave a little sob and hid her eyes in his

handkerchief. It was no use, she could not decry him even to herself. She loved him. She loved everything about him—the way he moved; the way he spoke; the touch of his hands and the warm insistence of his lips. She could think of nothing more perfect or more near to heaven than to be in his arms; to let him do as he wished to do and rain his kisses on her face and hair. She felt herself tremble at the very thought of it; and then, even as her breath came quickly, as her lips parted and her eyelids felt strangely heavy, she jerked herself back to reality.

She was engaged to Arthur; she was staying with Arthur's mother and wearing the clothes that had been given her as part of her trousseau. At home the wedding presents were collecting at the Vicarage and her mother was making plans for the wedding which was to take place in June. Had she gone completely crazed that she could think of turning her back on all that? Breaking her word of honour; shaming her family; becoming, in their eyes and in the eyes of everyone else, an outcast, someone of whom they would only speak with bated breath.

'It is mad, mad, mad!' Sabina said the word over and over again; but still she could hear that deep voice, with its wildly attractive accent, saying: 'I love you!'

'Why should this have happened to me?' Sabina asked aloud, and thought to herself that without it she would never have known what love meant. She had believed quite sincerely that she loved Arthur. She had thought when she came to Monte Carlo that she was the luckiest girl in the world to be marrying someone so important, so charming, so eminently suitable. What had changed her in that short space of time? She knew the answer—it was love!

She had thought that love such as this existed only in books. But even those more lurid romances that she and Harriet read in secret had not revealed to her a fraction of the truth about this strange joy which seemed to transform the whole world when he was near. They did not explain that she would feel breathless and on the verge of swooning and yet, at the same time, vividly alive because he touched her. She had not known that she could ever ache for the touch of a man's lips or feel as though a strange fire burned within her because his words had ignited it and the look in his eyes had made her tremble.

174

"I am in love!"

She said the words out loud and went to the window, only a moment later to step back, remembering that she was only in her night-gown and feeling that already, somewhere in the green undergrowth, two eyes were watching for that signal which would bring him to her.

'Can this really be happening?' Sabina asked herself. Could it be true that she, Sabina Wantage, the eldest daughter of the Vicar of Cobbleford, the dowdy, unattractive, unsought-after girl who had gone to London and been a social failure, was here in Monte Carlo, engaged to one man, in love with another, watched over by gipsies and, as their king had said, at the cross-roads of her life.

What was she to do? What *could* she do but marry Arthur as was expected of her?

She went through the day in a kind of dream. She went driving with Lady Thetford; they went to a luncheon party; they drove again in the afternoon, shopped, had tea with some friends and returned home to the villa to find a message to say that Arthur would call for them about a quarter to eight.

All the time Sabina had felt as if she remained detached, an onlooker at a strange play that was taking place around her. Now, for the first time, when she heard Arthur's name, reality appeared to present itself.

"Where are we going tonight?" she asked.

"We are dining with the Grand Duke Ivan of Russia," Lady Thetford answered. "He is a charming man and you will like him. He has recently built a villa in Monte Carlo and he entertains in great style and magnificence."

"Have you known him a long time?" Sabina asked.

"Quite a number of years," Lady Thetford replied. "He is another of my friends whom Arthur, to his surprise, finds quite acceptable." There was a little edge on her voice as she spoke and then she laughed. "I mustn't allow myself to get bitter," she added. "One must remember to be philosophical, especially as to the vagaries of one's children."

"Arthur is coming with us?" Sabina asked.

"Yes. When I told the Grand Duke that you were staying with me and that you were engaged to Arthur, he invited you both to dinner. I am anxious for you to see him. Someone once said that if he wished he could charm

175

a pigeon off a tree. I shall be interested to see what you think of him."

What was charm? Sabina thought to herself as she went upstairs to dress. Would Lady Thetford think that the gipsy king had charm? It was obvious that she thought her son had none. Sabina longed at that moment to confide in someone older and wise.

She felt suddenly young and helpless and terribly ignorant. What did she know about men, or any man for that matter? She had known so few and they had meant so little in her life. She had no standards to judge by and in her inexperience she might be making the fatal mistake of believing a man attractive and cultured merely because he was romantic.

And yet she was sure that the gipsy, whatever his breeding and his upbringing, was a gentleman in his own way. Harry had seemed to think so and almost instinctively he had called him 'sir.' It had not just been a gesture because the gipsy was doing him a service; it was as if he accepted him as an older man and someone in authority.

But Harry was young and inexperienced too. What would Arthur think of her vagabond friend? She gave a little shiver at the thought of Arthur ever finding out about him. She could imagine the coldness of his face, the note of angry rebuke in his voice.

Hastily Sabina began to dress. She wanted to escape from her thoughts; she wanted to drift back into the sense of misty detachment which had been hers all day. But it was impossible. Once again the problems of last night presented themselves. She was at the cross-roads. Which way would she take?

The Grand Duke's villa was, as Lady Thetford said, magnificent. There was nothing pretentious or overwhelming about its appearance from the outside, but once one had crossed the threshold it bore no resemblance to any other villa or indeed to any house that Sabina had ever seen before.

There were wonderful rugs from Persia, jade and ivory from China, silks and embroideries from Japan, sandalwood and spices from Arabia; and everywhere there were fabulous pictures, jewelled icons, carvings and crystal lights which bewildered the eye and made Sabina feel as if the stories of the *Arabian Nights* had come true.

But all of it was a fitting background for the Grand

Duke himself. Tall and handsome, with thin aristocratic features and tired dark eyes which seemed to light up when he smiled, he, also, seemed to have stepped straight out of a fairy tale. His courtesy and his fabulous charm made his guests feel at home however diverse their characters, however mixed their nationalities.

It was a large party, Sabina discovered, for they sat down over thirty to dinner, and she was delighted to find that Sherry was there and he came to her side immediately on her arrival, despite the fact that Arthur scowled at him and made it quite clear that he was none too pleased to see him.

"Don't be so disagreeable, Prosy," Sherry said to him, quite unabashed by his cold reception. "Going to talk to Sabina whether you like it or not."

"I haven't forbidden you to do so," Arthur said grimly.

"Better not," Sherry replied. "Shall take no notice of you. Dog-in-the-manger Prosy. Remember you were just the same at school. Never would lend me your cricket bat or even a fives' ball when I wanted one."

"I am not certain that I like being compared to a cricket bat and a fives' ball," Sabina said, laughingly.

"Arthur's most valuable possessions at the time," Sherry retorted. "Now he's got you he's going to be just as mean if he gets the chance. Have to be firm with him."

Sabina looked beseechingly at Arthur, but he was obviously not in the mood to be amused; and though Sherry continued to be lighthearted and gay, Sabina found, because of Arthur's attitude, the conversation was heavy and somewhat stilted until dinner was announced. To her delight she found Sherry was seated on her right, and the meal, with a long, elaborate number of courses, passed quickly in consequence.

"What's the matter with Prosy tonight? Like a bear with a sore head," Sherry said.

"Oh, do call him Arthur," Sabina pleaded. "He hates his nickname. He winces every time you use it. I am sure it makes him cross."

"Arthur then. What's wrong with him?"

"Is there anything wrong?" Sabina asked.

"Good lord! Mean to say he is always like this? Dead bore, that's what's the matter! Always has been."

"Sherry, you are not to say such things to me," Sabina rebuked him.

"Told you that. . . ." Sherry paused. "No, won't say it now."

"Say what?" Sabina inquired.

"What I was going to say," Sherry replied mysteriously. She could get no more out of him before she was forced to turn to the man on her left and engage him in conversation.

When dinner was over, the ladies moved into the drawing-room, which Sabina found opened on to a beautiful conservatory where an orchestra was playing and a fountain tinkled, crystal and iridescent amongst great banks of exotic flowers. She was so interested in everything she saw that she found it hard to listen to the chatter of the ladies, and when the men came into the drawing-room, she looked up to find Sherry standing beside her and realized that she had been far away with her own thoughts.

Sherry drew her a little to one side, ostensibly to show her some orchids, and then, when they were out of earshot, said:

"Not to be angry, Sabina, but Arthur's a bit foxed."

"Foxed?" Sabina queried. "Do you mean that Arthur has had . . . too much to drink?"

Sherry grinned at her.

"Wasn't entirely his fault," he said. "Not directly. Being extremely pompous and annoying, so told the Grand Duke what he was called at Eton and how jolly priggish he can be at times. Grand Duke entered into the spirit of it."

"The spirit of what?" Sabina inquired.

"One or two of us decided make Arthur drunk. When you ladies left the room, persuaded the Grand Duke to propose toasts. Drinking a toast Russian fashion means that a man must empty his glass. Grand Duke told servants fill Arthur's glass to the brim while we only had little in the bottom of our glasses. Of course, Arthur had to do right thing. Result he's really quite human."

"Oh, Sherry, how could you do anything so naughty?" Sabina said crossly. "It will upset Lady Thetford, and what is more, Arthur will be furious with you tomorrow."

"Not going to know it was my fault," Sherry said lightly. "Thinks we have all drunk the same amount. You're not to give us away, understand?"

"As if I should," Sabina answered. "Is he very bad?"

"See for yourself," Sherry said. "On his feet all right."

"I do not want to look," Sabina said agitatedly.

She felt suddenly nervous and frightened, and almost before she realized what was happening, Sherry had drawn her to the far end of the conservatory where a love-seat was half-concealed amongst the flowers.

"Let's sit here," he said. "Besides, want to talk to you."

"What about?" Sabina inquired.

"Want you to marry me."

"If that is a joke, it is not very funny . . ." Sabina began, and then realized that Sherry was serious.

"Can't marry Arthur," he said. "Won't make you happy! Never met a girl I liked as much as you. Marry me, Sabina. Have a lot of fun together."

"It is nice of you, Sherry; sweet of you, in fact. But I do not love you—and I do not really believe you love me."

"But I do. Besides, marrying Arthur without loving him."

"How do you know I don't love him?" Sabina asked, rather feebly.

"Good lord, got eyes in my head," Sherry replied. "No one could love Arthur! Don't imagine that he loves you either. Loves one person, that's himself—always has. Stands to reason won't alter now. Marry him and you'll only be a slave and a door-mat. Besides, he's a snob, and if there's one thing that I can't abide, it's a snob."

"You mustn't say all these things," Sabina protested.

"Marry me, make you happy?" Sherry pleaded.

"You know I cannot do that," Sabina replied. "And quite frankly, Sherry, I do no think I am the right girl for you."

"If you're not, no one is," Sherry said. "Shall go on asking you up to day you get married."

"Oh, Sherry! You are so kind to me and I like you so much, but one day you will really fall in love with someone nice and I shall be delighted—I shall really."

"What do you mean? Shall really fall in love?" Sherry asked. "In love with you, aren't I?"

Sabina shook her head.

"Not really."

"How do you know so much about it?" Sherry inquired.

Sabina was just trying to think of some plausible reply

179

when she saw Arthur approaching them. He walked a little unsteadily and there was a purposefulness about his approach, and a look of determination on his face which made it obvious that he had been searching for her.

"Ah, here you are," he said angrily, but he spoke rather more slowly then usual.

"Yes, here I am, Arthur," Sabina answered quietly.

"You're to come home, do you hear me? You're to come home at once," Arthur almost shouted. "I won't have you sitting about with this fellow—a wastrel at Eton, a wastrel now. You leave him alone and come along with me."

"But, Arthur ... where is your mother?" Sabina inquired.

"She's gone to the Casino," Arthur replied. "Told me to tell you you can join her there if you like. As a matter of fact I'm taking you home. All this gadding about is not good for a young girl."

"Now look here, Prosy ..." Sherry began.

Sabina put out her hand and checked him.

"I will do what he wants," she said softly. "Come along, Arthur. Let us go at once."

Sabina said good-bye to the Grand Duke, collected her cloak and moved with Arthur down the steps into the carriage which was waiting for them. She seated herself on the cushioned seat and when Arthur was beside her the footman laid a fur-covered rug over their knees. The door was shut and the horses moved off.

It was then, to Sabina's surprise, that Arthur put his arms around her and drew her roughly to him.

"I won't have you flirting with that fellow, Sheringham, do you hear me?" he asked. "You belong to me—let's make that quite clear. You belong to me!"

He bent his head and fastened his lips on hers. She was so surprised and so unprepared for his kiss that for a moment she could only let herself rest trembling and unprotesting in his arms. And then, as he held her closer and tighter, as she felt breathless beneath the pressure of his lips, she tried to struggle—but it was useless.

"You're mine," he said thickly, again and again. And now he was kissing her roughly, almost brutally, until she cried out with the pain of it.

"You're mine, and I'm not going to stand any damned nonsense."

He clasped her still closer until with an effort she managed to turn her lips away from him so that he was forced to kiss her cheek. He endured this for some seconds until, putting up his hand, he wrenched her chin round so that once again he could find her mouth.

"No, Arthur ... please, Arthur ... you are hurting me."

Sabina was frightened now, but he paid no attention.

"You belong to me," he said. He kissed her once again, so brutally that she could feel the blood on her lips.

"I ought to beat you for the way you've been behaving tonight," he said thickly. "One day I shall beat you."

"Arthur ... let me go."

Sabina heard her dress tear as she struggled with him; she felt his hands, hard and brutal, on her arms. Once again his lips seemed to hold her prisoner, to sap her will, to leave her helpless and trembling beneath his strength.

With a sense of utter relief she felt the horses draw up at the villa.

"I'm coming in," Arthur announced, still holding her but raising his head for a moment to see where they were.

"No, Arthur!"

"I want to talk to you," he said and his eyes were hard and dark with passion.

It was then that Sabina felt that she could bear no more. The footman opened the door.

"You cannot come in, Arthur," she cried. "I am tired ... I want to go to bed."

She knew that her voice was slightly hysterical, but somehow it didn't matter. Nothing mattered but that she should be free of him.

"I insist," she heard him say, and then again her own voice.

"No ... no ... I am tired."

She twisted herself free with a suddenness which took him by surprise. She scrambled somehow out of the carriage tearing the frill of her dress as it caught on the side of the door. And then, she was running up the steps of the villa and through the front door.

"I am going to bed ... Bates," she said breathlessly to the butler who was waiting in the hall. "I am tired and I don't want to see ... anyone. Do you understand? I am not to be disturbed whoever ... asks for me."

Bates looked past her to where Arthur was slowly, with some difficulty descending from the carriage.

"I understand, miss," he said. "No one will disturb you."

Sabina was already half-way up the stairs before he said the last words. She flung open the door of her bedroom and then shut it and locked it behind her. Then she stood with her back to the door, listening to what was happening downstairs. She could hear voices—Arthur's thick and angry, Bates's low and dignified. She could not hear what they said but after a long silence there was the sound of a carriage driving away, of the front door being closed—and then silence.

She moved from the door to sink down on the stool by the dressing-table. She put up her hands to her face and realized that her fingers were icy cold and shaking. For some moments she sat there, her face hidden, until at last, she raised her head to look in the mirror. Her eyes were wide and her face was drained of all colour. In the light of the candles she could see the torn lace hanging from her bodice, and red marks on her shoulder and above her elbow where Arthur's fingers had gripped her.

She touched her bruised mouth with her fingers and, taking her handkerchief, rubbed both her mouth and her cheek as though she would rub away his kisses. She could still feel the brutal impact of his mouth. He had been drunk—and yet she felt that was no excuse. There had been no love in the kisses he had given her, only a desire of possession, a lust that she recognized even while, in her innocence, she did not understand it.

Now she knew that she hated Arthur. She stared at her reflection wildly for some moments before rising to her feet, she ran to the little secret drawer in the table beside her bed. She opened it. At the back she had hidden the silk handkerchief the gipsy king had given her the night before. She laid it against her cheek, her lips moved against it, kissing it, feeling soothed and comforted by the softness of the silk.

'I cannot marry Arthur ... I cannot.' She said the words out loud and heard the tremor and the wildness in her tone. She looked down again at the handkerchief. This was the moment when she must decide which way she would go! Impulsively, as if she was half afraid of her own decision, she picked up the candle from the dressing-table.

Now she did not hesitate, and holding back the curtains walked out on to the balcony. She stood for a moment holding the candle high above her head, and then she set it down and tied the handkerchief over the edge of the balustrade. She stood looking out. It was very quiet. There was no movement in the garden and she wondered if there really were two eyes watching her, whether her signal had been seen, or whether that, too, had been but a part of her dream.

She waited. Nothing happened, and after a while she went in again to her room and set the candle down on the table. Now she felt as if the walls which just a short time ago had seemed a sanctuary, were stifling her. She was afraid, and yet she was not fearful. It was as if she stood on a high cliff and saw the waters swirling below her. They were waiting for her and she had not yet reached them.

Sabina took a lace shawl from the drawer and throwing it round her shoulders went out on to the balcony and down the steps into the garden. If he came to her, he would come through past the fountain and the pagoda, and she felt that she would rather wait for him there than in the house.

Now that some time must pass before he came, she felt again detached and apart from life, as she had felt all day. She could only wait! Wait, and feel the minutes going by while the fountain tinkled softly at her feet and the leaves of the palm trees whispered a little in the night breeze.

She was conscious that her arms were aching and she knew that tomorrow they would be bruised, but more vivid was the horror she felt within herself. Horror and a sudden hatred of Arthur such as she had never felt for anyone else in the whole of her life before. For a moment even her family did not seem quite real. Everything was out of focus save her fear of one man and her need of another.

Slowly, slowly, the time passed until suddenly, in the distance, she heard the sound of horse's hoofs. They stopped and a minute or so later she saw him coming towards her across the moonlit garden.

It was then that all her pent-up feeling, all the misery,

fear and fright of what had just happened, all her indecision and soul-searchings of earlier in the day and the relief and sudden piercing joy that she felt at the sight of him were merged together so that without conscious thought or decision she moved instinctively to where she wished to be.

She ran down the path, her arms outstretched, the shawl with which she had covered her shoulders flying out behind her. She did not think of anything save that he was here; and then she was in his arms and he was holding her as she had wanted to be held, and she was clinging to him, knowing that here was safety, here was security such as she had never known before.

"You have come ... you have come," she whispered. "Oh, hold me ... hold me tight ... do not let me go."

"What is it, my darling?" he asked. "What has upset you? What has happened?"

"Hold me closer!" she pleaded.

To be in his arms was like suddenly reaching heaven. She had no idea that anyone could be so strong, so gentle, and so utterly comforting.

"I was ... afraid," she whispered. "Afraid there was no one watching as you had promised ... that they would not tell you that I ... wanted you."

"I am here," he answered soothingly. "I came just as quickly as I could."

"You will not go away again?" she asked. "You will not leave me?"

She raised her face to his then and he saw, in the darkness of her eyes and the sudden sharpening of her features that she was really frightened.

"I won't leave you," he said quietly, "until you ask me to. I am here for as long as you want me."

"You promise you will not let him ... touch me? Never ... never ... again?"

"Who has touched you?" he began. And then he saw the marks on her shoulders and the torn lace of her dress. "Who has dared?" he asked, his voice fierce with anger.

"I cannot ... marry him," Sabina sobbed. "I cannot. I have tried to do what is right ... but I know now that I cannot ... marry Arthur ... whatever anyone may say."

She threw back her head suddenly, the tear drops on her lashes as she looked up at him.

"Take care of me," she begged. "Please ... please take care of me ... I cannot fight my heart ... any longer ... I ... I love you!"

CHAPTER ELEVEN

THE gipsy swept Sabina up in his arms and carried her across the garden to the seat under the pagoda where they had sat the first night. There he set her down although she murmured protestingly and clung to him.

"We have got to talk, my little darling," he said gently.

"There is nothing more to say," she answered. "I have made up my mind. Take me away with you ... now."

"Would you really come with me now, at this moment?" he inquired.

"I have told you so," she answered. "So please take me. I cannot stay here."

He said nothing for a moment. Then, as she looked up at him to see why he was silent, she saw there was a faint frown between his eyes.

"Are you coming with me because you wish to escape from the man to whom you are officially engaged," he asked, "or because you wish to be with me?"

"Because I wish to be with you," Sabina cried. "How can you question it? I have already told you that I ... I love you."

She said the words shyly and yet they were said. The words she felt must reveal to him the fullest depth of that surging, irresistible love which had swept her away so that everything else seemed insignificant and of no importance.

"If you knew what it meant to me to hear you say that," the gipsy said quietly. "I have dreamed, my English rose, since the first moment I saw you, of the moment when my love for you would ignite yours and when you would realize that we were meant for each other."

He lifted both her hands in his and covered them with kisses. Sabina drew in her breath and threw back her head as if she were ready to surrender her mouth to him, but he drew a little away from her.

"When you are happy, your eyes shine like stars," he said. "And tonight, because you love me a little, there is a warm glow beneath the shining glory of them. Soon, very soon, my beloved, I will make them stars of fire, and I shall know then that you desire me as I desire you."

"Take me away now ... at once," Sabina begged. But he shook his head and laid her hands down in her lap.

"For the moment I am not going to touch you," he said. "When I do, it makes it hard for me to think or to speak sensibly. I want so much to hold you close to me. I want, more than the hope of heaven itself, to feel your lips beneath mine. But first there is something I must say to you."

"What is it?" Sabina asked in a frightened whisper.

"I will not take you unfairly or at a disadvantage," the gipsy replied. "I love you, Sabina. I am ready to lay my whole life at your feet, to dedicate it to your happiness, to worship you as you deserve to be worshipped, to adore you and to love you while there is breath in my body. But because I love you so much, I must be sure that you realize what you are doing. You are after all only a child."

Sabina tried to protest, but he raised his hand and she was silent.

"A child," he repeated, "not only in years but in experience. I am older than you, ten years older, Sabina. And I am old, too, in the knowledge of human nature—especially of women. I will not pretend to you that there have not been many women in my life. I have loved them and some of them have loved me, but nothing and nobody has ever meant what you mean now. This is the moment for which all men yearn! The moment when a man reaches this goal towards which he has adventured for many years, through many strange and varied ways. Each man in his heart has his own ideal of perfection, and in you I have found mine."

Sabina drew in a deep breath. His words, the tone of his voice and the expression on his face, made the whole world seem almost too glorious to be borne.

"What is more," the gipsy went on, "I shall never in my life forget that in coming to me you give up everything."

186

"Everything?" Sabina questioned, almost beneath her breath.

"Yes, everything," the gipsy repeated, "that has mattered to you until now. You will have to choose, my heart's beloved, between me and your family. For it would be stupid of us to imagine that they will be pleased that their daughter, brought up as you have been—nurtured and cossetted in the quiet of the English countryside—should run away with a vagabond—a gipsy whom most people would despise and whom the majority will revile."

"They will ... understand," Sabina murmured. "I will make them ... understand."

There was a lack of conviction in her tone which the gipsy heard and he continued relentlessly:

"There are other things, too, which you will have to sacrifice," he said. "The balls and parties that you have just learnt to enjoy, the beautiful clothes which have thrilled you and which have made you, for the first time, conscious of your beauty. If you come with me, my sweet darling, those pretty gowns, with their frills and laces, must be left behind."

"Do you think they really matter to me?" Sabina asked. "I was delighted with them because I thought they made me look pretty, but when I have worn them I have wished only that you should see me in them."

"My precious!" the gipsy exclaimed. He put out his hands as if he would take her in his arms, and then checked himself. "There is still more I must say," he went on. "You, who have slept in a soft bed every night of your life will now sleep beneath the stars or in a wagon. You will have no place that you can call home, no friends save those you will make amongst my own people. Can all those things, Sabina, and answer this on your oath, can all things be lost without regret?"

"As long as you love me," Sabina replied, "none of them will ever matter."

He drew her into his arms and raised his head to the sky.

"May the heavens above witness that I vow myself to your service for all time."

There was such solemnity in his voice that it was almost as if they were in church. And then he looked down into Sabina's radiant face for a long moment before he kissed her on the lips for the first time.

She felt an ecstasy that was almost unbearable shoot through her. She felt as if he captured, possessed and conquered her, and at the same time drew her very soul from between her lips and made it his. It was as if their spirits swept away from the confines of their earthly bodies and soared towards the stars. It was as if the world about them was lost and forgotten and they were alone in a strange and glorious paradise—man and woman, yet joined indivisibly.

And because the joy and the wonder of it was too great to be borne, Sabina gave a little murmur and hid her face against his neck.

"I love you! Sabina, I love you! You are woman, child and angel all rolled into one. My love for you reaches to the depths of the sea and the heights of the sky, and still it is inadequate for what you are. Look at me!"

It was a command and yet Sabina hid her face. She was no longer immortal, but human and strangely shy of this wild tumult he had awakened within her. And now, because she was still reluctant, he raised her chin gently with his hand.

"So small," he murmured, "and yet you hold my whole life within your little hands."

There was a sudden sound as of a bough falling from a tree or of a bird rustling in the undergrowth, and Sabina started nervously.

"Let us go away," she said. "Suppose someone should come to prevent it."

"Are you still so fearful?" he inquired.

"No, but I want to be with you. I want to be really safe," Sabina answered.

"Because you feel like that you must still have the chance to change your mind," he answered.

"What do you mean?" Sabina inquired.

"I mean, my darling, that you must not come to me until another day has passed. It is hard to let you go; hard not to do as you ask of me; but I must be strong for both of us. As I told you before, my heart's desire, you are standing at the cross-roads, but you must not be persuaded into taking the wrong path. It must be of your own free will, your own choice, and without regrets."

"But I shall never change my mind. I have told you that I have chosen and I shall not go back on my word."

"I will still give you time to think and consider," he answered. "Tonight there is magic in the air, wild, crazy magic, Sabina, that is affecting us both. When the daylight comes, perhaps some of that magic will disappear. You will see me for what I am—a gipsy, one of whom it has been said that he carries his home upon his back. Will that be sufficient for you—not now, darling, when you are young, but when you are old? When that soft, golden hair of yours is beginning to turn grey and there are no longer stars of fire in your eyes. Will you still be satisfied with your choice? And make no mistake about it, Sabina, I will never let you go. If you come with me now, it is for all time and for ever."

"I shall never want to leave you."

"I want you to feel sure of that tomorrow morning when the sun is shining clear and bright through your window. When you can see your pretty gowns hanging in the wardrobe, and one maid-servant brings you your breakfast and another prepares your bath and helps you into your clothes. It is often the little things we sacrifice for love which hurt more than the great or tumultuous ones."

"How small and petty you must think me," Sabina cried.

"I think you are perfect," he answered. "A woman in many ways, a child in some, and only a baby in others. And yet, because you are all three and so much more besides, you have drawn my heart from my body; and if you do not come to me, then I shall be empty and lonely for ever—a man who has lost the power of loving, a man without a heart."

"I am coming to you . . . you know that."

For a moment they looked into each other's eyes, and it seemed to Sabina as if she grew older in that very moment. She saw all he was trying to tell her; she saw the difficulties, the tribulations, the discomforts that lay ahead. And yet still she wished to go with him! She saw that there would be times of loneliness, times when she would ache for her own people, for women of her own class, for people of her own blood. And yet still she knew that any sacrifice was worthwhile.

189

As if he read her thoughts and there was no need for words between them, he said after a moment:

"Very well, then. Tomorrow night at ten o'clock a carriage will be waiting at the bottom of the garden. Before this you will find hanging in your wardrobe the conventional dress and head-dress of a gipsy bride. You can bring nothing else with you. Everything else that you possess must be left behind. You bring me yourself—that is enough. I, too, must be enough for you."

"You will be waiting for me in the carriage?" Sabina asked.

He shook his head. "No, I shall not be there. You will drive alone to the camp. If at any moment on that journey you change your mind, you have only to say one word to the coachman, 'return'. He will have his instructions. At the word from you he will bring you back to the villa and I shall never trouble you again."

"It is cruel," Sabina said with a little sob. "Can you not trust me?"

"My beautiful darling, the breath of my life, it is because I do trust you that I am taking the greatest risk a man ever took. I am staking everything, my whole hope of happiness, in my belief that this love you have for me is real, true and unquenchable. But in every fairness to you, because of your upbringing, because you are English and I will always, in your eyes, be a foreigner, I must give you the chance to be free of me. If you come, my sweet Sabina, as I believe in my heart that you will come, then I swear to you before God that I will make you happy, that you will never regret what you have thrown away."

"I shall come," Sabina said.

He took both her hands in his.

"I dare not kiss you again," he said, a little hoarsely. "If I do, all my resolutions will be lost. If you only knew what it means not to pick you up in my arms now and carry you away, to take you while I have the chance, to hold you and possess you and make you mine, to make sure of you." His voice was suddenly raw and the passion in his eyes blazed down at her. "I love you, Sabina. I love you as never a man has loved a woman before. I want you. Dear God, how I want you—now and at once—as my wife, my woman, my queen."

He bent his head and she felt his lips, fierce and possessive, on her hands; and then, almost before she realized it, he had released her and was gone. He moved with feline, almost panther-like movements across the garden; and even as she tried to call after him, her voice half-strangled in her throat, he had vanished into the shadows and she was alone.

Slowly she raised her hand to her lips. She felt as if her whole body was singing aloud for very joy, and when finally she reached her bedroom it was to fall on her knees beside her bed and thank God for the wonder that had come to her.

She had thought it would be impossible to sleep and yet she must have been more tired than she knew, and long before she had finished recounting to herself the events of the evening, she had slipped away into unconsciousness.

She awoke with a feeling that something wonderful was about to happen, and when she remembered what it was she ran out on to her balcony. Was it really true that he had come to her, and that tonight he would take her away and make her his wife? She could hardly believe it was not a dream, until she saw, still tied to the balustrade, the silk handkerchief she had placed there last night as a signal. She lifted it to her lips and went back into her room.

How, she wondered, could she bear the long hours that must pass before it was night again? And yet nothing seemed to matter. Her whole being was poised, ready for flight, and everything else seemed trivial and of no importance. Not even the thought of Arthur could perturb her, and when she was dressed she sat down at the writing-desk in her room to compose a letter to him.

It was not hard to find words to tell Arthur that she no longer loved him and that she could not be his wife. It was far harder to write to Lady Thetford. Arthur's mother had been so kind and Sabina believed that the close affection the older woman obviously had for her had nothing to do with her relationship to Arthur. It was difficult to express her regret. It seemed ungrateful, but there was little she could say save to tell the truth. Finally she wrote:

I am in love as you once were in love, so you will understand that the world, and even the people I most care for, cannot matter beside the thought of being his wife.

She finished both letters and locked them away in the small drawer of the writing-table, of which she had a key. Then she began her letter to her mother. This was the hardest task of all. She knew how shocked, how surprised and hurt her parents would be. For the first time since she awoke she felt her happiness overshadowed. What would Mamma think of her?

They had been so proud of her engagement to Arthur. She had felt that even Papa, unworldly though he was, had realized what a social achievement it had been after years of being ignored or made use of by the Bartrams and by the other important families of the county, who seldom found it necessary to entertain the girls from the vicarage.

Sabina's face was set and pale as she began the letter. Soon there were tears running down her face and she was sobbing when finally she wrote over and over again the words: *Please forgive me.*

She had just finished the letter when a knock at the door interrupted her and she learned that Lady Thetford was ready to see her. Hastily Sabina wiped her eyes and went along the passage to find Lady Thetford sitting up in bed, the newspapers on the coverlet in front of her, a half-opened pile of letters at her hand.

"Good morning, Sabina," she smiled. "I have a note here from the Lady-in-Waiting to the Princess of Wales to say that their Royal Highnesses will honour me by coming to tea on Saturday afternoon and that they are looking forward to seeing the garden."

"How exciting it will be!" Sabina exclaimed. And then remembered she would not be there.

"You must wear that new gown in blue bengaline which arrived from Paris yesterday," Lady Thetford smiled. "Their Royal Highnesses will be bringing several members of their staff, and I shall invite Prince Charles to meet them, so we shall be quite a party."

"It will be lovely," Sabina said in a low voice.

She wondered if Lady Thetford would tell the Prince and Princess what had happened to her. She could imagine how shocked they would be. Perhaps, because of her bad behaviour, Harriet would not be allowed to be presented at Court. But no, she must not think of such things. She shook herself free of the little taunting devils which tried to disturb her, forcing herself to listen to Lady Thetford's arrangements for the day.

"Arthur is coming to tea," she said. "At least, that is what he told me earlier last night. And there are no plans for this evening. Is there anything you would like to do?"

"Nothing in particular," Sabina answered quickly.

"Perhaps that is as well," Lady Thetford said. "To be honest, I have a slight migraine this morning, and usually when I get one of these headaches it gets worse as the day goes on. Let us make no plans then, dear Sabina. If I am better, we might go to the Casino; and if I feel worse, you must forgive me if we retire to bed early."

"I think perhaps that would be best in any case," Sabina replied in a voice that she strove to make sound natural. "We were late last night."

"Ah, but you are young. I am sure you never feel tired," Lady Thetford said. "I only find late nights a trial when I get one of these headaches. There is no reason why I should have them, and yet I always seem to suffer from them in the spring."

"Will you not stay in bed today?" Sabina suggested.

"No, I have too much to do," Lady Thetford answered. "I must see about the flowers for Saturday. The Princess adores flowers and I want the drawing-room to look a bower of beauty. And I must speak to the chef as well. He will be in a great state of excitement at the thought of a Royal visit."

It was fortunate that Lady Thetford was so preoccupied with the thoughts of her tea-party that she did not notice that Sabina was often inattentive, or that she grew pale and dark-eyed, as if with an inner excitement, as the day drew on.

Arthur arrived for tea, and just before he arrived Sabina felt afraid. She felt she could not bear another scene, another battle of wills, just at this moment when all her nerves were tense and her whole being was concentrated on what was to occur tonight.

When he came into the room, looking smart as usual, it seemed to her that she saw him for the first time and wondered how, even in her wildest moments, she had imagined she could find happiness with him. She saw the coldness in his eyes, the tight, narrowness of his lips, and the obstinacy of his chin. He would be a bully when he grew old, she thought, and he would never, not if he lived to be one hundred, understand the real meaning of love.

He made what was a taciturn apology for his behaviour last night, not humbling himself in any way, but behaving as though it was, in fact, very generous of him to refer to the matter at all.

"I don't care for these parties given by Russian nobles," he said, a little pettishly. "And I must ask you, Sabina, to see as little of Sheringham as possible. I don't approve of him as a friend for my future wife."

"I like him," Sabina answered, brave enough to say what she felt because she realized that after today she would never have to listen to Arthur dictating to her again.

"Then I must deplore your taste," he retorted stiffly.

"Besides," Sabina went on. "I think it is a mistake for husbands and wives to choose each other's friends."

"You think it is a mistake!" Arthur ejaculated in astonishment. "Really, Sabina, you forget yourself. But anyway, I am not prepared to argue about the matter. Sheringham will not be welcome in our house when we are married, and under the circumstances it would be best for you not to encourage him now."

"But I have already told you, Arthur, I like him," Sabina protested.

Arthur got to his feet and walked across the room to the window.

"I said from the very beginning that it was a mistake for you to come here. You have changed, Sabina. You are not the same girl that you were when we first met."

"Are you suggesting that we should break off our engagement?" Sabina asked in a small voice.

"I'm suggesting nothing of the sort," Arthur replied firmly. "But I think it would be as well for you to remember my position and the fact that when you become my wife you promise to obey me."

"When I am your wife I will remember it," Sabina said quietly.

"You are young and innocent," Arthur continued loftily. "You must leave all decisions of any importance to me. You will find that my judgment will be for the best and that such dependence upon me will be well justified."

"That, of course, remains to be seen," Sabina retorted.

"Of course."

Lady Thetford joined them after this and there was no

further chance of an intimate conversation. Arthur kissed Sabina's check when he left and she thought as he did so that it made no more impression on her than if she had been kissed by a stone image. She was no longer frightened of him, no longer afraid of his violence or the lust she had encountered in the carriage last night. He could no longer harm her. She was going away from him, going where he could never reach her. She felt as if the chains with which he had bound her to him had fallen away, leaving her as free as the wind blowing in softly from the sea.

And still the day dragged on. Sabina almost prayed that Lady Thetford's headache would prevent their having people to dinner or suggesting a visit to the Casino. In case of the latter she was prepared to invent a headache of her own, but fortunately there was no need for her to lie. At six o'clock Lady Thetford announced that she would have dinner in bed.

"Just a bowl of soup, Bates, nothing else," she told the butler. "It is best for me to starve when I have these migraines. I shall take a sleeping draught as early as I can and pray that I shall be better in the morning. I am sorry, child, to be such a nuisance."

"But you are not," Sabina protested in all truth.

She escorted Lady Thetford upstairs and kissed her affectionately.

"I hate to see you suffering," she said. "If only I could help."

"You help me just by being here," Lady Thetford replied. "It will be a dull evening for you, Sabina, but I dare say you can find a book to read or some letters to write."

"You are not to worry about me," Sabina answered. "And thank you, dear, dear Lady Thetford. Thank you once again for being so kind to me."

"Silly child, you have thanked me quite enough," Lady Thetford protested. "I wish I were more cheerful company for you this evening. Good-night, Sabina."

"Good-bye," Sabina said softly, beneath her breath, so that neither Lady Thetford nor Marie heard her, and then she went from the room.

The hours passed slowly. She had dinner alone, waited on by Bates and James, the footman. After telling them that she would require nothing more that evening, she went up to her bedroom. Her heart was beating tumultuously. Soon it would be time to go. Soon she would see him again, hear his voice, feel his hands, his lips. . . .

She shut her bedroom door, crossed to the wardrobe, and paused for a moment. Supposing the dress he had promised was not there. Suppose the carriage never came. Suppose she had imagined it all—his promises, his love, the feelings he evoked in her.

With a sudden violence she pulled open the door, and then, in utter relief, felt weak and almost faint at what she saw there. Hanging amongst the glittering, shimmering gowns which Lady Thetford had given her from Paris, was a short coloured skirt embroidered in gold, a black velvet bodice and a white blouse, also embroidered with intricate and very beautiful patterns. Sabina laid the clothes on her bed. She could not even begin to think of how they had got there, she only knew that what he had promised he had performed. The carriage would be waiting and at the end of her journey she would find him.

Quickly she undressed. It took her some time to robe herself correctly in the many coloured petticoats she found beneath the embroidered skirt. The head-dress lay on the floor of the wardrobe. It was a coronet fashioned from gold thread, semi-precious stones and brightly coloured ribbons which hung down over her shoulders.

When Sabina was dressed she looked at herself in the mirror and smiled. She did not look in the least like a gipsy. Her skin was too white and her golden hair proclaimed her Nordic blood. She thought of the women she had seen round the camp fire; of their bronze skins, flashing black eyes, long dark hair, and their strange air of being primitive and untrammelled. Suddenly she felt afraid of them. Would they accept her or would they hate her because she had come amongst them and stolen the love of their king?

She remembered the dancer, sullen and sulky at her first visit, wildly antagonistic and angry at her second. Would she be waiting, ready in the dark to use the long sharp knife which every gipsy carried in her stocking? Sabina shivered at the thought, and then she remembered that he would be beside her. He would be there to protect her, to love her, to make her his wife, his queen. Nothing else mattered.

She went to the writing desk, turned the key in the

196

lock and brought out the letters she had written that morning. She arranged them on her dressing-table in a row. She saw now that when she had written the envelope to her mother a tear had fallen on the word Cobblefield, smudging it. It was symbolic, Sabina thought. It was fading from her life, but she knew that she could never entirely erase it from her affections or her memory. The big, grey dilapidated vicarage, with its worn stair-carpets and shabby walls, peopled with those she had loved to the exclusion of all else until this moment, would always mean home.

Yet she was leaving it all behind; she was destroying her parents' affection for her, humbling their pride and perhaps severing all ties with her family. And yet somehow it didn't matter. She loved him. She was going to him, and that meant all the world—and so much more besides.

It was then, as she set down her letters, that she remembered that she did not even know his name. It was as she thought of Papa that she remembered it. Recalling how he had said so often that when the time came he would marry her himself, in the small village church where she had been baptized and where she had worshipped since she was old enough to remember.

She had so often thought of herself standing there at the altar, dressed in white, her face covered with a lace veil. She could hear her own voice repeating the words, 'I, Sabina, take thee . . .' and now she did not even know the name of the man she was about to marry. She could hardly credit it, and yet it was true. She had thought of him always as the king, and somehow in their talks there had never been the occasion in which it had seemed easy for her to ask him his name.

Was she crazy she asked herself, to go away like this, to sacrifice everything to surrender herself into the keeping of a man who even now, at the last moment, was anonymous? And then she knew that, if she was to be told that he was the Devil himself, she would still go to him.

This was love! This was the irresistible rough sea of which he had spoken, the fire that Lady Thetford had said could both purify and create. Love had purified her of all desires, all ambitions, all snobbery. She wanted only to belong to a man because she loved him. It did not matter that her bed must be the hard ground, that she must have no possessions save those he could give her, that she must renounce everything and everybody which up to this moment had seemed important. She loved him and such love was irresistible, all-conquering.

She looked at the clock on the mantelpiece. It was ten o'clock! Quickly she blew out the candles. She had a last glimpse of her face, very pale, yet somehow almost spiritualized in its intensity. And then she was moving softly on tiptoe along the balcony and down the wooden steps. She crossed the garden, passed between the trees and came to the wall. Once again she found the stone on which she could raise herself to look over the top. Down below her was a carriage drawn by two horses.

Sabina had travelled in many vehicles during her life but never one that moved as swiftly as that sent for her by the gipsy king. The horses, she thought, must have been like the one he himself rode, for the long, steep pull up to the Upper Corniche Road seemed hardly to diminish their pace, and more than once, as the carriage swayed and rocked, Sabina was forced to hold on to the sides to prevent herself from being thrown on to the floor.

There was a wild exhilaration in going so fast, in feeling herself being carried away from the civilization she was leaving to the primitive life which waited for her. The window was open and she felt the sea breeze on her cheeks and rippling through the ribbons which hung from her head-dress.

Now that they were away from the town the gipsy driver was uttering strange cries to spur on his steeds, and more than once he broke into a song—the strange, melodious words seeming somehow in keeping with this whole adventure.

"A-ay, A-ay," his voice rang out into the darkness, and the horses galloped on while the wheels of the carriage rumbled over the rough road and Sabina felt as if she was tossed high on the waves of a storm.

"A-ay, A-ay," the gipsy cried again, and then Sabina saw ahead of her a crowd of shining lights. She could not guess what it was until they drew nearer and she saw that it was a procession of torches winding to the blazing light of a great fire.

The carriage drew up with a jerk, the door was flung open and a young gipsy invited her, in broken French, to alight She obeyed him and saw that she was expected to walk between the row of torches. Tonight there was no doubt about her reception. In the flickering light she could see that every man who held a torch was smiling—white teeth gleaming against dark skin and bright eyes apprising her not with anger but with admiration and pleasure.

Slowly she moved between them and realized that those she passed were following behind making a procession—moving on, on towards the great beacon of leaping flames.

It was then that she saw he was waiting for her. She felt her heart leap and it was with difficulty that she could force herself to continue walking slowly towards him. He was standing by the fire and she perceived that he was more gorgeously arrayed than ever before. There was golden embroidery on his white shirt, glittering jewels on his fingers and in his ears. There were precious gems, too, on the hilt of his knife, where it lay, partially concealed by the red sash at his waist.

She advanced towards him, and now, at last, he moved towards her, and the glory and the wonder in his face made her eyes drop before his.

"You have come!"

The words were like a paean of almost unutterable joy, and now her hands clung to his—needing his strength, asking his help.

"I have . . . come."

He felt that she was trembling and his fingers tightened on hers.

"My dream came true, my heart, my life, my love!" he said and his voice made her throb and quiver with an ecstasy beyond words.

Then he turned towards the gipsies gathered around them and cried out in a loud voice which seemed to echo and re-echo until it returned to her from the darkness. Sabina did not understand the actual words of what he said, but she knew that he presented her to his tribe. There was a great roar of voices, a shout of proclamation, and an old man, long bearded and wearing a chain of gold and precious stones, which Sabina guessed was a ceremonial jewel came forward with a knife in his hand.

She forced herself not to tremble or to cry out as he cut her wrist. She saw the red blood spurt forth, and then a cut was made on the king's wrist also and their hands were bound together—her right hand and his left hand—and as the old man said strange words over them, she knew that their blood was intermingled.

When this was done, they were brought a great earthenware flagon filled with wine. The old gipsy held it towards Sabina and she drank from it, and the king did likewise. Then, with a shout the flagon was sent crashing to the ground. Eager hands scooped up the fragments; Sabina was given a piece to hold.

"So long as we keep these pieces in our possession," the gipsy king said quietly, "our love shall remain."

"I shall never lose mine," Sabina whispered.

"Nor I mine," he replied. "Nor, you, my beloved."

Water was splashed on them then from another jar, with a gesture which Sabina guessed was to purify them from evil spirits, and at last, the ceremony was finished, their hands were untied, but still holding Sabina's fingers in his the gipsy king drew her to where a couch had been improvised before a clearing round the fire.

The music which had been playing softly ever since Sabina had arrived, now broke into a wild crescendo. A dozen dancers, both men and women, sprang into the open space. They danced wildly, with an abandon which was exciting and strangely emotional. The rest of the tribe marked time with their bodies, clapped with their hands and sang, if the spirit took them.

All the while wine was circulated amongst them. Sabina received hers in a great golden goblet, chased and embossed and decorated with precious stones, but at the same time so worn with age that she could only speculate rather than guess on its antiquity.

"The first time you came here, heart of my heart," the gipsy king said, "you told me that you had heard of the goblets which tribes like mine preserve for many centuries. Now you will see them."

There were gold plates on which they presented Sabina with fresh fruit; there were jewelled dishes on which they brought strange delicacies which had been cooked over the fire; and there were also flagons and goblets of every

200

shape and size so that her eyes were bewildered by them. And yet it was hard even with the dancing, the singing and the music, to notice anything but the man at whose side she sat. And she knew, too, that he was watching her; his eyes on her face, on her mouth and on the turn of her white neck.

"My life, my love, my soul," he murmured once, and she felt herself thrill at the depth and longing in his voice.

The dancers grew in number, the music swelled. Now there were few people to watch and all were partaking in the wild festivities of the wedding ceremony. The fire leapt higher and higher, more fuel was laid upon it until the heat itself was almost overwhelming and Sabina put up her hand as if to shade her eyes.

It was then that the king drew her to her feet.

"Come," he said.

She looked at him wonderingly, but obeyed. He led her away from the fire and through the circle of wagons towards the trees which stood at the back of the camp.

"Where are we going?" she asked.

"Where you and I can be alone," he answered, and she felt herself tremble at his words.

"Our people will dance until they are exhausted," he said. "There is nothing the gipsies love more than a wedding."

She felt there was no need for her to say anything. Now that her eyes had grown accustomed to the softer light of the moon, she could see clearly where he was leading her. The trees were tall and dark and the ground beneath them was soft and sandy. There was a scent of resin and pine and another strange, exotic fragrance she did not recognize, until a moment later they came to a clearing in the centre of the trees. Brushwood and branches had made a protective wall through which they passed, and then Sabina saw in front of her the strangest bedroom she had ever imagined.

There was a great couch on the floor, covered with a white bearskin. On it were cushions of satin and silk of many colours and enclosing it entirely from the outer walls of branches and brushwood were silks and satins in many and varied shades, giving the impression of patchwork and yet all blending miraculously together under the silver light of the moon.

There was a carpet on the floor, but the ceiling was the

star-strewn sky, with the tops of the trees silhouetted against it like protective sentinels. And then Sabina saw that the floor and the couch and everything, from the brushwood itself, was all strewn with flower petals.

She recognized tuberoses, tiger lilies and the sweet fragrance of night-scented stock, but there were many other strange and varied perfumes she did not know. And then, as she looked around her, she turned her face towards the gipsy king and forgot everything save that they were alone.

"My wife!"

He said the words very quietly as he took her in his arms, kissing her as he had said that he would do. His lips were on her eyes, on her cheeks and the pulse beating wildly in her neck, and the little hollow in her arms and at her wrists. He drew her down on to the soft fur-covered couch and his hands took the coronet from her head and released the pins which held and fettered her hair. It tumbled over her shoulders and he kissed it wildly, burying his face in it, drawing it like a veil across her face, seeking her lips through it.

"I love you! God, how I love you!"

She heard his voice, passionate, triumphant, elated; and she felt her whole being respond to him. She surrendered herself utterly to the touch of his hands, the desire of his lips. She knew then that everything was worthwhile, that she need have no regrets, no thought of what she had relinquished. This was life; this was love; this was happiness!

She had no thought of time. She only knew, as the hours passed, that her body thrilled and responded to him as an instrument thrills and responds to the master touch. Once, as he looked down at her, he said:

"Your eyes are stars of fire, as I promised they should be."

And then he was kissing her again and she felt herself burn with the flames of passion which seemed to consume them both. She could feel his heart beating against hers, her body close against his, her mouth soft beneath the hard insistence of his lips, until suddenly, he raised himself and looked up at the sky.

"What is it?" she asked.

"I love you," he answered, his voice very deep and

moved. "I love you, my perfect sweetheart, so I am going to ask you to trust me still further."

"Trust you?" she inquired.

"Yes. You will not understand what I am going to ask of you, but only trust me, as you have trusted me already. Do you love me enough for that?"

"You know I do," she answered. "You know I love you so much that I have forgotten that the world holds anything else but you."

"That is what I prayed you would say," he answered. "And now, my sweet, my beloved, my very precious wife, I am going to send you back."

For a moment Sabina thought she had not understood him aright. Slowly, in a voice that hardly seemed to be her own, she said:

"Send me . . . back . . . but where?"

"To the villa," he answered. "Tomorrow no one will know that you have been here—but I want you to trust me. All will be well, I promise you that."

"How . . . but . . . I do not . . . understand," Sabina stammered.

She thrust back her hair from her forehead as she spoke, but his arms were around her and once again his lips were on hers.

"I love you," he said. "And that is all you have to remember. That I love you."

He released her and reaching out his hand poured out a glass of wine from a golden flagon which stood beside the couch.

"Drink this," he said quietly.

"Please explain . . . you must explain. I must understand," Sabina said.

"Drink this first," he answered.

Obediently, because she was so pre-occupied with her thoughts, she did as he commanded. Only as she swallowed the last drops of the wine in the goblet did she realize that it was drugged. She felt a strange lassitude creep over her; she tried to speak, tried to ask him what he had given her, but his arms were round her and his lips prevented her from speaking.

Despite everything—her sudden doubts, the strange fear rising within her, the cloud which was descending on her senses and making them numb—she felt herself thrill

at the touch of his mouth. And then she was sinking deep
down into a darkness from which she felt there was no
return. . . .

CHAPTER TWELVE

SABINA came slowly back from a deep, dark oblivion. It
was like a heavy cloud through which she could barely
force her way. First the consciousness that she was herself
came slowly and insistently; but no other thoughts or
feelings troubled her, only an awareness, as if, like a plant
buried beneath the dark earth, she reached relentlessly
upwards towards the sun.

Slowly—so slowly as to be almost imperceptible—the
mists cleared, until at last to consciousness was added
memory. It was then that remembrance like a sudden,
piercing light seemed to strike, indeed to transfix her very
soul.

She opened her eyes. She was in the white-walled
bedroom which she had occupied ever since she came to
the Villa Mimosa. For the moment she could not believe
it was true. She closed her eyes as if to shut out the sight
of the gilt-framed mirror, the pictures on the wall, the
soft hangings of peach damask; but her whole being had
now roused itself to cry out in a sudden agony.

'Where is he? Where is he?'

She opened her eyes again. The golden radiance of the
room might have been the deepest and darkest dungeon
of some beleaguered castle, so horrible and so fearful did
it seem to her gaze. Was she dreaming or was this, indeed,
the truth?

And now she became aware that her body was
wrapped in a shawl. A big self-coloured shawl of soft
silky wool. It enveloped her whole body, holding her arms
to her sides, and as she struggled free of it, she saw that
her gold embroidered skirt and black velvet bodice had
gone. She was wearing only the white blouse with its
colourful embroidery and the full, silk petticoats which
rustled as she moved.

Someone had taken her shoes from her—perhaps for comfort. But nothing could have comforted Sabina at this moment. She looked down at the gay petticoats and for a moment her hands stretched out as if to touch them. Then, with a little cry of sheer, undiluted agony that seemed to come from the very depth of her heart, she flung herself face downwards on her pillow, hiding her face, striving, fruitlessly, to shut out the memories of last night.

She lived again that strange ceremony in the light of the dancing flames; and her lips sought and found the scar on her wrist. It still hurt a little and as she pressed it against her mouth she could taste blood—his blood and . . . hers!

They had been married then, married as their blood intermingled, and it was as his wife that she had walked with him out into the darkness to find that strange, yet beautiful, bedroom in the shelter of the pines.

Then throbbingly, as if she listened again to the wild cadenzas of gipsy music, she remembered those moments when she lay on the white bearskin, his arms around her, his lips seeking hers. She had not believed such happiness could exist. She had not known that her body could experience such rapture, such an ecstasy of emotion, so that thrill after thrill followed each other to leave her breathless and pulsating. Her whole being had ached for his touch, for the wonder of his mouth, for his kisses on her eyes and on her hair, for the hard pressure of his hands. And then his sudden unexpected gentleness.

She had belonged to him; she had offered herself to him body and soul. And yet, in actual fact, he had not possessed her. With a sudden agony now Sabina asked why he had not taken her as their desire for each other leapt high towards the stars and they had known that they were spiritually indivisible.

Why, why, had he let that moment pass? And why, above all else had he sent her back? She thought, as she pressed her face still closer to the pillow, that she reached the very lowest depths of humiliation.

He had conquered her and had not thought his triumph worth the taking. She had offered herself and been rejected! But through the depths of her misery she remembered his voice. 'Trust me,' he had said. 'Only trust me.'

Yet what could that mean? Trust him for what or for

why? She had gone to him; she had given up everything. She had been prepared to forfeit the love and respect of her family; she had thought the golden social prominence that Arthur offered her was easily forsworn. She had wanted only one thing—to love and be loved.

Sabina felt the tears running down her face; the slow, painful tears of disillusionment, of utter despair. What would happen to her now? she thought. Because nothing could ever seem the same. She loved him—loved him so unreservedly that she knew that, if he asked it of her, she would crawl barefooted across the world to be at his side. She loved him so much that she would go to him, asking nothing save that she might see him and be with him, that she could hear his voice and know that he was near.

She went down at that moment into a hell which was so dark and so black that it almost offered oblivion. . . .

A long time later she raised her head, and feeling choked went to the wash-stand for a glass of water. She felt the coolness of it on her tongue and remembered the glass of wine he had given her last night. It must have contained herbs, she thought—a gipsy brew—to have brought such swift unconsciousness.

She put down the glass of water and shook the shawl from her body, then picked it up again and held it against her face. It was soft as silk, being made of wool gathered from the sheep of Southern Europe. He had cared enough to wrap it round her so that she should not be cold. Had it been his arms which had brought her here? Or had he, too indifferent to be troubled personally with her return, handed her over to someone else?

'I shall never see him again,' Sabina cried despairingly. But she could not believe it. He had loved her, she was sure of that, if only for a short time.

And yet, what did she know of love? She put up her hands to her eyes and felt again the tears trickling through her fingers.

'Oh, Mamma! Mamma!' She murmured the words out loud—the cry of a child who has been hurt, the cry of a child who knows there is only one security in life, one person to turn to in trouble.

Even as she said the words, she remembered something else. She looked at the dressing-table. Her letters were gone! She had left them propped in a row—the letter to her mother, the one to Lady Thetford and the third to Arthur. They had gone!

It was then that Sabina went to the door to find it locked. She had turned the key herself last night before she stepped on to the balcony and ran down the wooden staircase to the garden. No one, then, had been in her room since she left it. No one save the man who had carried her here as dawn was breaking, to lay her, sleeping on the bed and then to go away alone.

Alone! The word hurt her to say it, to think it. He had gone and she was not with him. Had the gipsies already broken camp? Were their wagons rumbling away towards some unknown horizon, leaving nothing but the charred cinders of what had once been their fire. Was that all she would find if she went to the Upper Corniche Road?

'I cannot bear it; I cannot.'

She threw herself down beside her bed, but somehow she was past tears, past even the relief of abandoning herself to the tempest of her thoughts. Instead she found herself thinking that life must go on, although he had no further use for her. She wanted to die, and yet death would not take her as easily as that. She wanted to go in search of him—and yet how or where could she follow when only the wind knew the direction he had taken?

'Oh, God, help me.'

It was a cry from Sabina's very heart. A prayer more urgent than any she had had to make in her life before. She wished only that she had some pride to come to her rescue, that she could feel angry or incensed because he had promised her so much and then broken her very trust in him. But she could feel nothing but the hopeless misery of being a woman abandoned, a wife without her man.

Slowly she turned her hand over to gaze on her wrist. The cut was vividly red, a little smudged with blood. Sabina stared down at it.

'I love him. . . . I love him. . . . I love him.'

She said the words over and over again, until a sound from the clock on the mantelpiece made her glance towards it. To her astonishment she saw that it was nearly one o'clock. Slowly she got to her feet. What had happened that no one had come to disturb her? Had Lady Thetford given instructions that she was to sleep until she rang?

Lady Thetford! Arthur! Mamma! The girls! They were

all back in her life again. She, who had thought last night that she had left them all behind for ever. Slowly, moving as if she were old and stricken in years, Sabina went to the wardrobe. She took from it her white wrapper and taking off the silk petticoats, the white embroidered blouse, she put on instead a fresh nightgown and over it the wrapper. Then she unlocked the door and rang the bell.

Yvonne came hurrying within a few seconds.

"You are late this morning, *mademoiselle*," she said, cheerily, as she drew back the curtains and let in the sunshine. As Sabina did not answer, she continued: "Her ladyship has suggested that you should have luncheon in bed today. She thinks you must be tired to have slept so long, and when I heard your bell I was just instructing the chef what to prepare for you."

"Does her ladyship wish to see me?"

Sabina heard her voice come from very far away, as if it were the voice of a stranger. She was taking up her life again as she had left it. She was making the same ordinary, commonplace remarks that she would have made before last night, before she had believed that everything was altered, everything changed.

"No, her ladyship has gone out to luncheon," Yvonne replied. "She left a message for you, *mademoiselle*, to say that you were to rest today as there was the most important party for you to attend tonight."

"A party?" Sabina asked, dully, as if she had never heard the word before.

"Yes, *mademoiselle*, and I think her ladyship wishes you to look your very best. Get back into bed and after you have eaten your luncheon perhaps you will sleep again."

Sabina did as Yvonne suggested. She was too exhausted to argue, too stricken to even try to understand anything save the aching misery of her own heart. Yvonne brought her fresh pillows, arranged the bedclothes, put a small table by her side, and a few minutes later appeared with a tray laden with delicious dishes.

"Try to eat, *mademoiselle*," she begged, as Sabina shook her head, feeling that the very sight of food would make her choke.

Finally, to please Yvonne, she had a few mouthfuls of soup and then the tray was taken away again.

"The chef will be very disappointed, *mademoiselle*,"

Yvonne said reproachfully. "He tries his best to please, always, and he feels insulted if his dishes are returned to the kitchen untasted."

"I am sorry," Sabina sighed. It was an effort to say anything and she knew, even as she said the words, they were untrue. She could feel sorry for nobody or about anything save herself.

She felt now that her brain was on fire with questions which presented and re-presented themselves. What had she done? Had she perhaps offended him? Or worse still, had she revolted him in some fashion that she could not understand? Had he only wanted what was unattainable? Or was it because she was so ready and willing for his kisses—had indeed craved for them—that he no longer found her attractive? And yet, once again, even as the pain of such thoughts shook her physically so that her very hands trembled, she heard again his voice: 'Trust me. Only trust me.'

How, how—when he was not here? She lay back against her pillows and let the chaotic questions to which she could find no answers tumble over themselves in her poor, tired little head, until finally, to her own surprise, she slept. She drifted away into a dream in which he was with her. She knew again that sense of security that he always gave her. Her hand was in his—nothing else mattered save that he was beside her.

She must have slept for some hours. When she awoke, Yvonne was coming to the room.

"You have been asleep, *mademoiselle*!" she exclaimed. "That is good. You will feel better, much better now. See, I have brought you a pot of tea and the chef has made you some little cakes—fairy cakes he calls them. They are only a mouthful, but if you will only eat them, *mademoiselle*, you will feel better. It is not good to fast for too long."

"I will try," Sabina promised. She felt at peace within herself. Her dream had seemed so real and she had not been afraid or unhappy but only content, utterly and completely content, because he had been there.

To please Yvonne, and perhaps because she was, in spite of herself, a little hungry, she drank the tea and even managed two of the fairy cakes which the chef had made especially for her. She was finishing the last morsel of one when Lady Thetford came into the room.

209

"Are you feeling better, child?"

Sabina looked surprised at the question and Lady Thetford went on:

"Yvonne told me that you were tired and that was why I wanted you to stay in bed today. This is a hectic life for those who are not used to it."

"Yes, of course," Sabina murmured.

"But you have not much longer to be lazy," Lady Thetford went on. "We are going to a very grand party tonight, and I want you to look your best."

"Yes," Sabina answered mechanically. She thought for a moment of telling Lady Thetford everything, of saying that she could not go a party wherever it might be or by whoever it might be given. She wanted to confess what she had done last night; to reveal how she had gone from the house intending never to return. And then the hopelessness of trying to explain, of trying to tell a story to which there was no reasonable or probable ending, swept over her to keep her silent.

How could anybody understand what he had been like or what he had meant to her? How bald, how stupid it sounded to say—'I ran away with a gipsy'. And yet there was so much more to it than that. She had found the man who she believed had been her mate from the very beginning of time; the man who she loved to the exclusion of all else—more even than life itself—and now she had lost him! He had come into her life and he had gone, and there was nothing to show that he had been there—save a broken heart.

It was true, Sabina thought. Her heart was broken and some part of her that he had brought to life was dead. She knew now that without him she would never feel the same again. There was, beneath her breast, the cold hardness of ice. Her feelings, and her very heart, were frozen. She could no longer feel anything, not even the desperate, tearing agony which she had experienced at first when she knew she had lost him.

"Marie has got a new gown ready for you," Lady Thetford was saying. "I was keeping it for a very special occasion. But I want you to wear it tonight; and when you are ready will you come to my room? I have something to give you."

"I will come as soon as I am dressed," Sabina replied dutifully.

Yvonne prepared a bath for her and added a sweet bath essence to the water. The fragrance of it made Sabina feel she wanted to cry. It reminded her of the flowers that had lain on the floor of that woodland bedroom. But after a moment's agony she relapsed again into feeling dazed and numb. Nothing mattered any more. She was utterly divorced now from all feeling.

"I have died," Sabina told her reflection in the mirror, a little later. She murmured the words beneath her breath; but Marie, who was arranging the dress with Yvonne, asked:

"Did *mademoiselle* speak? Oh, it is *ravissant*, perfect, the most wonderful gown that *mademoiselle* has ever worn."

As Marie spoke she pulled out the frills of white shadow lace which cascaded out from Sabina's tiny waist to fall over a great stiffened bustle on to the floor in a small train. The tight bodice framed the sweet curves of her figure and the soft laces on her pale shoulders were nearly as white as her skin. Marie had swept her golden hair up on top of her head and pinned it there with big tortoise-shell pins. On top of each one twinkled a tiny diamond star.

"Her ladyship particularly wished you to wear these tonight, *mademoiselle*," she explained.

Sabina hardly heard her voice. All she could see was the dark emptiness of her own eyes, which seemed almost too big for the thin paleness of her tiny face. She was, indeed, so pale that she wondered if she would faint, and Lady Thetford, coming into the room, gave an exclamation:

"Goodness, child! You have been so long dressing that I wondered what had happened to you! Are you all right?"

"Yes, I am quite all right," Sabina answered, in a dull voice.

"Well, Marie must certainly put some rouge on your cheeks tonight," Lady Thetford said critically. "They will think I am bringing a ghost to the party, not a young girl." She waited a moment as if she expected Sabina to make some comment. Then as the latter said nothing she added: "Arthur is not coming with us, so you need not worry that anyone will detect it on this occasion. It is only that I want you to look your best."

"Thank you," Sabina murmured.

"And I have a present for you. I was keeping it for your marriage, but I want you to wear it tonight."

As Lady Thetford spoke she opened a velvet case that she held in her hands. Inside was a diamond necklace. It was made entirely of stars, graduated in size and beauty until they culminated in a large one in the very centre of the necklace. She took it from its case and it glittered and sparkled against the rounded beauty of Sabina's white neck.

Sabina stared at it dully, remembering that once, long, long ago, someone had spoken of her eyes as being stars of fire. She thought now that it was a fire that had been extinguished, that there was no sparkle of light in her face, only the dull, emptiness of resignation.

"*Mademoiselle* is more beautiful than I have ever seen her!" Marie cried. And Yvonne, too, exclaimed: "She is like a fairy princess!"

Sabina said nothing, but she thought that she wanted only to be the wife of a gipsy. She had not asked for exquisite gowns from Paris, or necklaces of diamonds, or stars in her hair. She wanted only the rough, dusty road beneath her feet, the trundle of wagon wheels jerking over the stones and the knowledge that she was with the man she loved and that—he loved her.

She realized suddenly that Lady Thetford was waiting, and remembered that she had not said thank you for the necklace. She put her fingers up to it, feeling the stones, cold and hard, beneath her touch. It was what her life was to be henceforward, she thought—her life with Arthur.

"Thank you."

She managed to force the words between her lips and add lamely, "It is very kind of you."

Lady Thetford seemed about to say something, perhaps to ask what was wrong, and then she changed her mind.

"We must go," she said a little sharply. "We have a long drive ahead of us."

Yvonne brought Sabina a cloak and wrapped it round her.

"Be careful of that wonderful dress, *mademoiselle*," Marie admonished her as she turned towards the door.

Sabina did not answer. 'I wanted rags and you have given me silk and laces,' she longed to reply. But what

212

was the point? Who would understand what she was saying? He had gone, and there was only emptiness—a vast, aching, emptiness stretching away into eternity.

A foot-warmer was put in the carriage for Lady Thetford and Sabina to rest their evening shoes on, and fur rugs were tucked securely round them by the footman before the doors were shut and the horses started up the hill. The sun was only just beginning to sink over the sea, and as they drove the dusk came swiftly and only a red glow on the horizon remained.

They must have been driving for nearly an hour before Lady Thetford said:

"You have not asked me where we are going."

"No, of course not," Sabina replied. "It is rude of me not to inquire."

"Not rude," Lady Thetford answered. "A little lacking in curiosity, perhaps, which is unlike you."

"I am sorry," Sabina apologized.

"Actually I think you will be interested when we get there," Lady Thetford told her. "Because you are about to meet a very remarkable personage and a great friend of mine. The Princess Rakoczi was one of the fabulous beauties of Europe thirty years ago. She is getting old now and is not always in good health, but she is still beautiful and still has an irresistible charm."

Sabina murmured something. She was not very interested in this princess whom she was about to meet. She wondered if she would ever be interested in anything again; if anything would seem gay, wonderful and exciting, or whether this terrible, frozen immobility within her breast would prevent her not only from finding things enjoyable, but also from finding them distasteful. Perhaps even Arthur would not affect her and she would not care what he did or what he said, nor even have to shrink from the touch of his hands.

"The Princess owns a castle in the mountains," Lady Thetford went on. "She likes the climate, that is why she spends many months of the year in this part of the world. And, of course, she has a vast number of friends."

"Yes, of course," Sabina murmured, because she felt she must say something.

Lady Thetford gave a little sigh and relapsed into silence. It was nearly dark now, but Sabina had a brief glimpse of turrets silhouetted against the sky, of a moat surrounding what had once been a walled castle, of gardens laid out formally but with great beauty, and of a bridge over which they passed into a great courtyard.

The servants ran forward to open the car and there was carpet over the steps which led them through a great Gothic doorway to a pillared hall. Maids appeared to lead them into a retiring room, where a fire blazed up the chimney and there were long mirrors and a dressing-table set with gold brushes and jewelled combs.

Sabina did not bother to look at any of it. She stood still and docile while maids took her cloak from her. Someone pulled out the flounces of her dress, another touched her hair with skilled fingers. She had a glimpse of the stars glittering at her throat, of the faint touch of colour in her white cheeks and of huge dark eyes, which even to herself seemed full of pain. Then Lady Thetford said:

"You look charming, dear, come along."

She moved out into the hall, Sabina following behind her; and now there were liveried servants with powdered wigs to show them down a wide corridor hung with magnificent pictures. There were double doors at the end and these were flung open and Sabina saw ahead of her a great *salon* filled with people.

She had a quick impression of chandeliers lit with hundreds of candles, of huge banks of flowers, which sent out a heady, exotic fragrance which seemed to scent the whole room. And then she saw that every woman present was wearing a tiara on her head and that the men wore sparkling orders and decorations on their uniforms and evening clothes.

The sparkle and glitter of the jewels and the brilliance of the whole company seemed to dazzle Sabina's eyes as she followed Lady Thetford obediently across the soft carpet to where, at the end of the room, a woman stood waiting.

She was, indeed, as Sabina could see, beautiful. She was exquisitely dressed and on her white hair, piled high above her oval forehead, there was a veritable crown of diamonds and pearls, while the same jewels fell in a heavy cascade from her throat to her waist.

She gave a little cry of delight at Lady Thetford's approach, and held out both her hands.

"My dear, dear friends," she said, in a soft, musical voice. "This is a very happy day for me."

She kissed Lady Thetford and then turned inquiringly to Sabina.

"This is Sabina, Princess," Lady Thetford said simply.

Sabina curtsied low and the Princess put out her hand and looked at her, she thought, in a surprisingly searching manner.

"I am so delighted to meet you, Sabina," the Princess said softly. She paused for a moment, still holding Sabina's hand, then added with a smile: "I think you have met my son, Michel."

Sabina looked up automatically. Someone was standing beside the Princess, dressed in a white uniform with the blue ribbon of a decoration slashed across it. He did not speak, he did not move, but suddenly Sabina was transfixed, staring at him with her eyes wide, her lips parted.

It was he! There could not be two people in the world who looked like that; How could she mistake the expression in his eyes, the twist to his lips?

Then, as the room whirled round her and the very earth rocked beneath her feet, she felt the frozen immobility of her heart melt and come to life again. She must have looked as if she were about to faint, for suddenly both her hands were in his. She was clinging to them, taking from them the strength and comfort which she had known in her dream.

"Oh, my little love, didn't I tell you to trust me?" he asked.

"Is it true ... really true, that you are ... here?" she faltered.

"That is what I asked myself when you came to me last night," he said in a soft voice.

There was no time for more. The Princess turned to speak to him and Sabina found her hand on his arm and he was drawing her down the centre of the room. On either side of them the guests curtsied as they passed and then followed in procession as they walked in silence and solemnity along the vast corridors of the castle, where every dozen yards flunkies stood holding lighted tapers in golden candelabras.

Sabina did not ask or even wonder where they were going. She only knew that her whole body was pulsating to the knowledge that she was beside him, that her hand was on his arm, that his fingers covered hers. At length the deep, low notes of an organ reached her ears, and the high, sweet voices of boys singing.

Then she saw in front of her the open doors of a high chapel and understood where they were going and why his guests were following them. There was the pungent aroma of incense, the light of high candles against a golden reredos; the priest, in his vestments, was waiting, and there were two white satin cushions before him.

Slowly they walked side by side to the chancel steps, and as they stood there, with the high notes of what seemed to be a heavenly choir filling their ears and echoing up into the arched roof, the guests filed into the seats behind them. Only when all were in their places and a breathless silence fell upon the assembled company, did the service begin and for the second time in her life, Sabina heard the name of the man she loved, the man to whom she had already been married once according to the gipsy laws.

"I, Sabina, take thee, Michel, to be my wedded husband. For better for worse; for richer for poorer; in sickness and in health. . . ."

She heard her voice reciting the beautiful words. And as he placed the golden ring on her finger she was conscious of the little red scar throbbing in her wrist. After that so much happened that she could hardly be aware of in what sequence the events followed one another.

She knew that the Princess kissed her and said kind and very sweet things. That Lady Thetford told her that she understood and was content that she should be happy.

"Michel came to see me this morning," she said. "I have known him since he was a child and I am as sure as he is that you were meant for each other."

Then there was a great banquet at which Sabina was offered many strange and wonderful dishes. Healths were drunk and toasts were proposed by one distinguished personage after another, each more noble in rank and more ornamented with fabulous decorations than the one before. If it had not been for the feeling that Michel was beside her, if he had not bent to whisper exciting and very loving things into her ear, Sabina would have thought she was imagining it all.

All the time she felt this could not be true, that she must be dreaming; and then she would feel her heart give a sudden leap and a little quiver of unexpected delight run through her body at his touch or at something he said which only she could hear.

When the feasting ended, the guests moved into a great gold and white ballroom where a gipsy orchestra played gay, wild melodies which made even the most staid person feel compelled to dance.

The Prince drew Sabina on to the floor, put his arm round her waist, and swung her round as he had done that night at the Palace, when he had dared her to dance with him. They did not speak now—there was somehow no need for words.

It seemed to Sabina as if she felt everything with an intensity which grew with every second that she was with him. The joy of dancing with him, of feeling her hand in his, of being close, of knowing that his eyes were on her face, was so intense that it was like a miracle that had come upon her unawares.

Still dancing, Michel drew Sabina out of the ballroom and into another room at the side of which was a small staircase. As they came to a standstill he held her close against his breast and looking down at her with a smile which made her heart turn over, he said:

"I think, my Heart's desire, this is where you and I escape."

He led the way up the staircase and opened the door at the top and they came into a high room. A log fire was burning in a stone hearth and the light from the flames revealed a huge four-poster bed with carved silver posts and hangings of turquoise blue satin. There were ostrich feather fronds on top of the draped canopy and a bed-spread of white ermine bordered with sable was laid across the foot of the bed.

And as her eyes grew used to the shadows and the leaping flames Sabina could see her own things laid about the room. Her nightgown and dressing-gown were on the chair by the fire and the bedroom slippers of velvet and swans-down which Lady Thetford had given her but a few days ago, were on the hearth.

But she had eyes for nothing but the man who stood watching her; and with the diamonds at her neck and in

217

her hair glittering in the flames she crossed the room to the fireplace to stand at his side.

"Why did you not tell me?" she asked.

"My beautiful, loyal darling!" he replied. "Need I explain that I had the absurd conceit to want you to love me for myself."

"But I would have loved you, who ever you were!" Sabina cried.

"How could I ever be sure? If you had known that I was a royal prince—the story of our love might not have been so perfect."

"But why . . . why were you pretending to be a gipsy?" Sabina inquired.

"I was not pretending," he answered. "I am, in fact, the hereditary King of the Zapak Tribe. My great-great-grandfather married the King's daughter many years ago, she was an only child and their son, my great-grandfather, became, in due course, the gipsy king. It has become a tradition in our family that for three weeks or a month of every year we give up our life of luxury and go with the tribe, wherever their wanderings may take them.

"I have been to many strange places and seen many strange sights with my gipsies; but this year, because my mother has not been well, I insisted that we should camp near Monaco. Perhaps it was some inherited intuition which told me I should be there waiting for you when you came; perhaps it was our fate. Whatever it was, my beloved, you came to me."

"If only I had known," Sabina sighed.

"Wouldn't that have spoiled it all?" he asked. "Can you imagine what it meant to me last night when you gave up everything that you held dear for a man who could offer you nothing but love?"

"And yet you sent me . . . back," Sabina said, and there was a little catch in her voice as she thought of all the misery and agony she had suffered that morning.

"I took you back," he corrected, "because I wanted to tie you to me by every bond and ceremony that exists. You have married me twice now, Sabina—there is no escape."

"As if I should want it," she said, her eyes shining like stars in the light of the fire.

"Don't look at me like that," he said a little hoarsely. "If you do, I shall touch you; and if I touch you, we shall

218

forget all the things that I have to say and all the explanations that have to be made."

She felt herself thrill at her power to move him, and because she was a woman she had to ask softly:

"So you do want me, after all?"

"In a few moments," he answered, "I am going to make you take back the doubt in that question. I shall prove my love for you—Soul of mine—until you cry for mercy. But now, let me tell you just one or two things more. First, I saw Lord Thetford this morning!"

"You saw ... Arthur!" There was something almost like horror in Sabina's voice.

"Yes, and I told him that you belonged, my darling—to me."

"What did he say? Oh, was he very ... angry?"

The Prince's eyes were twinkling, and he answered:

"Angry is not quite the right word. He was infuriated, insulted and, perhaps more than anything, astonished that you could possibly find any other man preferable to him."

"He did not ... mind losing ... me?"

"I think your behaviour in leaving him merely confirmed his already low opinion of your sex! But do not let us waste time in talking about him any more. He is no longer of the least importance and I am jealous of any man—yes, even of the self-opinionated Lord Thetford—if he engages your attention."

"I do not want to think about him," Sabina whispered. "I want to be sure that you are really here and that ... I belong to ... you."

"I will make you certain of that, my own true love, so that you will never doubt it again. But there is one other thing I must say. You gave up your family for me, little Sabina—or thought you were doing so. And so I will give them back to you. Harry shall change into the cavalry regiment he has always wanted. I have told him so today, and he is at this moment a very happy, excited young man. And Harriet, Melloney, Angelina and Clare shall all come and stay with us. As they grow older, you shall present them, my sweet darling, to your Queen at London and to my King, who is also my cousin, at his Court in Budapest. I want them all to be happy if it will make you happy too."

"Oh, how kind, how terribly kind you are!" Sabina

219

said, and there were tears in her eyes as impulsively she moved forward, her arms raised.

And now he reached out to hold her, pulling her close with a fierce possessiveness and a passion which seemed to burst through his iron control. His lips sought hers and they were joined together in an ecstasy of delight that was almost too wonderful to be endured.

At last he let her go, and looking down at her face, soft and glowing against his shoulder, at her lips, parted, and her eyes, half-shut with the passion he had awakened in her, he said:

"This is what I have waited for. You will never know, my dream come true, what it meant to me last night not to make you mine, not to take you when I held you in my arms, when we lay together under the stars and your wonderful hair covered us both like a cloud."

He reached up his hand as he spoke and pulled the diamond pins from her hair. It fell over her shoulders and then she felt his fingers on the hooks of her dress. A moment later he lifted her in his arms, holding her high against his chest, his lips seeking hers through the curtain of her hair.

"You are mine," he said wildly. "Mine by the laws of man and God—my gipsy wife, my love, my life, my Queen."

Barbara Cartland, the world's most famous romantic novelist, who is also an historian, playwright, lecturer, political speaker, and television personality, has now written over 280 books and sold nearly 150 million books over the world.

She has also had many historical works published and has written four autobiographies, as well as the biographies of her mother and that of her brother, Ronald Cartland, who was the first Member of Parliament to be killed in the last war. This book has a preface by Sir Winston Churchill.

She has recently completed a novel with the help and inspiration of the late Earl Mountbatten of Burma, Uncle of His Royal Highness Prince Philip. This is being sold for the Mountbatten Memorial Trust.

Miss Cartland, in 1978, sang an Album of Love Songs with the Royal Philharmonic Orchestra.

In 1976, by writing twenty-one books, she broke the world record and has continued for the following three years by writing twenty-four, twenty-one, and twenty-three.

She is unique in that she was one and two on the Dalton List of Best Sellers, and one week had four books in the top twenty.

In private life Barbara Cartland, who is a Dame of the Order of St. John of Jerusalem, Chairman of the St. John Council in Hertfordshire and Deputy President of the St. John Ambulance Brigade, has also fought for better conditions and salaries for Midwives and Nurses.

As President of the Royal College of Midwives (Hertfordshire Branch) she has been invested with the first badge of Office ever given in Great Britain, which was subscribed to by the Midwives themselves. She has also championed the cause for old people, had the law altered regarding gypsies, and founded the first Romany Gypsy Camp in the world.

Barbara Cartland is deeply interested in Vitamin Therapy and is President of the British National Association for Health. She has a Health and Happiness Club in England and has just started one in America where she has a selection of her own "Be Lovely" cosmetics, her Album of Love Songs, and many other things of unique and original interest. Her book *The Magic of Honey* has sold throughout the world and is translated into many languages.

She has a magazine, *Barbara Cartland's World of Romance*, now being published in the United States.